THE SURVIVOR'S REVENGE

War correspondent Nina Gillespie, physically recovered from wounds sustained in Dubrovnik, tries to pick up the threads of the life and job she has always loved. But she is haunted by memories of the bloodshed and takes a job as a local radio presenter. Following up a heart-rending tale from the adoptive parents of a baby from eastern Europe, Nina begins to uncover a cruel and complicated money-making scam. Nina is drawn back to eastern Europe to collect material for her programme, but there she encounters murder, terror, hatred and deceit.

THE SURVIVOR'S REVENGE

THE SURVIVOR'S REVENGE

by
Jessica Mann

Magna Large Print Books
Long Preston, North Yorkshire,
England.

British Library Cataloguing in Publication Data.

Mann, Jessica
  The survivor's revenge.

  A catalogue record for this book is
  available from the British Library

  ISBN 1-7505-1463-9

First published in Great Britain by Constable & Company
Ltd., 1998

Copyright © 1998 by Jessica Mann

The right of Jessica Mann to be identified as the author
of this work has been asserted by her in accordance with
the Copyright, Designs and Patents Act, 1988

Published in Large Print 1999 by arrangement with Constable
Publishers

Magna Large Print is an imprint of
Library Magna Books Ltd.
Printed and bound in Great Britain by
T.J. International Ltd., Cornwall, PL28 8RW.

For A.C.T.,
with thanks to Kate Adie and Fred Taylor
(26 April 1998)

1

1991

Nina Gillespie made herself a promise. Never again, I'll never do this again.

At the time she was crouching under a kitchen table with its owner, a woman who looked immeasurably aged but was probably no more than fifty, and beside the photographer from a weekly paper with whom Nina had scuttled into shelter when the bombardment began again. At the first familiar noise the old woman had beckoned the two strangers into her house. A sleeping baby of about nine months, its pale, damp face patterned with plasters and scratches, slumped in a battered buggy, with plaster dust settled on every sticky surface. A man in a leather coat and jeans squatted on a low chair.

Nina had only one thought, probably shared with everyone caught in the siege of Dubrovnik in that summer of 1991.

Let me out.

The noise.

The whole house, high and narrow in its ancient terrace, shuddered. A nearby building was collapsing. The roar of falling stones cascaded into their blocked ears.

The floor had recently been washed. A square of red tiles showed under the table, marked out in neat geometry by the flakes of whitewash still falling from the ceiling. Soup in an open pan on the surface above their heads was being thickened into a muddy sludge. How extraordinary that anyone could have been cleaning and cooking, Nina thought, suddenly unable to imagine a world in which such things were done.

Another shattering explosion. There were not words enough for the infernal sounds of the bombardment.

The man on the chair zipped his leather jacket and turned its collar up, as though clothes could armour him. His hand was not steady. The old woman said something and the man, staring at Nina, said in heavily accented English, 'She does not understand what is happening. This is her daughter's child, her daughter is killed, she has nobody. This is her home, she says she has lived here and her daughter too, now she can understand nothing, why this happens. Not again to go through such a thing in her life, she say.'

The old woman pulled her scarf across her face, holding it in place with dirty, shaking fingers, rocking the handlebar of the buggy with her other hand. Her dress was black, as were the cotton stockings wrinkled over skinny legs. Bloodshot eyes in lined and shadowed sockets stared upwards. Now she was speaking in a subdued monotone, in a rhythm that sounded like prayer.

Nina's shoulder bag contained the tools of a travelling reporter's trade, a notebook, a tape recorder. She rummaged to find a wadded paper tissue, which she carefully flattened out to spread over her mouth and nose. But she was still inhaling dirt, dust and smells, of sewage, bottled gas and stale cigarette smoke; and body odours—the woman's, and her guests'. We stink of fear, Nina thought. Once in El Salvador, unexpectedly under fire for the first time, her bowels, suddenly and uncontrollably, had opened. She had been literally shit-scared.

'It happens to us all, don't worry,' a veteran news reporter had assured her afterwards. Even here, even now, reminded of that instant when modesty had prevailed over terror, Nina was momentarily distracted by a hot wave of remembered embarrassment. But she was brought back to the cringing present by the whine and clatter of death overhead.

The innocent baby, orphaned, threatened —this can't be happening.

Zed, the photographer, obviously feeling the identical emotion, scooped the infant from its chair and cradled it under his chest, huddled over it as though his body could be an air-raid shelter.

Why's this child here, what am I doing here? Nina thought. Why did I ever come? It's not my war.

But then, they never were Nina's wars. Iraq, Kurdistan, Afghanistan, Belfast, Croatia, the Lebanon—she flitted from one alien crisis to the next, from guns to bombs, from roadblocks to booby traps, over bodies, through blood. Other people's blood.

Miraculously, considering the destruction and deaths she had seen, Nina had been wounded only once. It was three years ago during a riot in Jerusalem. She had paused in a shop doorway to change the cassette in her tape recorder and a stone meant for an Israeli soldier caught her on the forehead. It bled more than it hurt, but the photograph, snapped by a teacher watching prudently from behind the shutters of an upstairs window, was sold to several Western papers. The event had made Nina famous.

She fingered the scar, a tiny silvery mark under her fringe, which, in a perverse way, had been so lucky a wound.

Nina Gillespie, War Correspondent.

It sounded good too, for a while; only too soon, Nina became embarrassed by the title, finding it too self-congratulatory and vain in its implied dismissal of the suffering of civilians. Nina had come to realise that the only purpose in reporting war was to describe ordinary people in hideous situations. Babies and bombs. How could it ever have felt good to be out there in the middle of things as they were happening? But it had.

It was so important to make people understand that they shouldn't ignore what went on in the world. Nina's British listeners might be islanders, but they were not islands, none of them could ever be quite cut off from involvement. These events concern us all, she was telling them. She found the necessary images and right words to force others to share the feelings and pain that she had seen for them.

Now, hunkered here with her face on her knees, her eyes shut, her hands over her ears, Nina thought for the first time, Let this baby live, let me live, I must get out. I want out. I want to go home.

But it was not her real home, the Dockland apartment she shared with her husband, that flashed into her mind, but a vision of Dmitri's homely studio, the huge space, formerly a barn, in which brilliantly coloured constructions dangled from the rafters, where the air was aromatic with the scent of cut wood and anthracite glowed in the copper Pither stove. Nina used to sidle in there as a child to watch Dmitri work, and later on went back whenever she could, always finding welcome and advice. His bulk and calm were always comforting and the changelessness of the studio a reassurance in comparison with the restless, rootless, peripatetic life Nina took for granted with her mother. Dmitri, who never spoke of his life before arriving in Wales in 1946, where he had stayed ever since, might have lived through something like this himself, Nina realised.

She had never been chicken before. Nina was always the one of the media gang who ventured in further when the others, men and women alike, took cover or retreated. She had never fully felt her own vulnerability. Other people fell around her, their blood and guts splashed on the ground, their screams and groans filling the air, but impregnable Nina carried on with her mission—to observe and then to describe.

But this time Nina had moved from the audience on to the stage to be battered, petrified, defeated by the sound and fury. It must be because of that infant, whimpering now, as Zed rocked and crooned. What was he singing? 'Bye baby bunting, Daddy's gone a-hunting ...'

I can't take it any longer, let me out, Nina's mind screamed. She squeezed her eyes tightly closed for a little while, but the dark patterns against her eyelids seemed as threatening as the real world.

She, accustomed to being the outsider, free to look or free to leave, had become part of the nightmare, trapped, like everyone else, like that symbolic innocent,

15

that threatened infant, all together in a hell-hole.

We're here because we're here.

But that was where the difference lay. Nina had actually chosen to be here, as she had chosen to go to each of the trouble spots from which she had reported ever since her lucky break (unlucky for the local councillor who was blown to bits not thirty metres away from her) when, commissioned to report from Belfast on a city farm for pet animals, Nina had found herself reporting carnage and courage. The terrorists' bomb was a lead news story, and Nina had discovered a new specialty. Expert in belligerence and infamy, she could recognise weaponry like a soldier and describe its effects like the recording angel. Flying between continents at minimal notice, mugging up facts as she travelled from hastily assembled print-outs, she would arrive in strange countries to deliver authoritative reports within hours, on what was happening in them, to whom and why.

Nina had arrived in Dubrovnik the previous day, having been there with Carl on an Illyrian honeymoon only the year before, during the optimistic post-communist peace. When she checked into the hotel, she found herself joining a large gang of international aid workers and reporters, many of whom were old acquaintances. One, a BBC reporter always called by the single name, Roper, said, 'The vultures gather again.'

The Imperial was a degenerate Edwardian grand hotel which had been kept going under the communist regime. When Nina arrived it seemed little damaged by the current conflict. The barman pouring Italian brandy and sweet, vanilla-scented local vermouth wore a dusty dinner coat and black bow tie. A trio of elderly string players belted out the tunes of the 1930s. Nina's room was shabby and had evidently not been cleaned since the last several occupants checked out. She did not care; she could see the limpid sea and the town itself which, from above, was not the terracotta colour the posters showed, but as white and silvery grey as the bony landscape through which she had come from the airport.

No damage was visible from this angle, and there was no sound of fighting for the time being. The illusion of cultural holidays persisted.

'I'm going to take a quick look at the town,' Nina said. 'Coming, anyone?'

'Don't be ridiculous, this is a war zone,' Harry Anson snapped. If he had only kept his mouth shut Nina might have been more cautious. But Harry Anson's opposition was all it took. Harry was a member of the growing profession of itinerant international aid workers; Nina had met him several times, and taken against him on the very first occasion, about eighteen months previously, when they found themselves together somewhere in the Ukraine. It was not so much a war zone as a centre of universal unrest. Armed men leant shooting out of speeding cars while women, tightly wrapped in poppy-printed headscarves, hunched their way, under such cover as they could find, from food queue to shelter. Coming down the steps of the one-time Intourist Hotel, Nina found herself pushed to the ground by a strong arm almost before she recognised the sound of gunfire from which she was being protected. 'I can look after myself, thanks,' she snapped. Harry did not apologise. It was an automatic instinct for him to protect a woman in danger. When the shooting stopped, he

18

tried to pacify her with the country's sweet wine. He had straight sandy hair, blue, clear eyes under heavy lids, a sprinkling of freckles another woman might have found endearing, a self-confident, posh voice which commanded attention. He seemed amused by Nina, watching her mouth as she spoke, observing, noting her actions and attitudes. Nina decided he was arrogant and patronising, and he had not improved at subsequent meetings.

So Nina ignored Harry Anson's advice, and set off with Zed Lyons, the war photographer. They walked across the drawbridge where the great gate was guarded by boys in jeans and sneakers, with machine guns. Then they went past Onofrio's fountain on whose wide balustrade courting couples still sat hand in hand, and along the wide street. Weathered stains of ancient battles on the house walls were matched by patches of new, lighter-looking damage, but dark-haired men in leather bomber jackets still strolled along chatting as they had in peacetime. St Blaise's Cathedral was full of prayer and supplication while the enemy on the hillside drew breath.

Nina and Zed went into the Franciscan

monastery. The museum and treasury were locked, their doors and windows shuttered and shrouded in sheets of dirty polythene.

Zed had been here in '87, he said, with his partner, a sound recordist for The Voice of America. They had quarrelled. Yugoslavia was beautiful, he granted Nina that, nowhere more so, but the atmosphere had already been tense, with obvious aggression in the air. Those had turned out to be the last days of totalitarianism; he had recognised the hostility that everyone who had grown up under its dominion felt for the tourists flaunting their wealth and freedom. The locals, Zed remembered, had been openly jealous and full of hate. They held the West responsible for the troubles of the East. 'Actually,' Zed said, 'it hasn't changed. They still think it's our fault—mine. Yours. Collective responsibility. They're probably right. We are guilty too.'

Nina sat on a low stone parapet in the cloister, hazy sunshine warming her back, swishing her legs against the aromatic orange trees and jasmine. A flycatcher hopped from branch to branch. Last time I was here, she thought, it was with Carl.

'I can't get a grip on all this,' she said. 'It's as though there's something waiting, some much larger disaster. I have the feeling this may be the beginning of a cataclysm.'

'But this isn't Sarajevo, there are no archdukes to assassinate.'

'No, but I have a horrible presentiment about all this.'

'Are you going to say so? This is Nina Gillespie for Metromedia reporting the start of World War Three?'

Nina Gillespie said loudly, 'No,' and added sardonically, 'Goodness, Zed, how can you even suggest such a thing, whatever's happened to your faith in the peace-loving leaders of the Western world?'

'Who?' he began, but then the bombardment started again. First they heard random shots followed by shells falling in the vicinity. Together Zed and Nina ran out into the street which had suddenly emptied of people. As they paused, wondering whether to make a dash for the hotel, the old lady beckoned and shouted from her doorway. The incomprehensible language expressed a command. Take cover.

21

A familiar situation. But suddenly it was unfamiliar, because Nina had never felt as she did now, never before, never anywhere else. Not even when the pompous local politician disintegrated before her eyes, fragments of his bloody substance splashed and scattered all over her as she stood helpless.

Cowering under the old woman's table, Nina's hands trembled as she pushed the tissue in front of her nose and mouth and she thought, I've lost it. Lost my nerve. What shall I do?

'It's all right, baby, shh, shh.'

The old woman's prayer petered out. Her eyes were screwed shut in her brown, wrinkled face. She shifted to sit with her legs straight out on the ground in front of her, the checked slippers, the moment they were outside the protection of the table top, quickly covered by grey dust. Her skirt had ridden up to show pale hairy skin above the wrinkled stockings.

Another explosion, the loudest so far.

The old woman shrieked, a short, shrill ejaculation, and covered her face with her hands. Nina concentrated on those square, filthy nails, the thin gold ring, the distorted, lumpy joints.

'Daddy's got you, I'll take care of you, shh, shh.'

They were the last words Nina heard before the roof fell in.

2

Up the coast the shells sounded more like distant quarry blasting or thunder, but everyone knew what the noise was, although it was too far away to be an immediate threat. An Italian woman sobbed quietly in a corner while her husband made a pile of his glossy brochures, took out a Zippo cigarette lighter and set fire to his mini-pyre. Inspired by their example the representative of a German travel company began to fold and tear the contents of his newly obsolete information packs into narrow strips; after a while he began to plait them together. The local organiser, rousing himself from a paralysis of disappointment, went over to the bar and began to pour out whisky and gin. A man wearing the badge of a tour operator from Brussels said they might as well drink the bar dry because they knew nobody else would be coming to this resort any time soon.

'You don't look broken-hearted like the rest,' a man in jeans and a leather coat said to his neighbour. She was the director of a small travel agency, a pin-thin and needle-sharp blonde who had spent the day chain-smoking Egyptian cigarettes in a long tortoiseshell holder.

'It will mean some changes of plan,' she replied indifferently. 'What about you?'

'Oh, this isn't a disaster for me.'

She looked at him with more attention. 'Go on.'

'Conflict makes new chances for anyone who's got the nous to take them.'

'I'm interested.'

'There's good business to be done,' he said, looking at her sideways out of his almond eyes. As she held his gaze with her own sharp stare, he said deliberately, 'There will be commodities to buy and sell.'

'Such as?'

'If you're a trader, you don't care what—wherever there's a profit.'

'What about embargoes?'

24

'Like there was on alcohol into America in the twenties? Or opium in China a hundred years ago? One man's embargo is another man's opportunity.'

'Breaking the law doesn't worry you?' she asked.

'Listen, if I've got something you want, or you've got something I want, then I don't give a toss what the commodity is. Two satisfied parties and a profit. Where's the harm in doing a deal?'

She made an elegant business of putting a new cigarette in the holder, and he watched her white fingers and pearly nails as she watched him. Then she said, 'What's there to trade in a war zone, if that's what this is turning into?'

He leant forward with a light, which she sucked in with her hand holding his still. He said, 'They've got lots of things we want and we've got lots of things they need. Actually—' suddenly he sounded younger and less world-weary—'I've got some irons in the fire and I could do with a partner at the London end, as it happens. If you were thinking of a career move ...'

'We might do business together.'

25

3

1992

The Saturday of the ball, Claudia Anson had so much to get through that she set the alarm for half-past five in the morning and tiptoed past the dressing-room door so as not to disturb George. She was afraid things wouldn't go well, and nibbled absent-mindedly at her cuticles as she let the dogs out and fed them, drove to the village to fetch the morning papers, did breakfast trays for two of the wives, cleaned out and relaid three wood fires, put out the champagne and claret for dinner that evening, defrosted the Cumberland pie and cherry tarts for the shooters' lunch, filled three vacuum jugs of coffee and put crisp sausages and bacon to keep warm in the Aga, and telephoned Father Maloney to find out what tomorrow's lesson would be—the story of David and Bathsheba, from Kings 1—so as to be able to mark the right place for George, who would need to rehearse the names' pronunciation. Then she took her current volume of journal from its hiding place behind the cookery books and wrote an innocuous weather report. 'December 12, 1992, freezing, crisp, sprinkle of snow overnight.' She glanced back at the last few pages. Since it was only here she could give way to such emotions, apprehension and anxiety unbalanced the record. But in reality, she told herself, she felt them less than she wrote about them.

There was no time to write anything more personal now, though she wanted to record a visitation from the most regular of the phantom residents the evening before: the friendly shadow of some earlier Anson whose reassuring shape appeared to Claudia as it had to other residents in every generation. Claudia was sure that 'the tall lady', whose appearance was heralded by a swish of silky skirts, was one of her own forerunners, an earlier chatelaine who had loved and cared for the place as Claudia did. That was not the only ghost recorded at Ansons, but Claudia saw less of the others, one a hustling, bustling man who trotted through the reception rooms, another no more than a face seen from the corner of the eye. None was threatening or frightening. They just lived there too, welcome company for anyone who admitted their existence and could see them. George didn't and couldn't.

She heard George's door open, and was looking out at the snow, glittery on the dark yew hedge and the stone balustrade, and the starlit, still sky when he came down, a little before their guests. Claudia poured his orange juice.

'Coffee. Mouth like bottom of birdcage,' he grunted. No wonder, she thought but did not say, after a couple of bottles of claret and at least a quarter of whisky. He glanced at the headlines and buttered toast far too thickly. 'What's Mrs Potter's excuse this time?'

'Her daughter's had her varicose veins done,' Claudia said, hearing the placating tone in her own voice.

'So?'

'Joanne has to keep her feet up.'

'What's that got to do with us?'

'Mrs Potter has to look after the grandchildren.'

'Jesus wept, Claudia, I'd have thought the least you could do is keep this place going when I've got guests here, God knows

28

it's the only thing I ask of you, why you refuse to have servants ...' His grumbling was muffled in the next mouthful, but Claudia had it off by heart. She knew they could well afford to have efficient staff, but so long as the place was properly run, Claudia couldn't see why he cared who did it.

Claudia managed with relays of village ladies who were supposed to come in to help out, and mostly did. She had learnt to conform to the Ansons' way of life in most particulars but couldn't bear having resident help. Hard as she tried to lose or at least disguise her original self, she always realised that middle-class modesty still clung to her like a parasite. I'd go mad if there was always someone here watching me, she thought whenever George talked about the couples from the Philippines or Mexico his friends employed.

At least the arrangements for the dance were not Claudia's direct responsibility, except in so far as she felt responsible for everything that happened at Ansons. It was in aid of one of the good causes to which she had lent her name—a name she had been lent herself: Mrs Anson of Ansons. That name and the use of that house attracted money and goodwill; Claudia never conned herself into believing it was her own merits or abilities that brought in the invitations to join the National Art Collections Fund, the Red Cross, Macmillan Cancer Care, the Scanner Appeal, Action Aid for the Crippled Child and Claudia's latest good cause, Handyside's Bequest. Ansons was the regular scene of fundraising garden parties, Christmas bazaars, coffee mornings and bridge drives. 'Putting something back', as her mother-in-law called it, was part of the deal of being George's wife. Sometimes Claudia, clutching the bouquet she had just been handed, was lauded in speeches full of such words as 'tireless' and 'wonderful' but not all her obligations actually involved much work, and this ball was being organised by its own sub-committee, some of whose cars she had already seen coming up the back drive, as well as the florist's and caterers' vans. The sound system had been set up in the orangery the day before.

Claudia had not had a chance to talk to George since he had arrived home the previous evening with some of the house guests. One had to catch him early, before

the first snifter. Hearing footsteps on the staircase's polished boards she said quickly, 'George, you will be nice tonight, to Laurel Berryman and her boyfriend?'

'Who?'

'She's the charity's new administrator. You might take against her, she's very tough and ambitious, but—'

'Not another of those chippy ball-breaking females, you know I can't stand them.'

'Well, I suppose you might call her—good morning, Milly.'

George's sister, Milly Chandler, had never quite lost the patronising tone which had been in her voice in the first months, when Claudia was still learning how to behave. 'Morning, Claudia. God, it's cold, I hope you remembered to tell everyone about no central heating. Are you talking about the ball? I wanted to warn you about Beth Wood's mother.'

'Is that Peter's ex?' George asked. 'I saw him at Brooks's, over from Washington, he's in one of the Bush think-tanks. Tragic, really.'

'Is my bran here somewhere? Oh, got it—Peter could still make a comeback, I'd say. But listen, George,' Milly said,

31

pouring dry chippings on to yoghurt from the home farm, 'his girl Beth is Andrea's best friend, so she's coming tonight and so is Mary Ellen.'

'I met her once or twice with Peter.'

'She's changed a lot, according to Andrea, gone to a poly somewhere in East London and turned very lefty.'

'I can see it's going to be a jolly party,' George said with deep gloom. He went off to make sure everything was ready for the shoot and Milly said:

'Mary Ellen Wood was always very all or nothing, not one for taking things lightly. If she'd only ever learnt to turn a blind eye ...'

Milly looked quizzically at Claudia, who kept her features blank and bland, and said, 'Will you see that everyone's all right at breakfast? I'd better just check that everything's on track for the dance.'

Claudia crossed the courtyard to a beehive of activity in the orangery. Nobody needed her, that was clear. On the way back she met Ginny Carter carrying raffle ticket books and with a baby papoose-style on her bosom.

Claudia felt, and automatically tried to suppress, a pang of agonising, bitter jealousy. Why did this girl have a baby at last, when Claudia had empty arms? It had taken years for her to believe—never, never to accept—that she would not have her own child. If only George had been willing to compromise; but George would never co-operate in infertility investigations. Too afraid of finding he was the infertile one, Claudia's unworthy suspicion suggested, though in fact she feared she had brought it on herself. And he wouldn't even consider adopting. 'Someone else's little bastard inheriting Ansons, you cannot be serious, never let me hear the suggestion again!' Claudia would have done anything. Anything at all. For a while she'd had to keep clear of busy streets and supermarkets in case she suddenly gave way to the fierce temptation and grabbed someone else's child. Even now, when it was too late, Claudia's heart ached to have been a mother. And here was Ginny Carter, who must have suffered half a dozen miscarriages in as many years, but who was now holding her very own baby. Ginny's last pregnancy was not talked about at all to her or by her, even when it became obvious. She didn't want to tempt fate.

Claudia injected enthusiasm into her own voice. 'Ginny, how wonderful, I didn't even know you'd had it already, I'm so pleased for you. But weren't you away somewhere?'

'Yes, I've been visiting a cousin over in County Tyrone and the baby came so quickly I didn't even get to hospital!'

'My dear, how—'

'No, it was fine, my cousin used to be a nurse. So here's my wee Irish laddie. He's called Ian.'

'What a lovely baby, such gorgeous black eyes. He's not got your colouring, has he, or Tony's.'

'Tony's grandmother was very dark.'

'And isn't he a good size considering how early he must have been.'

'I know. I must have got my dates wrong.'

'You are lucky. Congratulations, my dear, I'm really thrilled for you.'

Claudia had developed a practised mechanism for burying her frustration. Back in the house she gave herself a moment to wander on her familiar path through the downstairs rooms, hiding her frivolous book—an unworthy crime novel—behind a row of leather-bound

34

Trollopes, smoothing her hand over furniture as she passed, twitching at cushions, minimally adjusting ornaments. So long as Ansons is safe and I'm safely here, she thought, then nothing else really matters.

One could, Claudia had found, throw off the outward forms and inward beliefs of the harsh religion she had been brought up in, but the attitude of mind survived. Being conscious of and enumerating her own good fortune—even if it was incomplete—was the equivalent of thanking a God she did not believe in any more. But what she worshipped now was the house she had fallen in love with at first sight, as she had with its heir.

Claudia had met George when she was eighteen, in the second year of a domestic science course at a London college. Her parents did not know that she had moved out of the students' hostel into a shared house; they did not know that she had hitched across Europe with two other girls the previous July, and spent six weeks sleeping under the stars, bathed in the scent of lavender, on the island of Korcula; they did not know that on her return home Claudia found she was pregnant.

In 'reading week' that October when the other students went home to wash their clothes and eat home cooking, Claudia had to think things out. She did not even know the surname of her baby's father, nor could she remember the unpronounceable name of his home town. Her own father would all but kill her if he knew she was pregnant. Her friends said she should have the baby. It could muck in with them in the shared house. But if she decided to have an abortion they would quite understand.

She planned to go and stay with the only relation she trusted, her great-aunt in Herefordshire, but got on the wrong bus by mistake—another of the little accidents and omissions which seemed to punctuate her life at that time—and found herself almost involuntarily tagging on to a tour of a historic house.

Ansons had few visitors so late in the season, and its only guardian was a young man in jeans who lay lounging on a deep sofa.

He looked up and smiled when Claudia came into the long gallery.

He was the personification of a romantic dream. Incredulously, she found that she seemed to be also. Claudia and George experienced the simultaneous illumination that her favourite fiction could only faintly reflect.

That was the first blessing in Claudia's enumeration, the shining, treasured memory of love at first sight, a happiness amply sufficient to blot out the trauma which followed it, of a quick, secret abortion. A decision for which God or fate had punished her.

Claudia Brown and George Anson were married the following spring in the chapel attached to a neighbouring castle, now used as a girls' school but still the place of worship for all the neighbourhood Roman Catholics. Claudia's family would not enter the chapel, which her father, a minister, called a place of idolatry and blasphemy.

They did come to the reception in Ansons. Colonel Anson conversed with Claudia's mother through monologue; always shy and used to being dominated, she did not try to interrupt as George's father described Claudia's future. 'Girl's got to learn, people like us, how we do things, cope with the place, let George alone—can't stand clinging women myself—boy's got to have his own life—no hanging round his neck, interfering, what?'

Meanwhile the hostile silence between Mrs Anson and Claudia's father was broken when she said, 'She should be a good breeder, that's one thing, good wide hips. We must be thankful for small mercies, I suppose.'

George's sister Milly Chandler patronised Claudia, who had been given Milly's daughter Andrea as bridesmaid and George's half-brother Harry as a grumpy page. Claudia had not invited any of her school or college friends, being quite simply unable to visualise them in her new environment.

Claudia and George began their married life in one of the estate cottages. They waited for babies which never came. Instead, there were disappointments and a slowly, reluctantly accepted sterility.

George, employed in the family bank, was regularly promoted. He didn't drink much, in those days. At first he commuted, but it was a long trip from Gloucestershire every day and after a while he took to spending more time in London. Claudia stayed at home. It was her period of apprenticeship. Gradually she learnt how to manage a great house; she watched the housekeeper supervise the care of the furniture, the butler clean the silver; she stored up the image of a properly laid table or the correct use of a napkin or handkerchief.

But old Mrs Anson was more interested in surfaces than what they concealed. When the time came for Claudia to take the house on she found it was in a dreadful mess. It was years before she had even looked inside every drawer and cupboard let alone tidied them out. Gradually she found treasures: ornaments and utensils once fashionable, later despised and now worth putting on display. There were bundles of discarded curtains labelled with the names of the bedsteads and windows they still fitted, the solar, the morning room, Lady Elizabeth's Parlour, Mistress Anson's Grand Bed. Claudia unwrapped clothes in fine fabrics from rustling layers of tissue paper and shook out their folds in envious delight. None was large enough for her to try on. At the back of a mahogany cabinet in one of the minor bedrooms she found, wrapped in a shrivelled, hardened, yellowed kid glove, a sapphire ring identical to that on the painted first finger of the Restoration Anson who rode into London behind Charles II and whose portrait by Lely hung in the dining room. Its square-cut stone was set in diamonds and curlicues of still-bright gold. Claudia put it on, finding that it exactly fitted her third finger, and wore it from that day on. She felt a kinship with its previous wearers and wondered whether they were included among her shadowy visitors.

Ansons' mellow stone and tiles, its impure glass and softened bricks exuded the vibrations of history. In every room, from the long gallery in which the ladies had taken their daily walks on rainy days, to the smallest larder outside the vast kitchens, one could feel the perpetual reminder of the daily lives of generations of other women. Whenever Claudia polished the ancient floors and antique furniture, or arranged flowers or stacked firewood, she was always conscious of being part of a precious continuum. When she caught sight of her own hand with the great ring on its grimy finger, she would hardly have been surprised to see it emerging from a lace cuff instead of her Guernsey sweater.

Ansons became Claudia's career, her love, her life. George, who had become a director of the bank, was happy for it to be so.

Claudia slept in a four-poster bed, high and hard, hung with Jacobean embroideries she had repaired herself. George often slept in his dressing room, so as not to disturb her when he came home late. To tell the truth—though it was one Claudia tried not to tell, even to herself—they were out of the habit of sleeping together; or even of living together. Claudia did not let herself think about it. Instead she counted her blessings, in an automatic way beginning with George himself, but more candidly continuing on to the house which was part of his identity, by inheritance, and part of Claudia's by heartfelt, passionate adoption. Pictures would flick through her mind, of the first morning sight, through a Tudor casement, of smooth lawns and pruned shrubs; walking down ancient oak stairs, across precious Persian rugs, through rooms which other people paid to see, sitting on chairs which would be roped off with twisted silk when the house opened to the public at half-past ten (but still jumping up with a guilty mien if the salaried curator caught sight of her).

For this weekend, with guests who had come down for shooting and the ball,

41

the barriers were removed, the druggets lifted from the trail the public followed, and places laid for real meals. The scene was set for use by a junior government minister, an American Supreme Court judge, one of George's associates from the bank and their wives. By Milly Chandler, her boring husband and their daughter Andrea.

Harry had promised to come himself and invite the famous Nina Gillespie, but he'd rung two days before to say he might just make the ball, but not to count on him. 'He's stuck in one of his sink so-called states somewhere in the old Soviet Union,' George reported.

Harry was ten years George's junior and very different in personality. Harry conversed where George sat silent; Harry was interested in the world and in other people, even interested in Claudia. She knew nobody else was. In George's eyes these days she hardly existed, except as a domestic convenience. With practised determination, Claudia turned her mind away. Think about Harry instead, remember how kind he'd been as a little boy when she was still putting her foot in it right and left. He'd make little signs across the dinner table—'Use the other fork' or 'Don't cut your bread, break it.' He'd come with her to see gardeners or craftsmen, easing the awkwardness. She took him to the cinema.

Harry had never conformed, and called himself the one who got away. He had a brief stint in banking after Oxford, hated it and left. Now he worked for a United Nations funding organisation which tried to inject financial expertise into formerly communist economies. From the head office in Geneva he made forays into countries known by rival names depending to which of the warring factions within them a speaker belonged.

Harry was the sort of man who had once given the British Empire a good name. A century earlier he would have been sitting under a palm tree dispensing justice to natives: real justice, without fear or favour or thinking of his decision's effect on himself. He was a man without cynicism, far too prone, Claudia had once told him, to believing in the essential perfectibility of humankind. He'd looked surprised and asked, 'Don't you?' But Claudia, child of an ostentatiously religious but fanatically puritan and repressive manse,

43

had, painfully self-taught, learnt cynicism. She believed in keeping up a good outward show and leaving motives unannounced and unexamined.

House parties at Ansons were always a good show. Or show-off, as Harry had once remarked.

Breakfast in the breakfast room. Coffee on the hoof. Lunch in 'the shooters' barn', a cosied-up hilltop shed with a view over three counties. More coffee. Tea (crumpets, fruit cake, shortbread biscuits) in the library, drinks in the long gallery, dinner, with ten extra guests, in the dining room. The kind of weekend Claudia had learnt to manage. Mrs Anson of Ansons, hostess and chatelaine. The object of envy.

4

Six months after being wounded in Dubrovnik Nina Gillespie had gone back to work at Metromedia, signed off her sick leave with the advice to start work gently. 'No bangs or pop guns. Go and cover some garden fêtes,' the doctor advised.

A rival who worked on the gossip programme and couldn't resist clever cattiness, said, 'You're like the Edwardian courtesan who married a millionaire. After the hurly-burly of the *chaise-longue*, the deep deep peace of the double bed.' *Ellen Terry*

actress

Nina, who felt her brain had turned into cotton wool, didn't get it.

'After the hurly-burly of reporting hard news you've sunk back into the peace of the features department. Isn't it a bit beneath you?' He had never hidden his jealousy of Nina's fame.

Having recovered quickly from most of her injuries, Nina retained physical and mental scars. Her hands trembled, her concentration wavered, she jumped at sudden noises. She could feel her heart beating all the time, thud thud in her chest, as distracting as a loudly ticking clock. Once she'd dived right under her desk at the sound, exactly like a shell bursting, of a filing drawer slamming. And when the camera pointed, Nina froze. In spite of the thick panstick and powder she became suffused with fear, shame and self-disgust. Even when she made a fly-on-the-wall documentary, asking disembodied questions, she had to force the words.

45

Everyone told her that the fine but jagged line running from eyebrow to jaw bone was inoffensive but she couldn't believe them.

'It'll fade,' Carl told her.

But something deep inside Nina was in mourning. 'I've always taken my looks for granted, honestly, I don't think I was vain—was I, Carl?'

'No.'

'But this feels like—like a deformity. I've never been sorry enough for people who are disfigured, it serves me right.'

Carl was brisk. But Nina observed his eyes sliding away from the left side of her face. She was damaged goods.

'I can't see anything else, like I was branded, I must be being punished, maybe I've been too detached, watching others suffering, always a dispassionate reporter, serves me right.' When she looked in a mirror the rest of her face seemed to be shrouded under a mist: what use were dark curly hair, very white skin and eyes the colour of light, clear amber, once they were so marred?

Even the gentle domestic stories she was covering defeated her. 'I can't do it. I can't!'

The company doctor's modish diagnosis

46

was 'stress' though Carl thought a phrase from an earlier war fitted her condition better; he said Nina was suffering from shell shock. Shaking all over, she would hide in the bedroom whose red walls now looked like blood instead of the imperial Chinese lacquer the decorator had matched. In that hot room, Nina crouched under the muffling feather duvet where nobody could see her disfigurement, on the pompous bed matching one in the Duke of Devonshire's palace at Chatsworth, which Carl had commissioned to mark their wedding. 'A new decade, a new way of life, a new job,' he'd said at the time, having been head-hunted by an American conglomerate, though Nina could never see much difference between life as partners and as a married couple. It was inevitable—wasn't it?—that sex would become more reassuring than thrilling, that a calmer, less uncritical affection would replace the first consuming passion. And Carl would seem surprised and mournful, as he never had been before, when there was nothing to eat in the fridge and no ironed shirts in the cupboard, even though Nina was as busy as ever herself.

Back on sick leave again, she had no excuse for squalor and indolence, but she couldn't face doing anything and could hardly bear even to see her visitors—women friends, her mother down for the day from some commune in Cumbria, Zed Lyons with Daisy, the orphaned baby he had rescued from the chaos of Dubrovnik. He was having trouble with immigration officers and the social services but so far had managed to fend off interfering authority and Daisy had become a lively, rosy, happy little girl, snatched, as Zed romantically said, from the jaws of death.

But Nina's congratulations were half-hearted at best. She had lost interest in life, zest for her job and heart for her relationship with Carl. That, at least, was mutual. Nina, no longer in the public eye, was not a trophy any more. He had loved her worldly success and fame, the glances that followed them, the image of a glamorous couple. Without all that there was nothing left. This was not the domestic, for-better-for-worse, till-death-do-us part marriage Nina had always wanted, let alone the in-sickness-and-in-health one.

So at the beginning of 1993, Nina went home to Wales. Back to square one, on which, when Nina was eight years old, her mother alighted at the travellers' camp near Cardigan. They had come from Glastonbury, and before that Stonehenge, and before that—an unknown place. 'Who knows? Who cares?' Pam Gillespie would whisper in her frail, die-away voice. 'We float with the wind, like flower seeds.'

They had drifted from tent to caravan to squat to cave; from lover to guru to friend. Nina was seven before the school attendance officer caught up with Pam. After that, wherever they went, Nina managed to get herself to school. She adored the stodgy meals, the tidiness, the cleanliness, the organisation; she loved reading and getting sums right and collecting the information for her projects and finding explanations. She was endlessly curious about other children's lives, so different from her own. What she would really really like, Nina told Pam, would be to live in a house in a street and for Pam to wear clothes like other mummies and send her off in the morning with sandwiches and crisps and an apple, and best of all, to *watch television.*

The first thing Nina would ask in a new place was where she was going to go to school. Luckily some of the children from the camp went to the local primary so all Nina had to do was tag along with them on day one, while Pam was still sleeping off the night before. She told the teacher she had come to school. That teacher was called Mrs Wartski. And Dora Wartski changed Nina Gillespie's life.

Dora and Dmitri Wartski lived in a shabby, generous house on the outskirts of Cardigan. They had no children of their own, but had fostered several, both officially through social services departments, and casually when friends had begged them to invite a problem daughter emaciated from anorexia, or an errant son who had got into bad company. There was something about Dora's invincible trust and Dmitri's peering interest which got through the hardest outside shell.

In Nina's case, it was nonconformity to which she did not want to conform. In the Wartskis' house she found the books and conversation and regular, companionable meals which, without recognising it, she had craved. When Pam Gillespie set off on her travels again Nina stayed with Dora till the end of the school year. The next summer she was invited back for the holidays. After that she went back regularly and for longer and longer visits, and at sixteen moved in with the Wartskis to go to the nearby technical college. Home, for Nina, had nothing to do with peripatetic Pam; home was a place where the background noise was the tap-tap-tapping of mallet on chisel and the whine of polisher on stone, where the rough garden was dotted with tall, inscrutable sculptures and the cream-painted walls were gaudy with the work of Dmitri's painter friends, where enchanting birds could be seen on the nearby cliffs and Dora identified them when Nina couldn't.

Dora lived long enough to see the Berlin Wall come down, having been there when it went up, working on the staff of Save the Children. She sat in front of the television screen weeping for joy, went to bed with a stomach ache and was dead within the year.

So it was with Dmitri alone that Nina took refuge after leaving Carl. Dmitri had become seedy without Dora there to nag him to bath and shave, but he was working more passionately than ever on his columns and spires of granite or slate. He didn't seem to be selling many. Nina realised that he was living on his old age pension while the rambling house crumbled about him.

There were fewer moments now when Dmitri was 'with it', and when he was, he had become much less benign than when Dora was alive. He welcomed Nina, but not uncritically, and one evening, the first she had felt able to stay up late, he grunted, 'About time you joined the real world. The trouble with your job, you're always on the outside, patronising primitive people—it's a kind of imperialism.'

Nina was dismayed, hurt, indignant. But Dmitri meant what he said.

'Western observers,' he hissed. 'Flying in from another planet like spacemen, knowing they're inherently superior to the savages they make myths about. Watching us like zoo animals.'

He's been there, Nina suddenly thought, he's been on the other side of that fence. She tried to change the subject but Dmitri growled on. 'Take the Balkans, as you Brits would say'—but he was naturalised nearly fifty years ago, she thought indignantly—'That's where you put your fantasies and adventure stories. It isn't real for you, just a place to exploit, for fun, for trivial entertainment all full of stereotypes, brigands and vampires and romantic royalty.'

Remembering her teenage delight in *Dracula* and *The Prisoner of Zenda*, Nina could not disagree.

'Well, there it is,' he grumbled. 'Just remember they aren't an alien species, the people you go and watch and never get involved with.'

His acerbic comments, which echoed the self-criticism other people had jollied her out of, perversely made Nina feel better. She had at least been wounded in an alien cause. The next day she got herself a job. During those fallow months she picked daffodils, helped in a catering business called Pixy's Pantry, drove a minicab, a badly paid and dangerous job but one that forced her to learn something about self-defence. Then, a come-down for her, a coup for it, the local radio station took her on as a reporter. It was the first step on a long road back.

5

As far as Mary Ellen Wood was concerned, the offensiveness of the evening at Ansons was happily redeemed by George Anson's behaviour, which made a highly entertaining side-show for anyone who was not personally involved. Beth Wood had insisted on her mother coming to the ball. 'Just this once, Mum, you've really got to. Mrs Chandler says you can bring your own partner.'

Mary Ellen had not spent much time with suitable partners since her marriage broke up so she invited her professor to come along instead, the man who, when she applied to study psychology because she had always thought she was interested in what made people tick, sighed and said, 'We get Brownie points for taking mature students.' Looking at Mary Ellen's long limbs under a neat blue skirt and high-buttoned blouse, a careful but misjudged choice of clothes, he added, 'And extra funding.'

Kevin Reardon was an academic whizz kid whose education had been at the comprehensive school in Sunderland where his father owned a corner shop, and Oxford. His accent, though modified, still sometimes seemed impenetrable to southerners but everything he wrote was lucid and trenchant. At first he was wary of Mary Ellen, an outsider who seemed both posh and self-confident, but she quickly changed her style, leaving off the low-key cosmetics and jewellery and throwing herself into student life as whole-heartedly as she had once performed her part as The Member's Wife.

Kevin's field of special interest was social history as revealed in fiction. He had published books on attitudes to sex, poverty and—an unexpected best-seller—royalty. The next book was to be on class distinction and mobility.

Kevin was as sharp as a Stanley knife, and a good teacher. He told Mary Ellen to lighten up.

'I feel such a fool. I can't cope.'

'Half the battle's just hard work.' He looked like a soppy, sympathetic dog, like the spaniel Mary Ellen had when Beth was small.

'You really think I can do it?'

'Sure you can. Trust me.'

'I need the qualification, it looks as though I'll be needing to earn my living sharpish.'

As part of Mary Ellen's 'clean break' settlement from Peter she had been made a member of Lloyd's of London. Members, otherwise known as 'names', underwrote insurance risks through their professional agents. They lost if too many claims were made but received as income the premiums paid by those who took out insurance.

'It sounds a bit of a gamble,' Mary Ellen had said when the system was first explained to her by Peter's accountant.

'Not at all. It's been profits all the way for years. Nominally you accept unlimited liability, liable down to your last cufflink, as they say, but in fact you're making one lot of money earn two lots of income. It's very tax advantageous. Everyone does it.'

Mary Ellen signed on at a series of ceremonies during which formally dressed men intoned ritual and incomprehensible speeches more like a marriage than anything else. Do you, Mary Ellen Wood, take this organisation, Lloyd's of London, to be yours, for better for worse, for richer for poorer ...?

She wrote her name a dozen times with a golden pen and instead of a ring was given a plastic card which was evidence of her entitlement to enter a glass and tubing building designed by Richard Rogers and have lunch in a basement called The Captain's Room. As she left beside her 'agent', she saw a row of other novices waiting with their sponsors for their induction.

Since then Lloyd's had done badly. There had been losses. When Mary Ellen rang her agent his voice was soothing. Win some, lose some, next year you'll be coining it. Meanwhile there were claims to meet: air crashes, oil spills, hurricanes, asbestosis, catastrophe years. The explanations were plausible and always twinned with encouragement about the up-turns and bonanzas to come. So Mary Ellen wrote cheque after cheque to Lloyd's. She moved to a smaller flat when Beth and Andrea Chandler took a flatshare in Notting Hill, handy for the crammer in South Kensington where they were supposed to be retaking failed exams. In fact both girls slept until lunch time and stayed out all night. They went to cocktail parties and dances, watched rowing, racing and tennis, bought clothes and were prettified. Mary Ellen was surplus to requirements, except for the Ansons ball. Beth had nagged and eventually wept. 'It would look so awful if my mother's not there.'

So Mary Ellen put on a dress left over from her previous incarnation and took Professor Reardon, who said it would be useful field-work for the new book.

The dance was preceded by dinner in a scarlet dining room painted with *trompe-l'oeil* grottoes. Mary Ellen was placed beside a boy whose parents had lived in the constituency. He was a bond dealer in the City now, earning a huge amount of money and, according to Beth, hooked on cocaine. 'Lots of them are, Mummy, they can't keep up the pace without it. Do you know what, soon their noses collapse, like lepers or something, isn't that the yuckiest thing you ever heard?'

When the smoked salmon mousse was replaced by boned and stuffed quail, her neighbour turned to Mary Ellen. She talked to him about student politics and compulsory union membership. He looked at her as though she were mad and told her about his new wheels (a Porsche), his new flat (in Chelsea), his next holiday (in Martinique) and the size of his last bonus. He was riding high. They all were. This dinner alone probably cost the Ansons more than Kevin Reardon earned in a month; enough to fund half a dozen students through college. Only three years earlier, when she was still married to Peter, Mary Ellen would have taken it for granted, but having dropped right out of this particular world she felt like a visitor from another planet.

She could see Kevin Reardon making mental notes: uniformed staff—though Mary Ellen knew, from former experience, that they were hired from a catering company for the evening—gilt and silver, exotic flowers and precious porcelain, and women who had got family jewels out of family safe deposits, flaunting wealth that ten years earlier, in Mary Ellen's hearing, they had strenuously denied owning. Milly Chandler was already tipsy, making a sexual come-on—surely, Mary Ellen thought incredulously, not to common Kevin?—of raising her golden goblet, its outside beaded with condensation, her arm stick-thin, smooth and brown, but with a hand which was pitiably immune to plastic surgery.

Harry Anson arrived late, bringing with him the frisson of fame. He had become well known as a television authority on Third World problems, always on the news. He was smaller and less gingery than he looked on the screen, though still a burly, wide-shouldered man whose light eyes met others' in a ready, confident gaze. His cheek met his sister Milly's before he hugged and kissed Claudia. 'Nina couldn't make it,' he said.

'Nina Gillespie,' Milly said to anyone listening. 'The TV lady.'

'Is she still around? I don't seem to have seen her on television for a long time,' George remarked.

'Don't you love the way her voice swoops up and down, always so enthusiastic,' Milly said.

'Lost her looks, I heard,' shouted the Ansons' only surviving great-aunt, now in her nineties, who had dressed herself up in maroon velvet and staggering diamonds. She was sitting beside Kevin Reardon nodding her head up and down, thin hair and pink scalp gleaming through a bejewelled net, and went back to telling him about her own time as a débutante when she had danced with Edward Prince of Wales. 'I never thought to see all this in my lifetime again. Who would have thought I'd live to see this day.'

'You and Nina Gillespie must be such friends, Uncle Harry,' Andrea said sentimentally. 'You saved her life.'

'Actually I don't know her at all well,' Harry said shortly.

'But Mum said you were going out with her, she saw you at—'

'Well, I'm not,' he interrupted. 'Your mother asked me to bring her, that's all, and she can't come because she's tied up with a legal case.'

'Is that the one against Zed Lyons?' Kevin Reardon asked.

'That's what she said. He's charged with assisting in illegal immigration and the child's been made a ward of court.'

'Shocking case,' Kevin said. 'A bad law and inhuman officialdom, always a disastrous combination.'

'I do so agree,' Mary Ellen said, backing up her mentor. 'He was right on, saving that baby, it wasn't a crime.'

'But the law says it was,' Harry told her.

'Whether it would have been invoked if he wasn't gay is another matter, of course.'

After dinner they put on furs and wraps to walk across the lantern-lit courtyard to a ballroom hung with swags of aquamarine silk. Tables round the dance floor were garlanded with unseasonal white roses. There was a band and a disco, and more meals, supper and breakfast, as well as a running buffet. Expensive prizes had been given for the tombola. Winners might get a holiday for two in Bali or a box at the Royal Opera House.

In an obscure corner under a blown-up logo of Handyside's Charitable Bequest, a dowdy woman sat by a display of photographs showing events in Yugoslavia. There was the bombardment of Dubrovnik, its fountain hidden behind protective planks and sheets of iron, and (perhaps chosen with forethought, to hang here in his family's home) the famous, dramatic picture of Harry Anson carrying the unconscious Nina Gillespie out of the devastated town. There was Zed Lyons' own photo of the orphaned baby who had become the rope in a tug of war between him and the authorities. Underneath was a newspaper cutting. Zed had told a press conference that he lived in dread of her being taken into care. 'We're family now, me and Daisy. She hasn't got anyone else.'

The last set of pictures showed the fate from which Daisy had been rescued: she had escaped becoming one of the maimed and hungry children for whom funds were being raised. As the revellers passed most averted their eyes. 'That's really gross,' one girl said, and her friend agreed.

'They shouldn't put that sort of thing here, it spoils everything.' There was a collecting bowl on the table containing some small denomination coins.

Mary Ellen stood watching with a sociologist's or even an anthropologist's dispassion. She thought how much she would rather be in her flat writing her essay and felt no twinge of envy or memory, as though her own time of being part of this other world had never occurred. 'Roll on the revolution,' she said to Kevin, but he wanted to dance. Later, passing Mary Ellen on his way to the buffet, he said cheerfully, 'I love it.'

'It's disgusting. Over the top.'

'Don't worry, it won't last, retribution always strikes in the last chapter. Any minute now somebody will be ruined by a financial scam. The South Sea Bubble or the Wall Street Crash.'

Kevin flung himself about to the music, eating, drinking, once or twice making a surreptitious entry in a small notebook.

Speeches were made. First Milly Chandler, the chairman of the ball committee, thanked George and Claudia for the hospitality of Ansons, and referred to her own childhood games played in this very room. She presented the charity's administrator, Laurel Berryman, a pretty woman with a tower of golden curls above pink and white skin and a black velvet dress; she looked rather like the Gainsborough portrait of one of George's ancestors. While Laurel made a quick, crisp speech about Handyside's day-to-day work, Claudia remembered her first sight of Laurel, at the job interviews for the charity's first full-time director. She'd already impressed the interview panel with her looks and good sense. Then, asked on whose side she would be, she'd made a statement. 'That's exactly what caused all the troubles in the first place, defining people by races, groups, sub-groups, religions, sects. Turning them into Jews or Aryans, black or white, Muslim or Orthodox. I'm going to get food and medicines to human beings who need them. No more, no less.' Everyone on the interviewing panel had applauded and soon afterwards Claudia had gone out to the waiting room to bring Laurel back and offer her the job; she'd never regretted the choice, for Laurel was devoted and efficient. Claudia was rather frightened of her and tended to do what she said, knowing it was bound to be right.

Milly presented Jake Konin, one of the charity's workers, and her half-brother Harry who had organised vital support for the survivors.

The charity's patron spoke. She was a Montenegran by birth who had first come to England as the daughter of a Yugoslav diplomat, become a film starlet and married a racing driver who was later transmogrified into a television personality. Her accent was not good, considering she had lived in London for twenty years, and when, as on that evening, she was agitated, it became even more difficult to understand her.

So many women raped, children starving, men, women and children killed, tortured, suffering. She'd been there. She saw it, she saw and spoke to the people it happened to.

Her audience was sympathetic but impatient. Not an evening went by without everyone seeing televised scenes of real horror which, if they were fiction, would be censored from family viewing.

Claudia Anson stood by, hardly listening. Her mind was on smaller anxieties. Was her dress all right? It was a flowered taffeta from Harrods' designer room, but Claudia feared it needed a less insignificant-looking wearer than she was, a taller and thinner woman, who could do justice to the Anson rubies and whose mousy hair did not keep escaping from its jewelled clips. Someone had broken one of the irreplaceable plates in the early Derby dinner service. Andrea Chandler was stoned. The lavatory in one of the guests' bathrooms was blocked. More snow was forecast; what would she do if the ball guests couldn't get away?

And then, George. Could he be relied on not to pass out? At least he'd been really nice to Laurel Berryman, expanding with pride as she gushed about the glory of Ansons: what a wonderful house for a party, and how marvellous it must be to live surrounded by all this heritage.

'The West must do something, we've got armies haven't we, all we haven't got is the will. We should go in, just send the troops and stop it all, that this should be happening in Europe fifty years after the war, it's perfectly unbelievable ...'

Milly Chandler said there were collecting bowls coming round. A bevy of pretty girls, Beth Wood and Andrea Chandler among them, sidled between the tables, with beribboned baskets.

Introductions.

Beth, by Claudia, to Jake. Mary Ellen, by a gooey-eyed Beth, to Jake, who greeted her in the kind of accent her student friends used, a glint of plebeian camaraderie in his black eyes. We're both playing a part, his expression implied. Jake had a very dark European complexion, and a startling white streak against his liquorice black hair. He looked gorgeous, Beth's mother thought, but dangerous, and she was relieved when Laurel Berryman came up behind him, and ignoring Mary Ellen put her hand familiarly on the back of his neck, and slid it round to a ballroom dancing position on his shoulder. 'My turn,' she said. Closely embraced, they danced away.

Beth went off with the corners of her mouth turned down.

Later Claudia saw George go up to Laurel and, by now more than slightly drunk, kiss her hand, goggle at her uplifted bosom and sweep her away from her table, back on to the dance floor.

About midnight, when she was sitting alone behind a pillar, Mary Ellen heard Ralph Chandler on the other side of it introducing Kevin to a duke. They conversed knowledgeably about soul music.

Milly, temporarily sobered with coffee but holding a tumbler of whisky, apologised to Claudia for foisting poor Mary Ellen Wood on the party. 'She's an awful warning, isn't she, what happens to women who lose their *raison d'être.*'

'She doesn't look too bad.'

'In some filthy poly with yobbos and druggies and dragging herself down to their level.' Milly took a large swig of her drink, swayed a little, and stepped back to lean for a moment against the wall. 'She even said she's a socialist now. What's my brother doing with Laurel Berryman?'

'Harry?'

'No look, George.' George, red-faced

and sweating, was holding Laurel in a night-club shuffle, his mouth pressed on to her white, bare neck. Milly announced, 'He's all over her. I must say I wouldn't have thought she was his type, he usually goes for bimbos.'

'I wouldn't know,' Claudia said.

'Quite right, very wishe ... wise, see no evil, hear no—'

'Excuse me, Milly. I'll see you later.'

Mary Ellen set off on what must have been her tenth or twelfth circuit of the ballroom. Standing by the photograph display, she said, 'Do you get asked much about the charity at this sort of do?'

'I don't think people want to be reminded, not when they are having a good time.'

Mary Ellen watched two couples, one young, one old, walk past with averted eyes. 'No, they don't seem to,' she agreed.

Suddenly aggressive, the other woman said, 'Well, do you?'

Mary Ellen looked at the all-too-familiar images of emaciated children, bandaged limbs and crutches, skeletal grins. 'But it's what it's all about.'

'Look, we're all the same. We might read

about what's going on over there, we see the pictures of bombing or concentration camps or people who have been wounded or mutilated. Maybe we'll say it's awful and send off some money. And then we forget all about it. That's human nature.'

'But you're doing something.'

'I'm not achieving any more than you did when you handed over some cash for expensive ball tickets. It buys the same food or blankets as the money I collect. Money salves all our consciences, that's all. It's a long way away, we didn't make those people hate each other, we didn't arm the war-lords.' Her voice was thin and derisive, its accent tight. In her dowdy incongruity she was like the skeleton at a feast, the reminder of death and judgement.

George Anson lurched round a pillar towards them, half dragging, half leaning on Laurel Berryman. His puffy face was wet and red, the front of his shirt stained with wine. Laurel's laugh tinkled as she whispered into his ear. Then, visibly reverting to professional mode, she said, 'Yvonne, I don't think you met our kind host. George, Yvonne Day's one of our most devoted supporters, she works so hard—'

70

'Whatever turns you on.' Like many experienced drunkards, he spoke with exaggerated clarity.

'Turns me on?' The woman seemed bewildered.

'Get your kicks out of good works. Ever so virtuous. Like my sainted bloody wife.' His voice had risen, so that others had turned their heads and were watching the exchange. 'Tell you what,' he roared, 'it's all a con, a con trick, swindle—what's the good, eh? Eh? What's it for?'

'George ...' Laurel maintained a social smile, but her hand, on George's arm, was white-knuckled.

'Is it my fault if wogs and niggers kill each other? Abroad. Abroad's bloody and foreigners are fiends, s'what my old father always said.' He waved his hand at the fascinated audience. 'Bet you lot agree, only too mealy-moushed—mouthed—too mealy shay it.' George Anson made a gesture taking in the pitiful pictures, the pathetic bowl of cash. Claudia Anson was nowhere to be seen—knows better than to tangle with a husband who's sloshed, Mary Ellen thought—but Harry was pushing his way towards his brother. 'I ask you,' George hissed. 'All this compassion, everyone oh so sympathetic. They're all savages. Barbarans. Barba—what's the world, barbarians. Killing each other. What's it got to do with me?'

6

1995

Nina's interview was nearly finished when her attention was distracted. What was that woman doing? Someone had left the remains of tea on a table, with the money to pay for it. A tired woman with cheeks a greyish shade of pale and faded sandy hair, wearing slightly old-fashioned, though once-expensive clothes, slid on to one low chair, quickly draped her coat and bag over another, and in the same, smooth movement scooped all the coins off the bill and into her pocket. She poured tea into the used cup, adding milk and three spoonfuls of sugar, and lifted the cup to her mouth.

Nina felt an obscure discomfort, a rush of hot shame or regret, without quite knowing why. This woman was associated with something uncomfortable in Nina's mind, as though some trespass, never redeemed, was on her conscience.

The waiter came past with his pad and pencil without seeming to notice that the pale woman was not the original occupier of the table. The lounge was full of people coming and going, as always at these railway hotels, so no foreign, overworked temp was ever going to distinguish between the numerous respectably dressed middle-aged ladies who ordered tea and cakes.

Nina dragged her attention back to the business in hand, to her subject. Her target? Victim? Quarry?

'I'll do anything,' she said. 'Anything it takes.'

His eyes rested on her face, cleverly paled, on her shaking, tightly clasped hands and the narrow white-gold wedding ring.

'You're my last hope. Can you help me?' she pleaded.

Strangers hardly ever recognised Nina any more. Media fame is brief and transitory, and it was three years since she had last appeared on television, four years since she was wounded in Dubrovnik. As for her voice—it was probably distinctive enough to anyone who listened to talk radio though it seemed pretty unlikely that this man ever listened. All the same Nina had unearthed a checked skirt and Barbour, instead of wearing her usual black trouser suit and white shirt, and she had switched into the broad rustic burr of her childhood; she was calling herself by a friend's name, Polly Lowther, and using the details of her life as a teacher, a wife and a victim of fertility treatment at three different clinics.

This man, who had introduced himself as Cliff Jones, was the last in Nina's chain of informants. He looked clever. He looked, she suddenly thought, dangerous. But he could have no idea that she was not what she purported to be, a woman desperate for a child, so desperate that she would break the law and brave any risk.

After a long pause he said, 'You know the fee.'

'Twenty thousand pounds.'

'In cash. Sight unseen.'

'Yes.'

'Course, I'm not a cowboy like some others in the business I could mention.'

'Others?'

'Nah, you don't want to know about

them, you struck lucky, finding us. We'll
do all right by you. And you won't have
trouble with the law neither, not like that
photographer bloke.'

He meant Zed Lyons. His appeals had
gone all the way to the House of Lords,
but unsuccessfully. Daisy had been taken
into care and placed with a foster family
and now the social services department
of his local council had offered her for
adoption—but not by a single, gay man
called Zed, no matter how loving and
caring he might be.

'That was awful,' Nina said.

'Yeah, well, stick with me and you won't
ever see no social worker at all.'

'I can't tell you how grateful I am,'
Nina said, clasping her hands emotionally
together.

'There's no going back, you know that.'

'As if I'd want to.'

'For better or for worse.'

She gazed into his eyes. 'I am counting
the days,' she said.

'And you'll keep quiet.'

'Not a word to anyone, I swear it.'

'You'd better mean it. 'Cos otherwise ...'
He didn't finish the sentence, but it was
an open threat. Nina lowered her eyelids,

submissively acquiescent.

There was another silence. Then he said, 'Well, that's that then. I've got your number.'

And I, Nina thought triumphantly, have got yours: your words on tape. Your offer to sell me a living human being.

For a moment she sat remembering the unseen man who had put her on to this story. Call me Bill, he'd said, but it wasn't his name. We've got a right one here, the studio manager whispered through the headphones, her thumb making a sign of triumph.

Bill wanted to talk about his wife. Bronwen. That was her real name, Bronwen, he'd added. About Bronwen and their baby. You remember, Nina, you were talking about adopting babies last time I listened in. And saying people of my age were too old, we hadn't a hope. Well, we knew that, me and Bron, by that time. It took so long. She'd had our first—stillborn—and then she lost another and then they said she had to have a hysterectomy. Desperate, she was. Suicidal, really, Bill whispered. Past it for adopting, nobody would look at you if you were over thirty-five. Everyone we knew breeding like rabbits, and rubbing salt in as hard as they could, moan moan about how tired they were, and tied down. They asked us to baby-sit.

So they leapt at it when someone suggested another solution; really leapt at it, Bill and Bron did. Wouldn't you have? He was a benefactor. Our fixer, doing good by stealth.

Take a child with nothing, hungry, uncared for, a kid without a future, and give it a happy life and a good home. Illegal, chancy—yeah yeah, so what. A *baby*.

A baby, it turned out, that would stay babyish. Not just 'learning difficulties'. No politically correct words for its state. To be blunt, it was congenital idiocy, an IQ too low to measure, plus a list of physical ailments that began with Aids and went down the medical dictionary to syphilis. Inherited, inevitable, recognisable illnesses.

Trace the number, Nina scribbled and underlined it and held the paper up to the window.

'They knew,' Bill said bitterly. 'They knew all right. Didn't care, though. Got us over to Strabane for the handover and just landed us with—that. Took the money and ran.'

No going back, Cliff Jones had said.

Last Christmas Bronwen had delivered the two-year-old to a residential home, fixed the vacuum cleaner's hosepipe to the Volvo's exhaust and breathed in the fumes until she was dead.

And Bill wanted revenge. 'You get them, Nina. Expose them. Blow them out of the water.' And then he'd added as an afterthought, 'But take care. These are not nice people. They aren't doing this out of kindness. I wouldn't want you to get hurt.'

Through the window the producer could be seen clenching his fists in the air. Bill's bad time made great broadcasting. Sad, but great. And one with a follow-on story. Now for Nina to investigate.

Nina sat unmoving as the man calling himself Cliff Jones strode out of the room. Polly Lowther lived near Bristol, a train journey home from Paddington. It was important to play out the legend because they were surely watching. The hotel lounge was crowded, some people on their way home after a long day, others who'd arrived too early for a night out on the town. Somebody would be there to check on her, she thought, wondering who it was. That man in pin-stripes who had been taking such a long time over the *Times* crossword puzzle? The young Asian businesswoman with her palm-top computer? The two women who were showing each other their purchases, Christmas presents for all the family?

It was surely not the tired woman, who was now slowly and luxuriously eating the rock bun, buttered scone and small iced sponge that had been left on someone else's plate. Nina watched closely as the woman savoured their freshness and sweetness, and asked, the next time one of the waiters came within earshot, for some more hot water.

At a table to the right a mumsy woman was being interviewed for a job. No, not a job, for voluntary work. She had apparently applied to drive a vanload of relief supplies across Europe.

'Unpaid, I'm afraid.'

'Oh, of course. Good works. I quite understand.'

There were two interviewers. One was taking notes, a well-maintained woman with an expensive colour and cut job on

79

her mid-brown hair and a conventionally flowered silk suit. She came in the category of 'must have been pretty once', with the small snub features and time-expired look of innocence which probably made her the belle of the A level year. But that look of unsophisticated girlishness never wore well. She was with a man who was tall, painfully thin, with a large Adam's apple and rough, red hands with which he fiddled with himself almost continuously, stroking or twitching his hair, running the little fingernail around his ear, adjusting his woven tie, rubbing his palms up and down the rough tweed of his suit, retying the laces on his desert boots. 'It can be dangerous in former Yugoslavia,' he said.

'Dangerous?' The applicant was a country woman, up in town for the day in her tartan skirt and waxed waterproof jacket, surrounded by shopping. On the table she had a list in large, round handwriting, with pencil ticks. Curtain fabric Peter Jones, Laura Ashley, party frock.

'Not much law and order out there, you know,' the man told her.

He's putting it mildly, Nina thought, unconsciously fingering her cheek. More journalists and aid workers had been killed in that Balkan maelstrom than ever before in any one of the world's trouble spots. And the death toll, or roll of honour, was lengthening by the week.

The woman said, 'But I'd heard … when I asked at the charity shop they said …'

'You didn't speak to the administrator?'

'Who …?'

'Mrs Berryman. Laurel Berryman. She usually has a word …' the man said.

'No, it was someone else. I'd have recognised her voice, she's on television, isn't she, I didn't realise …'

'Nobody with young dependants, they are supposed to say. You should have been warned.'

'No, they never told me that. I didn't know. If that's the position …' She began to gather the carrier bags together. 'I'm very sorry but in that case … I think I've made a mistake.'

'It's all right. We understand. People need to be keen.'

The applicant gathered up her packages and went off down the long corridor to the mainline station.

Her interviewer and his companion looked at each other and shrugged. She said, 'Well, Dennis, thanks for all you've done today.'

'I suppose we might have guessed she wouldn't do, when she said she could only fit in seeing us here before her train home.'

'I know, we've got to have people who will put themselves out. They need to know things can get tough. I couldn't do the job, I'd be terrified. I do admire them.'

'Are you catching a train here too?' the man called Dennis asked.

'Yes, the five thirty-five. Don't wait though.'

'Well, if you don't mind ...'

'Not a bit. See you at the next committee meeting. Waiter! I'd like some more tea, please.'

The tired woman, the cuckoo in the nest woman, was reading her predecessor's original bill with careful attention. She put some of the coins back on the table and waited for the change. The interviewer had been watching too, her mouth agape. Now she pushed her chair back and walked across to the other table, saying, 'Mary Ellen, is it really you?'

Mary Ellen, Nina thought. That's who she is. Mary Ellen Wood.

Suddenly transported back to the 1980s and her very first assignment as a news reporter, Nina for an instant felt herself to be again in the crowd of ravening newshounds as they surrounded Peter and Mary Ellen Wood. She remembered how the thrill of the chase drowned any pity for the hunted creature that Mary Ellen had suddenly become, how an ordinary stranger had been transformed into Nina's raw material. It was the first, but not the only episode of its kind during that period when Nina was working her way up in a competitive profession, and the memory of them all was uncomfortable.

'Will you be getting a divorce?'

'Mrs Wood, did you already know about it?'

'Are you going to stand by him?'

'How did you feel when you saw the photo?'

'Can you forgive him?'

'Mr Wood, will this make a difference at the next election?'

'Peter, what did the Prime Minister say when he found out?'

'Are you going to resign?'

'Do you still love him?'

'Hey, Mary Ellen, look this way a minute.'

'Hold his hand, Mary Ellen, look up at him.'

'Smile.'

Mary Ellen Wood looked straight at her questioners, met their eyes, smiled at the millions of people who were her audience.

She smiled towards Nina Gillespie, who saw exactly what the hastily convened damage-limitation experts had arranged for her and the rest of the world to see. Peter Wood's arm was like an iron bar placed diagonally across his wife's back, his hand, firmly on her hip, holding her in place. There he was, the strong man of the party, a man of destiny, tall, muscular, aquiline, with black straight hair flopping down over his forehead; clear blue eyes, regular white teeth. A dish. A pin-up. You simply couldn't blame a man who looked like that for straying from so mousy and insignificant a wife: a tall, plump, soft-skinned woman with bushy hair once presumably red and now artfully apricot, triangles of blusher standing out against her cheeks, unphotogenically small eyes and an old-fashioned rosebud mouth. She was dressed in suitable blue.

She looked terrified. Had she been cowed into submission by the bully at her side? Was she dazed by the sudden exposure of his unfaithfulness? Was she baffled by this change from previous public appearances, all, invariably, triumphant?

The Woods had displayed themselves together before many crowds since the first time Peter stood for Parliament and was triumphantly elected at a by-election in 1975.

The bride, the newly elected Member's wife, the Minister's wife, the Secretary of State's. Proud but modest, she always deflected attention on to the man at her side. Now she was the centre of attention herself.

As she jostled and craned with the reporters who had lain in wait outside the Woods' London flat that freezing afternoon, Nina Gillespie had thought, The woman might as well be in the stocks and all these people throwing rotten eggs. Or stand in for the old wooden Aunt Sally at the midsummer feast on the recreation ground. The schoolchildren always threw mud at it.

At the time, Mary Ellen Wood represented no more than the raw material of Nina's chosen career: a good story for one of her first outside assignments. Nina had no sympathy to spare for a woman of privilege. Mary Ellen knew nothing about pulling oneself up by the bootstraps from the bottom of a heap, and turning from an office junior into a professional reporter who'd taught herself to speak an octave lower and in a different accent. For the first time Nina had a chance at a story that could be really called a story, because a flu epidemic had decimated the reporting staff.

The news had broken that morning in a tabloid, and was quickly copied for later editions by all the other media. The Right Honourable Peter Wood MP had been pictured in bed with Rosalba Suarez, a Brazilian transvestite. He, she or—as some reporters said—it looked like a buxom woman but was said to be still, or before surgery to have been, male, and a prostitute most recently and most notoriously seen in company with the Maltese owner of a West End casino and an Italian racing driver.

The photograph and the accompanying

quotations from Rosalba left no doubts and few secrets. Another juicy scandal. Nina, desperate to do well, had speed-read her way through a cuttings file. Mary Ellen Wood was a prize-giver, fête-opener, canvasser at elections, taker of telephone messages; a home-maker, housekeeper, carer or caretaker. Mrs Wood's life had been measured out in job descriptions.

All these years on, Mary Ellen Wood, who had separated from her husband within a month of that day of revelation, was wolfing down the cakes left on someone else's plate.

The other woman had plumped herself down on the chair facing her. 'Mary Ellen, don't you remember me? It's Claudia Anson.'

God, Nina thought, that's Harry's posh relative. The wife. Nina had heard the gossip about the husband and listened to it because of Harry. The story was circulating in what was no longer Fleet Street: journalist's tattle, waiting for some evidence to print it with. Claudia's husband, Harry's boozy brother George, having a walk-out with some dazzling career woman, mumsy mousy wife left behind in the country.

'Yes. Hallo, Claudia.'

'I haven't seen you since that ball at Ansons, it must be ...'

'Three years.'

'Weren't you a mature student? Have you finished the course? English, wasn't it?'

'I had to give it up. I never qualified for a grant, you know,' Mary Ellen Wood obscurely explained.

'So what have you been doing, are you ...' Claudia lowered her voice. 'Are you all right?'

'I get by.'

'But surely Peter ...'

Peter Wood, Nina knew, had been forced to give up his political career, and had actually been pictured drawing the dole. Hadn't he gone to America for a while after that? But now she'd heard he was touting himself round the television companies hoping to get a chat-show.

'What about Peter?' Mary Ellen sounded hostile and distant.

'Well, my dear, surely he didn't leave you completely ...'

'Destitute?'

'Well, has he?' Claudia demanded.

'He provided for me when we were

divorced. He made me a member of Lloyd's.'

'Oh my dear, what a disaster. Are you badly hit?'

'Ruined, actually.'

'And doesn't Peter ... no. No, I can see he wouldn't.'

Watching Claudia Anson take this in, Nina saw her face perceptibly pale, her lips and hands quiver. She looked terrified. Why? Was it the sudden warning, 'there but for the grace of God go I'?

The effort of pulling herself together was like an acting lesson, the clenched fists, the deep breath, the unconscious settling of the shoulders. Then Claudia leant across the table and put her hand on Mary Ellen's dry, worn skin. 'I tell you what, I'm really pleased to see you, I'll take the next train so we can have a snack together before I go. Waiter!'

'I don't need your charity,' Mary Ellen Wood snapped. Nina realised that this woman, destitute and outcast, seemed far more self-confident and 'together' than the pillar of society that Claudia Anson must be.

'Actually I'm starving too, it's been an exhausting day. We've been trying to find

89

drivers to go out with the convoys. You know, it's Handyside's Bequest, the one we had the ball for. Ah, waiter, we'll have—would toasted sandwiches suit you, Mary Ellen? Several toasted sandwiches, and I'll have a scotch and soda, and my friend would like ...'

'A glass of red wine would be—'

'A bottle of red wine. And some—oh, nuts, crisps, that sort of thing. Thank you so much. I must say, I could do with a drink. Now, Mary Ellen, do tell me, how's your Beth?'

'She's fine, though we don't manage to see each other very often. She married a Spaniard in the first year at college and they moved to live in Chile. On a ranch.'

'You must really miss her.'

'Yes.'

'Goodness, I do admire you. How d'you manage, all on your own?' Claudia Anson asked with, Nina thought, real wonder in her voice.

'I get by. You could say I beg, borrow and steal, I've become remarkably resourceful.'

'But it must be so difficult to lose your place in the world. And having to be so self-reliant, too—I simply couldn't.'

'A lot has to go,' Mary Ellen explained, chewing as she spoke. 'Inhibitions, hesitations, guilt, bad conscience—I don't have anyone else to worry about, you see, it doesn't matter what anyone else thinks any more. I used to be terribly worried about doing the right thing but now I don't have to explain things or justify myself—it's OK, actually.'

'Well then!' Claudia Anson clapped her hands together. 'I've had a brilliant idea. You can drive, can't you?'

'Of course.'

'So you can go with one of our convoys. You're exactly what we need, a sensible person, not too young or old, someone responsible—you'd be perfect. It's only a couple of weeks, all found, don't worry about money, the charity covers all the expenses so you don't lose anything by it, and it's such good work, so valuable.'

'Are you going, Claudia?'

'Oh no, I'm afraid I can't possibly. Of course I would if I could, but it's difficult to get even a day away from Ansons. I do try to help as much as I can with the work but there are limits. I sometimes feel as though the whole place would collapse if

I wasn't there.' It was, Nina realised, said in a tone of pleasure, almost of love. 'No,' Mrs Anson affirmed complacently, 'there's no way I could ever manage it. Look, Mary Ellen, let me give you all the information, I've got a folder here, you can read it in your own time.'

Mary Ellen Wood looked dowdy, her body flabby, her face puffy, like a different order of being from the carefully maintained Mrs Anson. Mary Ellen was wearing a respectable but indefinably time-expired suit and her shoes were scuffed, a rig, presumably, left over from the now quite distant period when she had been The Member's Wife.

When the waiter brought the food Claudia had ordered, Mary Ellen grabbed and bit into the toast and oozing cheese as though it was the first hot food she had seen for months.

Nina watched her with painful compunction. That's what the media achieved, she thought. She had never before thought of herself as a force that changed lives, let alone a destroyer, but now she wondered, Is it my fault? Did I do that? And then she wondered whether one of her colleagues might do the same thing to

Claudia Anson, make her feel driven to leave the husband whose infidelity she could ignore so long as it wasn't talked about.

What went on in Claudia and George's marriage? One could never tell from the outside. Nina suspected that Harry didn't like his brother much, and she wondered what he felt about Claudia. He hadn't mentioned her to Nina since they met again when she came back to London and they'd embarked on a cautious, noncommittal progress towards—she was not sure towards what. A friendship? A relationship? A love affair? She'd been in Harry Anson's company not much more than a dozen times, and that included their first, inimical meeting all those years ago and the uncomfortable public handshake when Nina, in the presence of numerous cameras, thanked him for saving her life. A few drinks and dinners on, Harry Anson was still a private idea in her mind, one she avoided visualising too clearly for fear of pricking a bubble. He was usually abroad. The possible, tentative, uncertain future seemed like a special goody to be saved up for later. There'd be time.

7

Claudia always intended to read the committee papers thoroughly and well in advance. They would arrive in their large recycled envelope, stacks of neatly word-processed information, with figures galore and arranged in bold or capitals, upper case, lower case or Roman numerals, bullet points, brackets, paragraphs, clauses and sub-clauses; the passive mood, the third person, the reported speech all as formal as if it were Hansard, and no matter how determined her attention or good her intentions, Claudia inevitably found her eyes glazing over and her mind distracted. She'd highlight a phrase here or a section there, never remembering later what she'd meant by it; and when it came to chairing the meeting, she felt like someone groping her way through a dark thicket. The director would do it much better, Claudia suggested, but Laurel insisted in her clear, self-assured voice, 'No no, the chair must take the chair, it goes without saying.'

This time Claudia had meant to read the documents on the train journey to London. She opened the first page: 'Your attendance is requested at the seventeenth meeting of the Executive Committee of Handyside's Bequest, 21 November 1995 at 11.00.' Her eyes wandered to the *Argus*, and a profile of Laurel Berryman. The accompanying picture was a three-quarter face portrait. Laurel looked beautiful, an archetypal English rose, standing by the open doors of a fully loaded Handyside's lorry. Her fair hair was tied back in a black velvet bow, she had small pearl drop ear-rings and was wearing a businesslike pin-striped trouser suit buttoned over a low-necked lacy vest. The momentary pride in knowing someone who was the subject of a newspaper profile had been followed by the fear of what it would say.

But Laurel had managed to be discreet, even with an interviewer who was known as one of Canary Wharf's piranhas. Mercifully she'd refrained from biting too hard on someone whose celebrity had been won in so worthy a cause. Laurel was described as a tenant farmer's daughter from Derbyshire. 'It was a small hill-farm and things were never easy but it was a good place to grow up. I'd come home from school and bring the cows in or milk them, and my mother taught me to cook and housekeep at her knee the way she'd learnt herself. It's been useful in my career because it means I do understand something about living close to nature and being at the mercy of elements outside your control, the weather, that sort of thing.'

Was she equating the subsidy-cushioned existence of a British farmer with the war-torn peril of Yugoslavian peasants? 'Of course not but it did teach me one can't always be in complete command of things.'

'She seems entirely in command of herself,' the journalist observed. 'I admire her two-piece which doesn't look like the usual dowdy uniform of a charity-worker, and she tells me it's Jasper Conran and she's going on to a reception at the Banqueting House. Watching her in the cocktail bar of the Ritz Hotel—her choice of meeting place, not mine—I observe that she's perfectly at home in the company of rich people, politicians and opinion formers and ask how she made the leap from a small farm to high society? Her answer consists of a cagey recital of the facts

96

in her publicist's hand-out: comprehensive school, Oxford Polytechnic, a first job with a conference organiser, then on to the travel trade before moving sideways into charity administration. But when I ask anything more personal Laurel clams up. She hasn't let me inside her home, though she tells me it is a doll's house in Chelsea, and no boyfriends or emotional entanglements are admitted, though newspaper archives show photos of her hand in hand with various men. I mention rumours about her relationship with a stately-home owner, but the only reply is a change of subject. Laurel says she thought I'd come to talk about her work, not her private life, and launches into an account of Handyside's Bequest.'

Claudia had read the article as soon as she got on the train, pulse racing with apprehension. But Laurel had left things unsaid, she hadn't mentioned Ansons and Ansons' owner. Claudia sank her face in her hands, forcing herself to breathe deeply. So long as nobody knows, she whispered, so long as they keep it quiet. A bubble of anger rose within her—why did there have to be this thing to keep quiet, why was George ... why did he ... why had he ... Forcing herself not to put it into words, even in her own thoughts, Claudia made herself stop hating him. Or resenting Laurel. Ansons is all that matters, she told herself.

'Are you all right, Mrs Anson?' The doctor's mother. Claudia spoke to her, asked about her arthritic hip, agreed it was perfect weather for a day trip to London. Then she reread the article more calmly, thinking how little she'd known about Laurel. That farm, the comprehensive school—she looked like a girl from Roedean. Claudia had always assumed she had a private income to supplement Handyside's meagre salary. If only Laurel didn't always manage to make her feel such a weed.

Only too soon Claudia was at the head of a long polished table in the long wood-panelled room, her homework not done. The committee meetings of Handyside's Charitable Bequest took place in the former offices of one of its benefactors, a solicitor who had become a High Court judge. He seldom came, which was a relief as under his eye Claudia would have felt even worse. As it was, she had come to dread the quarterly meetings at which the trustees received efficient, impersonal reports from the director about fundraising and what the funds were spent on. Claudia entered the pompous room with reluctance, uncheered by its hunting prints and the view out into gardens. She twitched uneasily at the neck-bow of her own mid-blue dress, aware, as soon as she saw Laurel's pelmet-length black skirt, endless black-stockinged legs and fitted scarlet jacket, that she'd got it wrong again, and that unlike Laurel's disciplined hair, her own was rustically messy.

Ginny Carter had brought Ian, now a tough toddler. 'He'll just sit and draw, won't you, darling,' Ginny said. 'No, don't do that, your hands are all sticky, oh goodness, Laurel, sorry, your lovely skirt, here, let me rub it ...'

Laurel stepped back, brushed her own hand over the sticky patch and said with steely self-control, 'Hadn't we better get started, Claudia?'

Apologies. Welcome to new member— the photographer Zed Lyons, introduced by Nina Gillespie to Harry and by Harry to Claudia, who had accepted his offer to get involved with Handyside's. Minutes of the previous meeting. Matters arising.

'Item six, Claudia, oh sorry, madam

chairman, I mean, where it says we were going to send a load of medical supplies, I thought Jake told us they needed powdered milk more and that's what we decided. Where is Jake, anyway? Oh Ian, that's a lovely pussy cat, my clever one, now do a bow wow for Mummy.'

Above the injured roar, as Ian made it clear that his picture was not a cat but a lion, Laurel said, 'Jake's away on a delivery run, he's going to double-check, but we heard the babies were all right for food and it seemed sensible to send what's really needed without bothering you all with convening another meeting.'

'Believe me, they need the lot,' Zed Lyons interjected.

'Of course, you've seen the worst, Zed,' Laurel said. 'You'll know how badly they need antibiotics, and immunisations.'

'Well, let's move on,' Claudia said. How silly it all is, she thought, Laurel's going to do whatever she decides whatever anyone here says; and a good thing too—nothing would ever get done if it was left to any of this lot. Zed, all angry and passionate because of his suspended prison sentence and that little girl they took away, Dennis, so jumpy and ineffectual, Ginny, so soft and pink with her die-away voice, preoccupied with that dynamo of an infant—doesn't look at all like her or Tony, I wonder if they went in for donor insemination in the end—or me. I'm not doing much good here.

An item on fundraising—another ball, an auction of promises, a new onslaught on business sponsors. 'George—the chair's husband—said he'd introduce us to some useful new contacts,' Laurel said. Claudia sensed people watching her and managed to stop herself showing any reaction. All the same, how dared she? If I died she'd move in that very day, Claudia thought.

Sourcing of supplies: British manufacturers, a supermarket chain, a Dutch organisation. 'Want to be careful in Holland, centre of European smuggling,' growled Major Bancroft, an ex-soldier who saw conspiracies everywhere. He produced a cutting from his wallet and began to read aloud. '"The Charity Commission has frozen the bank accounts of a charity which raised millions of pounds for orphaned war victims after allegations that one of its trustees arranged to deliver military uniforms, camouflage nets and handcuffs to friends in former Yugoslavia."'

'Should we move on?' Laurel suggested.

Volunteers and the requirement not to overburden them. Mary Ellen Wood was proving to be worth her weight in gold, a reliable driver. Laurel floated the idea that committee members might set the example and an effusion of excuses followed.

'What about you, Claudia?' Laurel suggested.

Wouldn't she just love to get me out of the way for a bit! Claudia thought. Carefully she said, 'That's an interesting idea, Laurel, of course, but I've got so many commitments at Ansons, there's just no way I could manage it.' And don't want to anyway, she didn't add aloud. Getting more actively involved was not Claudia's line, she had never wanted to be hands-on in the causes she lent Ansons' name to; she frequently had to suppress the feeling that they weren't her own, her personal, heartfelt concern. Intellectually persuaded of their value, she found her emotions limped behind, out of sight. I want to be on my island, she sometimes thought, not involved in mankind at all. But the privilege of that island of peace and beauty and history brought with it the duty of benevolence—up to a point.

The lease of the London premises. Suggestions for additional board members. Major Bancroft knew a field marshal who might be interested. Ginny suggested a new young singer. Publicity—always a contentious subject as the charity never managed to get as much press coverage as it needed. But Laurel had arranged to have lunch with the features editor of the *Independent*. 'Even if it's only another profile of me, it'll get Handyside's into print.'

Drivers, volunteers—at this point Ginny, who had been darting between Ian and her place at the table, slapped her hand on to the mahogany. 'Actually, I want to say something.'

'Go ahead.'

'I've been reading this book about World War Two, did you know about the concentration camps? You wouldn't believe the things they did, I'd no idea—but listen, there was a chapter about something called Children's Transports. People like us went and fetched kids here to safety, thousands of them. And I thought, that's what we should be doing now. All those children, wounded and hungry and going without education, and here we are with so much to give them. I mean, look at Ian, he's so bonny and thriving, aren't you my precious, and then think about the poor little things over there in the refugee camps—actually it doesn't bear thinking about—well, all I'm saying is, we shouldn't just be sending bits and bobs we can spare, we should be rescuing them. Anyway, that's what I think.'

'Shall I take this one?' Laurel murmured to Claudia. 'Ginny, I think you know we'd all like nothing better than to be able to do as you suggest, but we couldn't get visas, it's not possible.'

'What d'you mean?'

'There are laws about immigration, who's allowed to settle here and so on.'

'Vicious laws,' Zed said. 'I should know.'

'You poor thing, I think it's awful, the government's awful, we shouldn't—' Ginny said.

'Well, of course, it can be a problem, caring for immigrants and paying for them to stay in hostels and then, with so much unemployment—' Claudia began.

'We're only talking about kids,' Ginny cried. 'When there's so many couples desperate to find babies to adopt, frustrated parents who'd pay everything they had to if only they could be allowed to care for a baby, it's all really ridiculous, I don't believe we couldn't get round those silly rules.'

'Hear hear,' Zed said quietly.

'When you think, people would give anything—anything at all—oh Zed, I'm sorry, I'm rubbing salt in the wound, I shouldn't have reminded you of poor little Daisy,' Ginny gabbled. And so they would, Claudia thought, they'd give anything. I'd have paid every penny I ever had, I would even have given Ansons itself for a child of my own.

'Rules are rules, my dear,' Major Bancroft said.

'I tell you what I think about wicked rules like that—' Ginny began.

'I move the next agenda item,' said Councillor Ashton, opening his mouth for the first time that afternoon.

They limped through to the end of the agenda. Afterwards the members who had not hurried away stood chatting. Ginny said defiantly, 'Rules are meant to be broken, that's what I think, if it's in a good cause.'

'Well, I'm sure we do, sometimes,' Claudia said.

'Do we? Which ones?'

'Perhaps Laurel should answer that. You know all about the rules, don't you, Laurel?'

'Actually, Claudia, I have no idea what you're talking about.'

'Ian, not that cup, my precious, put it on the—oh dear, I'm so sorry ...'

Gradually the room emptied of committee members. Claudia began to collect up coffee cups until Laurel said, 'Really, the mess! Don't bother about it, Claudia, we have a cleaner.'

'Perhaps I should be getting back, George has an American friend coming for the night.'

'Oh, sorry, Claudia, I should have mentioned it before. George told me to tell you he's had a change of plan, he won't be down till tomorrow, we're going to Covent Garden—you don't mind, I hope?'

'Why should I mind?' Claudia said, the phrase repeating itself like an echo in her brain; why should I mind if you steal my husband and put me to shame? 'Of course I don't mind, you're welcome,' she said. And only unvoiced did she add, 'to everything except Ansons.'

8

1996

When Nina came back from Wales her
first job had been at one of London's
commercial radio stations, hosting a day-
time phone-in with listeners measured in
five figures. A few months later the
listeners had multiplied and Nina had
started another programme, which had
no regular slot but was often picked up
by the networks and heard by a national
audience. In *Private Ear* Nina investigated
scams as though she were a private eye
and then made them into lively reports.
She'd covered such subjects as pyramid
selling, car servicing, the export of live
animals and telephone cold-calling. Radio
was so strapped for cash that Nina often
had to be her own researcher, secretary,
editor and sound recordist. She regarded
the programme as her own particular
property and enjoyed the luxury—rare
in the broadcast media—of deciding for

herself what subjects to cover. And she felt as secure as anyone could in so chancy a job; at least she knew her ratings were rising and the reviews were good. Under the mostly benevolent eye of her station manager, Brian France, Nina would have a free hand until she screwed up.

Her own qualms were the restrictive factor. Harry implied, even if he never said, that she was wasting her time and talents on trivialities.

'What does it matter if some whining publicity seeker hasn't got the sense to come in out of the cold, compared to the genuine problems of the world?' he asked after one of Nina's half-hour of vox pops.

It was impossible to justify that particular, unsuccessful programme; win some lose some. 'I wish you hadn't heard that one, I know it didn't work. But they often do,' she said weakly.

'I know, I always listen,' he said. 'My radio's set to tape them if I'm away.'

'Really, truly? I'd no idea.'

'Some of them are heart-rending. The one last year, that bloke who adopted a brain-damaged baby, he was unforgettable. You should follow that up, you know.'

They were having a picnic lunch in

Kew Gardens, making the most of a perfect early spring day. While she spoke about sensible subjects Nina was also making word pictures of the pattern of light leaves against the lacquer red of the pagoda, and Harry's pleasantly contrasting sandiness. His company was ... what was the word? Comfortable. A flitter of unease crossed her mind. Wasn't that a quality appreciated in middle age? Carl, she remembered, had been exciting. But what good had that been? At the same time Nina was carrying on a serious conversation. She assured Harry she was still working on the babies-for-sale story.

'It's too important for a rush job, and frightfully difficult to find people anyway, though I'm asking around. I need someone who's actually got away with it but I don't know how to set about finding them. If you've conned the world into believing a lovely healthy baby's your own, you're hardly going to broadcast the truth.'

'So what will you do?' Harry asked. 'I've never known how journo researchers find people.'

'Gossip. Ask around. Tell people what you're looking for—like I'm telling you.'

'I heard some gossip along those lines

the other day—now what was it ...'

'Tell me if you remember. All one can do is ask and check.'

'Actually, it sounds dangerous to me,' Harry said soberly. 'You could do a lot of damage.'

Nina could not bring herself to describe to Harry, hardly even to herself, the roadblock in her mind that was obstructing her research. She was afraid of this story. But when attacked, Nina invariably, automatically, hit back.

'What about the harm to those babies? And their real mothers? I've talked to social services departments, social workers are full of stories of middle-class parents who just want babies as accessories. And think how awful for people to grow up not knowing who they really are, embedded in a nest of lies.'

Harry didn't want to argue, merely remarking, 'Of course if you can do good you can do harm too,' and turned the conversation on to his attempts to help get an electronics factory going in Somalia. But Nina did feel—what was the word? Unworthy, she thought. Like school reports, could do better. All the same, the baby-scam had to be followed up. So long as she was careful how she used any material.

Nina was living in a flat in Hampstead in the same house as one of Dora Wartski's friends, a child psychologist called Fidelis Berlin, who, just when Nina was planning to move back to London, had happened to mention to Dmitri that the apartment above hers was on the market. Both women had trod cautiously, nervous of getting too involved with an inescapable neighbour, but by this time it had become clear that neither would turn into a millstone round the other's neck, so their friendship was maturing.

Fidelis was an efficient, trim, tall woman in her early sixties, always impeccably dressed in unconventionally elegant clothes, with her grey hair perfectly cut. She had retired from her university post, but still wrote articles and books and still undertook private consultations. Nina admired Fidelis, once joking, 'I want to be like you when I'm grown up.'

Fidelis had drily replied, 'I could find you a better model, if you need one.'

Harry went to Somalia the day after their Kew Gardens lunch. The still-beautiful weather had drawn Nina out again, and

111

she met Fidelis by chance in a café in Hampstead High Street, where Nina was reading a long piece about the ITN reporter Michael Nicholson who had taken an appealing small girl called Jelena Mihaljcic from a Sarajevo orphanage, written her into his passport and flown her to London with him. Natasha Nicholson, as the girl became, had since been adopted by the Nicholsons and was growing up in the family house in Surrey, with a pony and a private pool. Unlike Zed Lyons' baby Daisy, Jelena was allowed to stay with the Nicholsons and her adoptive father was never prosecuted. It was a useful addition to Nina's growing dossier.

'That story's got a happy ending of course, but you know, Fidelis, I've come across examples of—well, you can only call it baby smuggling. Of course it turns out to be pretty nasty if there's something wrong with the baby, though there could have been with someone's own baby too, it's just bad luck, and if there is a family around, then it's dreadful. But there isn't always, and then I don't quite see who loses by it, even if some gruesome types are gaining.'

'No, the espresso's mine,' Fidelis said to a dithering waiter. She seemed to be dithering herself a little, opening her mouth and closing it before deciding to speak. 'Perhaps you didn't know, Nina, that my particular professional interest has been in maternal deprivation?'

'No—oh, I'm so sorry, Fidelis, don't talk shop, if you don't—I mean, I know what your fees must—'

'No, that's not what I meant. I was wondering if you knew why I'd specialised in that aspect of child psychology?'

'No idea.'

'It was because I was a pre-war child refugee from Nazi Germany myself. Mother substitutes were very relevant to me.'

'No, I never knew that, Dora didn't tell me.'

'Actually I first met her at a summer camp for children who'd lost their families, just like me. She'd been in Germany after the war with the United Nations Relief Administration working with war orphans from displaced persons camps. In fact that's where she and Dmitri first saw each other, he'd walked west from Lithuania and found a job as a hospital orderly, and then he became Dora's translator because he had four languages—his father had been

113

a diplomat before the war. Anyway, Dora was one of the organisers of that summer camp, and she inspired me—I was in my teens by then. It was near where we lived in Wales so I got a holiday job helping out.'

'It must have been a painful reminder of what happened to you.'

'No, I've never been able to remember anything that happened before I was four.'

'What happened to your own family?'

'They vanished without trace. I don't even know who they were.'

'So were you adopted?'

'Fostered, by very good, very nice people. I had a perfectly satisfactory childhood and as you know, life's been good to me. So I can say from personal experience that such adoptions may not do harm. But from professional experience, and years of contact with disturbed children, I can say they may also do great harm. Take your pick.'

Nina walked home to her own flat, identical in floor plan to Fidelis's below, but with nothing else in common. Nina had wanted something quite different from the warm wildness of the Wartskis' house and the luxurious extravagance of Carl's apartment, so where Fidelis had colour and ornament, Nina had sparse white space. The ever-changing shadows of the tall trees outside made pattern enough, and the birds in them gave endless entertainment. Her few chairs were black leather or bleached ash, her table and desk were made of glass. She did not even have mirrors, preferring not to see her own reflection, and hardly needing to, now that she always wore black. Even her books and clothes were hidden behind louvred panels. The emptiness made her feel free.

Nina added to her fattening file of notes on the babies-for-sale story. It was, she knew, a really juicy story, a story with legs, but it was leading her into an area she dreaded. Babies stolen, transported, sold. Lost boys. Lost girls. Children from Russia, from Yugoslavia, the Balkans, from places which even thinking of made Nina's body and soul shrivel in terror, her hand cupped round her scarred cheek. Stop, Nina, calm down. Think about something else.

She turned the page of the paper in front of her, unseeing at first and then recognising in the gossip column a face she knew.

'It is not often we hear of aristocratic do-gooders doing much practical good. But Mrs Claudia Anson, wife of the stately home owner and bank supremo George Anson, shown here at Royal Ascot with curvaceous Melanie (Melons) Lockyear and charity organiser Laurel Berryman, is setting off at the wheel of a five-tonner ferrying emergency humanitarian supplies to former Yugoslavia.'

The same story about Claudia Anson, in more or less snide form, appeared in all the papers, which implied that some efficient public relations campaign had been mounted, advertising the good works of a woman who only a few months previously Nina had heard insisting that she would never, ever, in any circumstances be able to drive relief supplies herself.

9

They met at the depot of Handyside's Bequest, far east in London's Docklands. Jake Konin, with more grey hairs than when Claudia had last met him three years before, was cheery and ebullient. He kissed Claudia's hand, hugged Mary Ellen and insisted on lifting their luggage into the cab of the van. 'I brought jazz this time,' he said, 'I hope you ladies will like it, we'll be dancing all the way.'

'Sorry, chaps,' the despatcher said. 'The tape player's on the blink.'

Early as it was, Laurel Berryman had turned out to see them off. She and Jake exchanged a cheek-to-cheek and Claudia remembered they had once gone out together. But now Laurel was too grand, too smart for a man like Jake. He still had the aura of a student, with an expectant, inquisitive expression and an unfocused wildness about him, while she, as perfectly dressed as always, was every inch the *grande dame*.

He's attractive, Claudia thought, rather to her own surprise, for she was not used to noticing that in a man. But he did not look as if people who came in the category of 'older women' would attract him.

Claudia was wearing flannel trousers and a pink cashmere sweater under a Barbour. Her bobbed hair was held back by a velvet Alice-band. Mary Ellen Wood had battered trainers on, and stained denim jeans and

117

a quilted, khaki anorak with unravelling stitching. She had fastened her straggling sandy hair into an elastic band. Her skin was so pale as to seem almost green, her eyes bloodshot. She'd greeted Claudia without surprise.

'Laurel said you'd be along the next time. Checking up on us?'

'No, no, not at all.'

'Doesn't George mind?'

With a candour born of terror, Claudia admitted that he'd hardly notice she was gone.

'Can we get on?' the despatcher said. Observing the information sheet's pronouncement that 'Handyside's Bequest is a non-hierarchical organisation', the man made no pretence of deference to the chairman. 'So you've decided to see life at the sharp end at last, Claudia.'

'Yes, I suppose I have.'

'You don't sound very keen.'

Laurel said, 'You could always back out now, if you're too scared, Claudia, you've said yourself we need willing volunteers.'

Claudia, who was a deeply unwilling conscript, almost leapt at the offer. Then she realised it was impossible. All the arguments that had forced her into actually doing as that ill-informed gossip writer had claimed she would do raced through her head again. Once it was in print that Mrs Anson was going herself, it had all inescapably followed: the heavy goods vehicle driving test, the interviews with reporters, accepting the compliments, deprecating the praise. I want to go home, she thought. But there were invisible chains preventing her. I can't get out of this. I'm trapped.

'You've checked everything, Laurel, haven't you?' Jake asked.

'I've still got to make sure,' the despatcher said, holding on to the sheaf of papers to check each carton and item off. He opened the rear doors to reveal the van's load space, which was already crammed full of crates, marked with the charity's logo of Dürer's clasped, praying hands. These were the supplies to be conveyed across Europe.

A customs inventory form listed the details of a mixed cargo of food, warm clothes and blankets, babies' nappies, first aid kits and cuddly toys which, all coloured fluorescent pink and wrapped in transparent film, were used as padding between the stacks of boxes. Claudia remarked that it looked like a den for deformed, garish livestock. She tried to undo a carton to see what was in it.

'Don't do that,' Jake Konin said quickly. 'It's all complete and carefully packed. Don't disturb anything now.'

Claudia heard Laurel murmur to Mary Ellen, 'All OK?' and receive the reply, 'Everything under control.' Rather to Claudia's surprise, the two women embraced.

'So I'll see you back here—' Laurel said.

'Yup. Soon.'

Then they climbed in, belted in together on the front bench, its slippery covering dotted with small triangular tears through which crumbling grey foam bulged out. The passengers' feet were planted on their luggage, Claudia's leather case, Mary Ellen's nylon sausage bag, Jake Konin's grip. In the cab they also carried a cool box and three sleeping bags. They had a package of sealed mail for the field workers and open letters on the headed paper of Handyside's Charitable Bequest, exhorting anyone it might concern to help them on their way. They had a copy of the regulations which required at least two co-drivers on each journey. They had a programme showing their stops at pre-booked accommodation, in Rotterdam, near Munich and in Split. The following day they were to pick up a local escort, and, at a designated point closer to their destination, were to join up with other vehicles to form a convoy. The emptied vehicle should be returned within a fortnight.

When they went for coffee on the ferry, Mary Ellen said, 'Have you got any aspirins?'

'Aspirins, Kleenex, nail file, extra strong mints.'

Mary Ellen swallowed three of Claudia's aspirins and accepted a paper handkerchief, saying, 'I think I'm getting a cold.'

The next time they stopped, for petrol, she took a sleeping bag into the back and made herself a kind of bunk out of boxes on which she lay with her eyes closed.

'Is she ill?'

'She must be tired out, poor thing, she's such a committed worker, this is her third trip since the New Year,' Claudia said.

Jake didn't seem to be the sort of person who talked when he drove, so, with the radio and tape player on the blink, the journey was monotonous. It was raining, there was a lot of traffic. Claudia had never been in a vehicle that had to stay in the slow lane, at a uniform snail-pace. We can't sit like stuffed dummies all the way, she thought, driven as always by the fear of doing the wrong thing, or—just as bad—not doing the right thing, and began to put forward the laborious social pawns of the 'getting to know you' game. He spoke in a kind of standard modern English accent, which was rather as Claudia had once herself spoken, and so carefully amended, but she supposed, with that name, that he was not originally British, and asked where he'd come from.

'London,' he replied.

She asked what he did.

'This and that.'

And where did he live?

'Here and there.'

She laboured on. He did not admit to hobbies, or a wife or partner.

I sound like the Queen, she thought. Or like the person I've become, the chairman, the *grande dame*, being nice to the people who do the dirty work, showing an interest. Does he think I'm patronising him? And then she thought, perhaps I am.

He took off his coat and rolled up his sleeves, revealing thickly furred arms and releasing an acrid, feral smell, overlaid by some musky cosmetic. When she fell silent he began to hum in a smooth tenor voice.

It felt like a long time before they stopped at a service station.

The two women went together to the lavatory. Claudia didn't often see herself stripped bare, but that morning it had seemed unsuitable to apply her usual layers of cosmetic disguise. She looked with horror at the unadorned result, moderately lined, intermittently blotched, uniformly pale. This is the face I've earned, she thought, marked with the stigmata of my silly insecurity and anxiousness. Maybe Jake Konin despises me, maybe that's why he's so quiet.

She twitched at her newly shortened hair and stroked her mouth with lip salve. Only two weeks, she thought. But oh, how she already longed for the sanctuary of home. Why had she ever left it? What a muddle, what a mistake.

Mary Ellen came out of the cubicle and Claudia said, 'Are you all right?'

'I'll live.'

'I'm sure you'll be feeling better by tomorrow.'

'I've had worse.'

'D'you suppose Jake's always so gruff?'

'Just doing the job. I've been with him before, he's OK, he never talks on the road.'

'Where do you think he comes from? I wonder if he was a refugee himself.'

'What's it to you?' Mary Ellen asked.

'Well, nothing really, I was just interested.'

'He'll be waiting.'

Driving was slow, but they did reach Rotterdam that first night, where they had been booked in at a motel with a lorry park. It was not full so they were given separate rooms for the same price as shared ones.

'It's all in a good cause,' the proprietor said, and promised that his boy would keep an eye on the lorry. He was a member of a Reformierde Kirke group that collected supplies for the British convoy; more cartons would be loaded under his supervision. Meanwhile he provided Mary Ellen with cold-cure pills, and brought drinks for them all on the house. After a couple of glasses of wine, Claudia slept like the dead for most of the night, momentarily disturbed by voices coming through the wall from Mary Ellen's room. Sleeping again, she dreamed voices disjointed, half heard, Mary Ellen and Jake talking about the journey, Split, hotels, hospitals. Jerked briefly awake, Claudia thought indignantly that Mary Ellen wasn't anywhere near ill enough for that. Sleep overcame her. Again, the lullaby of half-heard conversations. Passports. Laurel Berryman. What had she said? Laurel, her hair brighter and bushier than ever, her nails red talons, her clothes tight and dark, smiling smiling, big white teeth, what did she want? Claudia must run to find out, hurry naked through the streets never catching up, never getting there. An insecurity nightmare, very familiar in type if not in detail, and only too easily explicable. The thoughts and images she kept at bay in waking hours pursued her down the night hours in distorted form.

They were all bleary-eyed in the morning. They opened the van's rear doors, saw that everything was properly packed and stacked and agreed there was no need to check it further. It was Claudia's turn, so, careful not to grind gears or jerk the clutch, she drove. Mary Ellen closed

125

her eyes, Jake Konin watched Claudia. What was he thinking? Still dopey from the disturbed night, she tried another conversational feeler to keep herself awake, for they'd better create some semblance of social harmony. She spoke of their destination: how dreadful it all was, how helpless they felt.

Claudia said a few days were not too much to give. A short break, a small sacrifice, before it was back to the comforts of home.

10

Nina was sometimes invited to lecture to students so went to Cardiff as guest speaker at a seminar for students on the radio journalism course. They wanted to know about technology—what gear did she take, what gadgets should they acquire?—and job prospects. She, perhaps pompously, wanted to talk to them about theories. 'We can't change things, we shouldn't become part of the story, often we can't even explain what's happened or happening. Chaos can be incomprehensible.'

'What are you there for, then?' a boy called.

'As a witness. And to neutralise history.'

'What's that supposed to mean?' the course tutor asked aggressively. He was a man who had once been senior to Nina, but lost his professional way and ended up as a lecturer when it was clear his days of doing the job were numbered. He'd traded on their acquaintanceship to invite Nina to his college but still resented her for overtaking him.

'History is the survivor's revenge.' Nina quoted an expression whose provenance she had forgotten, but whose truth seemed self-evident. 'We're there to record the lives of those who didn't survive to tell their tales.'

'Like Richard III?' one of the students asked.

'Sorry?' said Nina, who had never done any period before the Industrial Revolution at school, although she had been taught about Spinning Jennies and Luddites several times over, owing to her mother's frequent moves round the country.

'He never did anything wrong but the accounts were written by his enemies, so it

127

was all propaganda and he's remembered as a wicked hunchback. But the winners wrote down lies.'

'I'm not saying that couldn't happen now,' Nina said. 'We all know perfectly well that it can and does. But it's our job, mine and yours, to give the other side of the story. Tell it how it is, not how posterity wants it to have been.'

Driving back to London the next morning, Nina decided the weather was too lovely to stay on the motorway. The soft spring air was tempting her into the countryside. She'd take a detour, maybe go for a walk, have a sandwich in a pub. Driving slowly along a winding road she noticed a brown 'tourist attraction' sign. The word 'Ansons' was written beside a symbolic picture of a stately home. Nina was irresistibly tempted to follow the signs.

Harry never mentioned his childhood home, which would not fit well with the classless image he adopted. But then, Nina thought, neither of them talked much about their backgrounds. When they were together they lived in the present—which restaurant or film to go to, or, equally often, who would cancel the booking because one of their jobs had disrupted the diary. There was no talk of a more distant future except in the most impersonal terms—the prospects for peace in some trouble spot, the financial future of a tottering economy somewhere in the Third World. And they steered clear of talking about their own lives. Theirs was a bizarrely old-fashioned courtship, if it was a courtship at all, or perhaps it was just an equally old-fashioned loving friendship. Part of the pleasure in the relationship was its leisurely, tantalising nature. Were they in love, either of them? Were they going to fall in love? If and when they did, the time would come for Nina to tell Harry all about Carl and to hear about Harry's own emotional adventures. But she wasn't sure she really wanted to know.

Ansons, though, must have formed Harry just as Nina's own rootless, unfocused childhood had formed her into a woman with a driving ambition to achieve worldly success. I'd like to see what he's reacting against, she thought. Is it nosy of me? Would it be an intrusion? No, it's open to the public, after all. I'm just another tourist. And anyway, he needn't ever know.

The entrance was guarded by two lodges

and gates with winged lions on top of their high stone posts. The drive ran for three-quarters of a mile between dignified old trees. Rounding the final bend, Nina saw Ansons before her, as neat and symmetrical as a doll's house. If there had not been lots of other cars in the visitors' car-park Nina would have driven straight away again, but she could see she would be safely lost in an anonymous crowd so followed the arrows along a wheelchair access to the ticket booth, and saw that a tour would be starting in five minutes.

She found herself in a group of early-season visitors dressed in beige or grey and a generation older than Nina. They behaved rather like church-goers, low-voiced and respectful of the antiques and works of art which constitute the twentieth century's objects of pilgrimage. Nina felt little of their awe, but for the fact that Harry could ever have taken for granted life in such a palace; nor did she share her companions' admiration. In fact she found the lavishness and formality of Ansons' appurtenances almost repulsive. What was it about places like this that made the great British public drool? She wondered why so many women had castles in the air instead of smaller dream homes. Yet she knew people would kill to achieve something like this. But Nina couldn't begin to imagine how anybody could live, nowadays, in so archaic a setting. She thought indignantly that it didn't look like any change had been made in this house for the whole century or more. The dining room, laid up as though for a banquet, the stiff and formal drawing room, the library in which no book could have been read for decades—it was all fossilised. Set in stone. An incitement to class hatred and revolution, she thought; no wonder Harry had repudiated it.

But at the very moment her thoughts reached that point, passing through a gallery hung with ancient portraits, Nina saw Harry himself, dressed with unfamiliar formality in a dark suit and black tie. He appeared through a door at the far end of the long room. Seeing the party of tourists he made to retreat immediately. But then he caught sight of Nina. She felt her cheeks flaming with mortification, and dropped her eyes. When she looked up again he had gone, but lagging at the back of the group as it was conducted on to the back stairs on the way to see the old kitchen, she found he had come round through another door and up behind her. As the last of Nina's companions disappeared down the stairs, Harry said softly, 'Good afternoon, Miss Bennet.'

'Who?'

'Don't you remember in *Pride and Prejudice,* when Elizabeth is being shown round Pemberley?'

Automatically on the attack, Nina said sharply, 'I don't see any likeness between you and Mr Darcy.'

'Quite right, there isn't really, if only because I'm not the owner of Ansons. I had to represent George at a funeral.'

'Oh, I'm sorry.'

'No need, he was ninety-two, one of my father's old retainers and I never liked him much.'

'I was just passing,' Nina said with feeble truth. 'I wasn't being nosy, Harry, I just thought I'd have a look.'

'And what d'you think of it?'

'It all seems very grand, but I don't have much experience of stately homes. Is it all like this?'

'Like what?'

'So like a museum.'

'In that it's well preserved and never updated, yes, I guess it is. Come on,

132

I'll show you the private bit. Oh, don't worry, my brother's not here and Claudia's away too.'

'But, are you sure?' Nina felt uncharacteristically awkward and embarrassed. What must he think of her, poking her nose in like this? She followed Harry along chilly polished passages and through tidy, impersonal rooms, unable to imagine that any of them could ever feel like a normal human being's home. Could Harry possibly see it as such? And if he did, how could she ever have supposed they might have other things in common?

Stopping at a leaded bay window he paused for her to look down at an enclosed courtyard across which the tourist party was being shepherded towards a chapel.

'Is there a private chaplain too?' Nina asked.

'Not quite, but the rest of the family's still very piously papist—well, George has to be observant, it's in the terms of the trust, but that's another reason I couldn't ever inherit.'

'Are you the one that got away?'

'Something like that. I wouldn't live here to save my life, the whole thing would go straight to the National Trust if I ever had any say in the matter.'

'Don't you feel it's home, then?'

'Not really, I've always been uncomfortable with the whole exclusivity bit. You've either got to get out from under or swallow the legend whole, like Claudia did. She's run the place for years, but I don't think she's done anything to please herself at Ansons in all the time she's been married, everything's in keeping, part of the tradition, restored or replaced but never new. God knows what her own taste would be.'

'Don't you like her?'

'Oh yes, I'm really fond of her, she was lovely to me when I was a kid—I was only ten when she married George and she was a better sister than my real one, but when she moved in here to take the place over it's more like it took her over instead.'

'Running a historic house must be very absorbing.'

'Consuming, I'd call it. She's always been shy and unsure of herself, so she hid out here and turned into a kind of handmaiden to the legend, it's like she's lost her real self and become an archetype called Mrs Anson instead. Ansons has eaten her alive.'

Following Harry through the house Nina couldn't help noticing how many of his ancestors had been like him, burly, sandy men with uncompromising, heavy-lidded eyes. Having no idea from whom she was descended herself, it made her uncomfortable to recognise this package of inherited qualities. How could he have cast off all this history, all these people, the weight of their gaze? And if he didn't, and they got together properly, then she—Nina stopped her thoughts in their tracks.

'Is it haunted?' she asked.

'Claudia thinks so. At least, she used to say so when I was a kid. But I noticed she only ever mentioned ghosts that were in the records. She probably wanted to see them so much that she thought she did.'

'Ladies with their heads under their arms? Knights in armour?'

'I wouldn't know, I don't have any feeling for the supernatural, you can read the books if you want. Come on, we'll see how they're getting on with the kitchen.' They went through a pantry into a stone-flagged room with a vaulted ceiling, a scrubbed table that would seat twenty, a porcelain sink big enough to bath a toddler and a six-oven Aga.

135

Two men in paint-stained overalls were at work and Harry said warmly, 'Edgar, Donald, good to see you. Nina, meet Edgar, he's been the carpenter here since long before I was born, and Donald's my old sparring partner, middleweight champion of the Midlands, knocked me for six more than once.'

The two men regarded Nina with unabashed curiosity, before Edgar said, 'Seeing as you're here, Harry, take a look at this, might be rot, Don thinks, but I don't know whether your brother ...' The three men squeezed together into a cupboard to one side of the stove. Nina looked round at the forbidding size of the room, felt the impossibility of ever producing a meal in it herself and glanced at the shelf of cookery books beside her. She took out one which had no name on the spine, wondering what sort of recipes Claudia Anson would collect and copy, and read, 'December 10, fog all day. G rings to check all ready for w/end. How unreal he seems to me these days, as insubstantial as his visiting ancestors and less relevant to Ansons than they are. A puppet going through the motions of an English gentleman.'

Flushing with sudden shame Nina

realised she was reading someone else's private diary and replaced it quickly hoping Harry hadn't noticed.

'Mr George said to leave it, but I don't know,' Donald said.

'Better check with him again, then. And the colour too, I thought Claudia said this room was going to be blue.'

'Blue's what Mrs Anson wanted right enough, but the other lady thought mushroom when she came at the weekend and that's what your brother told us to do. She's coming back later to see if we got it right.'

'Today?' Harry exclaimed. 'I must go. Tell George I couldn't wait, will you, Edgar? And I'll see you soon. Look, Nina, we'll go out this way.'

He led her at a trot through a garden so perfect it looked as though the flowers were artificial. As she hurried behind him Nina grabbed a white petal from a green copper pot. There was a spotted woodpecker. Not silk: real tulips, real apple blossom. A nut-hatch. Real grass like billiard table baize. It made the place seem all the more unreal.

As they reached the car-park Nina gasped, 'What's the matter, Harry, why the rush?'

'I don't want to see my bloody brother. Bringing that woman here, letting her get her mitts on the house, countermanding Claudia, what's she supposed to think when she comes home?'

'Are she and your brother going to break up, then?'

'Not if he wants to keep the loot, divorce is a big no no. Claudia must know he's been going out with Laurel—'

'Laurel Berryman?'

'Yes, why, d'you know her?'

'No, but I know who she is, there was a piece in the *Argus*—'

'I saw. Its only redeeming feature was that George wasn't mentioned. Claudia introduced them herself at one of her fundraisers. I think she's a perfectly ghastly woman, but she's managed to get poor George wound round her finger.'

'Without Claudia knowing?'

'She's never mentioned it, and of course she's shut away down here most of the time, but I'd have thought she must have realised something's going on. Oh God, let's forget about it.'

In a couple of hours Nina had learnt more about Harry's family than in the previous couple of years. No wonder he hadn't talked about them before.

Harry said, 'I came by train and cab, why don't you give me a lift and I'll give you dinner. Let's get out of here, back to the modern world.'

Modern men and women in the modern millennial world did not go in for slow motion courtship. Even as she enjoyed the glances and touches, retreats and reticences that had characterised their relationship so far, Nina had also felt a little uneasy. She had been used to the moves in what the original inhabitants of Ansons would have thought the reverse order: sex first, then love and (for those who wished to) children, and last of all, if at all, marriage. Always between her and Harry there had hung unmentioned a kind of detached amusement at the unconventionality of their behaviour. They'd been to dinners and dances, outings and stayings-in; they'd talked and argued and even flirted and kissed. But only today, as she stopped at the kerb in front of the modern block of flats in which Harry had a bare but light-filled penthouse, and he said, 'Coming in?', was it suddenly clear to them both what she was coming in for.

The only mystery was why they'd waited

so long. Or how Nina had done without it for so long. In the morning she felt like a statue brought to life as though she'd been petrified during those months, no years, several years of celibacy. And to think I told myself I didn't miss it! she thought, grinning secretly into his hot chest. Her body was relaxed and yet simultaneously enlivened, with deep pulses of pleasure still echoing through it. She felt slight and narrow against his breadth and strength. She breathed in ... what was it? Something spicy. His hand moved and she quivered against it, her nerves leaping to his touch.

Later they drank coffee, he made scrambled eggs, they sat at a table together just like they'd been doing for months, but oh, how different the understanding between them. Language, words, all were enhanced by another kind of meaning.

'How long would it have taken us to get here if I hadn't been nosy about your background yesterday?' she asked.

'Or if I hadn't lost my temper about my idiot brother and his gold digger.' She looked a question, and he went on, 'Laurel Berryman's got her hooks into

George but she's two-timing him with her old boyfriend, I've seen them together.'

'Who is he?'

'Some man she had in tow when I first came across her—which was the time she met George too, as it happens, there was a fundraiser at Ansons three years ago. Come to think of it, I was supposed to bring you to it. Just think, we could have got together ages ago if I'd done as I was told.'

'Do you ever do that?'

'Try me.'

11

They spent the second night in a hotel so simple it should have been called a hostel. They had cafeteria food, over which Jake made conversation, as he had the previous evening, about music and films. Claudia was impressed that Mary Ellen knew all the student jargon and could follow the contemporary references. Claudia didn't understand much, and tried not to be shocked by the vocabulary both the others took for granted.

They were given narrow beds in tiny cubicles. Claudia heard Mary Ellen coughing through the thin wall. Claudia found it hard to sleep. She lay tossing and turning under the lumpy, skimpy quilt, and at last turned on the light to make notes in her journal. She wrote, 'I'm really hating this, I must have been mad to come, I could have got out of it somehow. Just because Laurel said I'd been committed. God knows where on earth the papers got that story. Even if it made everyone expect me to come I shouldn't ever have given in to moral blackmail. God, what a coward I am. I don't even dare get a taxi tomorrow morning to the nearest station and go home. But I dread to think what's going on at Ansons without me. Or to me away from it.'

Claudia woke up feeling battered. She was forced to listen to every moment of Jake Konin's ablutions as he brushed and spat, shaved and shat in an uninhibited explosion, and when they met at the lorry he croaked, 'I'm feeling really rough.'

'You look all right.'

'I ache all over.'

'Maybe you've caught Mary Ellen's cold.'

'I'm OK, I'll drive,' Mary Ellen announced.

Jake immediately lay down on the bed of boxes and was soon loudly snoring.

The two women looked together at the map and itinerary, Claudia forcing herself not to draw back from the other woman's filthy breath, and feeling, as they bent together over the paper, an almost fierce heat emanating from her skin. We aren't up to this, she thought, why don't we just stop here in safe, civilised Germany. Or we could fly home. I can afford it.

But Mary Ellen had started the engine. She knew the way from the hotel to the autobahn. Nothing deflected her. They drove south, pressing on behind other, bigger lorries and road trains with several huge trailers, muddy, wet, greasy, noisy. Claudia felt shaken in her skin, her back ached. I hate this, she thought. But she endured, drove and endured. Much much later, towards the end of one of the longest days she could remember, they approached Rijeka. Claudia looked in the package of documents. 'I can't find the ferry tickets,' she said.

'Jake has probably got them.'

He was deeply asleep, as though he'd

been knocked out by some drug.

'Oh Lord, I do hope he's not really ill,' Claudia said. She pulled his leather jacket from under his head, which did not wake him, and found his wallet. As she riffled through the papers, not knowing what the ferry tickets would look like, she could not resist glancing at what was in it. 'God, he's loaded,' she said, as she took in the details of a bank draft for eight thousand pounds. And there were Dutch and German notes, photographs, several of Jake himself, one in front of a church Claudia recognised as Dubrovnik's cathedral, one cheerfully arm in arm with Laurel Berryman. Letters in a language Claudia did not know, a foil pack of pills.

'God knows what these are—oh, thank goodness for that, here's the ticket. Oh no, it's not.' Holding it away from her long-sighted eyes, Claudia realised she was looking at an air ticket, Split–Zagreb–Heathrow, which must have been extravagantly full price and changeable because it was dated the end of this week.

'What's that—give it here!' The truck swerved a little as Mary Ellen snatched the folder out of Claudia's hand.

'Careful!'

'You distracted me.'

'D'you s'pose Jake's not coming back with us, then?'

'Oh for chrissake Claudia, mind your own bloody business, what's it got to do with you, stop farting around, we need the bloody ferry tickets.'

'But they aren't here, what had we better do?' she said.

'Listen, I've got enough on my plate without you—wait a minute, I know what he always ...' Mary Ellen pulled down the sun visor. Clipped to the back of it was a European Community passport and a small folder. 'Here they are, I forgot, that's where he puts them.'

At Rijeka they had to wait for hours, queuing for the ferry, to get through the formalities, to be slowly processed.

'God, it's slow,' Claudia muttered, and Mary Ellen said, with a kind of glee, 'Slow is how most of life is for most people, Claudia, they wait and queue and are expected to be grateful. I've had to learn that.'

A tank was being loaded into the hold of the ferry, a slow and dangerous-looking process. It was followed by more heavy goods vehicles than seemed possible, the Handyside lorry coming almost last, parked by hundreds of minute wheel turns under the furious eye and deafening shouts of an unshaven seaman in a vest. Yawning and speechless, Jake got out and went up the companionway.

Claudia prepared to follow him. 'At least we can go on deck and get some fresh air now,' she said, but Mary Ellen answered:

'Don't be daft, Claudia, this is a war zone. Once when we took this ferry it came under shell fire.'

'My God.'

'You must have known what you were letting yourself in for. Or didn't you, all those months ago when you got me into it?'

'I'm awfully sorry, Mary Ellen—'

'Didn't anyone tell you, not even dear Laurel? Tough.'

'I expect you know how long we're going to be on this ship,' Claudia said humbly.

'It's overnight. There's one stop on the way.'

Night three: a foretaste of hell. In her journal, Claudia noted no more about it than just that. Much of day four was spent at sea, because the ferry was delayed,

146

having stopped for hours at Zadar while the hold was emptied, in order to unload the tank. Then all the vehicles were slowly, petulantly reloaded.

In the afternoon they reached Split. Claudia had seen it before during an expensive Mediterranean cruise and had always remembered the glory of what remained of Diocletian's palace, lit and visible across the twinkling sea. It was not floodlit now and they went to the cheapest possible hostel, well inland in reeking slums, where Claudia and Mary Ellen shared a four-bedded room, both fully clothed and with a scarf over the pillow to avoid any contact with grimy linen. It all compared unfavourably with the luxuries that had been available to rich foreigners in the early 1980s.

The next morning Jake Konin was really ill.

He'll have to rise above it, Claudia thought, there were more important things to think about than how they felt. No doubt the people to whom they were ferrying these supplies felt ill all the time.

But he was delirious and had a fiery rash.

'I don't think he's got a temperature,'

Claudia said dubiously, wiping a towel over his forehead. Tucking the sheet round his naked shoulders, she noticed a lily tattooed on his upper arm.

Mary Ellen said, 'We need a doctor.'

The hotel's manager was a dispirited, swarthy man called Enver who had come home from Australia after communism and before the war. All the time he'd spent in the South Pacific the Adriatic coast had been his lost paradise, but now he yearned for Melbourne. 'You been to Oz? No? You wanna to get yourself out there before it's too late. God's own country. This dump's been ruined.' In the intervals of condemnation, Enver said he would get Jake to the local hospital.

'No, that won't do, we can't go on without Jake,' Claudia said firmly.

Enver wanted to be rid of the two women. The lorry was in the way in his yard, he needed the rooms and any road, he didn't want bloody Brits in his hotel any longer than he could help. Brits weren't exactly popular round here, and he could do without any trouble.

Mary Ellen seemed to have taken charge. She said, 'I'm not shifting myself or the van till he's seen a doctor. One who speaks English.'

Waiting for the doctor, Claudia tried to telephone England. There was no answer from the charity, but then, Claudia realised, it was only six in the morning there. Laurel can bloody well wake up, she thought, dialling the director's home number, but only the machine replied. Claudia left an angry and self-pitying complaint, wished too late that she could cancel it, and dialled her own number at Ansons. George would probably still be incoherent after a usual night's boozing, but ... one, two, three, four ... her machine was set to pick up after eight rings. After seven it was answered. Hearing a woman's voice, Claudia absent-mindedly thought it was her own and prepared to leave a message for George, before realising it was not hers but another woman's sleepily saying, 'Hallo? Who's there? Hallo?' Claudia slammed the receiver on to its rest. Who? How ... Stop it, she told herself as she so often had before, don't think about it, don't even wonder. George probably has people for the weekend, that must have been Milly, she's got every right to stay at Ansons and answer the telephone. All the same, she didn't

149

try again, instead uselessly readjusting the blankets round Jake, and then going to the small window and starting some breathing exercises, deeply in, strongly out. The sun was shining in a pale blue sky but the air smelt of chemicals and sewage. This is dreadful, she thought. What on earth am I doing here? How did this all happen?

The doctor came in the end, a haggard young Slovenian who said he, like many of his compatriots, had done a year's postgrad in England. Jake stirred at his arrival and the two men shook hands. 'We have met, our families have been connected,' the doctor said. He moved his hand to Jake's pulse.

'So Jake's a Yugoslav himself?' Claudia asked.

'No. But his family was, I believe, from Vitez.'

'Does that mean he's a Muslim?' Claudia wondered whether it might explain his hostility to women, but the doctor said:

'That I would not know. None of us had religion in those days.'

'What's wrong with him?'

'I cannot say, although he is quite unwell. He cannot continue with you on your journey.'

'But he can't be! What are we to do?'

The doctor was implacable. There was no way Jake would be driving another metre. He couldn't even sit in the van. Good nursing and time was what it would take.

'Nursing! But we can't—'

Enver broke in, using his own language but decorating his peroration with gestures that made it perfectly clear what he was saying, and after a few minutes the doctor made a gesture of surrender, and turning back to Claudia said, 'OK, so I admit him, I take him now in my car.'

Claudia looked at the two strange foreigners in this strange place. Steadying her voice, she said, 'There's still the problem of the lorry. If I could arrange for another driver to fly out ... I'd better call London. But we were supposed to be meeting up with a convoy. I don't know if I can get in touch with—'

'You will drive on, my niece will go with you,' Enver said with firm finality.

'No, that's impossible,' Mary Ellen exclaimed.

He said, 'I arrange this,' and left the stuffy little room. Claudia stood there in a kind of despair.

'This whole thing was a mistake,' she told the doctor, but he was wrapping the oblivious Jake in a blanket, and, in a kind of debased fireman's lift, heaved him towards the stairs. Mary Ellen stuffed his gear into the expensive grip: a gilt wet shave razor in a soft leather bag, the expensive tubes of shaving cream and aftershave, the tortoiseshell tooth and hair brushes.

When the doctor had gunned his rusty Lada away, Mary Ellen and Claudia assembled their own few belongings. Claudia was struck by the contrast between Mary Ellen's mangy brushes and slimy sponge and the opulence of Jake's gear. An odd man. She still couldn't make him out.

'I never knew he was a foreigner himself,' Mary Ellen said.

'He isn't, any more than I am.'

'Come again?'

'My mother's parents were refugees from Lithuania,' Claudia said, surprising herself at the utterance of a personal detail she never mentioned, if only because it had never been mentioned in her own home. Claudia's mother had escaped to England with her family in 1939 when she was eleven. At fourteen she was baptised, and at seventeen she married the minister who had taken them in. Their two daughters were brought up in a closed, fierce world of prayer and self-denial, and it was not until their mother died that they discovered her history. Claudia wished she had not spoken, the last thing she wanted was that sort of information circulating at Ansons, and wished it more when Mary Ellen made the pin-prick reply:

'Yup, so that's how come you don't look English.'

Enver came in, followed by a young woman with black eyes and hair, tanned skin and an air of physical confidence. She wore jeans and a T-shirt with a stick pin, showing a golden flower on a blue background, the lily of Bosnia, stuck into the material. She spoke like an escapee from *Neighbours*.

'But you're Australian,' Claudia exclaimed.

She said, 'I surely am, Sheila Kazaz, and I've got a brother called Bruce, would you believe? He's up with the BIH.'

'The what?' asked Claudia, not being able to tell one warring faction from another, or wanting to.

'The Bosnian army. We've got to fight for ourselves, for sure no one else is going to.'

'Is all your family here, then?'

'Nah. My old man was dead set on making real Aussies of us, he nearly killed us when we both came back last year.'

'Did you come back to—' Claudia stopped herself from using the word fight. 'To help?'

'Yup. There's hundreds of us here, second and third generation.'

'Really, so many?'

'It's 'cos there's been such a lot of emigration, all through this century, Bosnians and Croatians and Montenegrans and Slovenians and Albanians and those pigs of Serbs, all settling in other countries and sending money home, or going abroad to study—you'll find no end of people who've lived down under, or in the States or Germany. Not so many from Ukay, you won't let them in.'

Claudia examined the girl curiously but with a sense of inevitability. No matter what the girl seemed like, whether it was a good idea or not, Claudia saw that this was about to happen. She would not escape home to normal life, she would carry

on with this reluctant journey; she and
Mary Ellen Wood, of all people the most
unsuitable to trespass in a battle zone,
would drive on with this unfriendly, alien
young Sheila Kazaz.

Not, it seemed, if Mary Ellen had
anything to do with it. 'No way we're
taking you, it's not on.'

'Why?'

'The charity can't take unauthorised
passengers, there's the insurance and the
permits, it just can't be done.'

'I won't be a passenger, I'll be a driver,
and an interpreter.'

'We couldn't go on without her, Mary
Ellen,' Claudia said.

'You're such a wimp, Claudia, of course
we can.'

'Listen, I know when I'm not wanted—'
Sheila interrupted.

'No, no, Sheila, we do want you, really.
Mary Ellen didn't mean it. There have
to be three drivers and you know the
territory, we'd be really glad of your
help.'

'We don't need it,' Mary Ellen insisted.
'I know the way, it's all fixed—'

'Well, I'm the chairman of Handyside's,'
Claudia said. 'I'm making this decision.

We'll go together.' There was a heavy, difficult silence as the girl adjusted a black robe above her clothes and began to wrap a veil around her head. In an artificially social tone, Claudia asked, 'What made you come back?'

'I wanted to help. Still do. Stop those bastards, I mean. You know, when your own people are being wiped out and starved and tortured you can't just not join in.'

'It must seem like some change from— where did you grow up?'

'Sydney.'

'Doesn't it feel very strange here? I mean ...' Claudia broke off before saying this seemed a primitive place in comparison with the gleaming antipodean city she had once visited.

'It surely is different, for one I'd never heard a bomb before, even if the only terrorism down under is the Serbs and Croats letting off their bombs. But I've learnt a lot here.' She swung herself into the cab. 'Better hit the frog and toad.'

'What?'

'Hit the road. Get a wriggle on. Want me to drive first?'

'Can you drive a lorry?'

'Sure I can so long as the Muj don't see me.'

'Muj ...'

'You must have been warned about the Mujahedeen? They don't think women should be driving.'

'Fundamentalists,' Mary Ellen interposed.

'Arabs, Baluchis, Afghans, Saudis. They've come to join in but they're all fundamentalists, they'll shoot at anything they think's Western,' Sheila said. 'You should hear the doctor talk about them, he learnt to like a drink in Ukay and he's been in Germany too, he fancies frankies and wienies too, but the Muj'd shoot at the sight of booze or sausage.'

'Aren't they all Muslims?' Claudia asked.

'Yeah, sure, but at least the locals'll drink beer. Those Muj are all raving nutters, they don't think females are human.'

'Is it all right for you to come along, then?'

'I'm only coming to make sure you meet up with the convoy, then I'll get a hitch back. But we'll have to keep our eyes peeled 'cos if they see me or you at the wheel there'll be dead trouble.'

12

Nina's boss was a jovial-seeming man, soft-skinned, always a little sweaty, with a ready smile and a way of seeming apologetic and easily wounded. Vulnerability was a disguise Brian France wore over adamantine decisiveness. He used phrases to preface what sounded like suggestions: would you mind, and I wonder whether, and not unless it's convenient. Each was a command. Do it or else. Even his idle comments carried a hint of menace to those who worked for him. There was an atmosphere of tension in any organisation he commanded.

His office was reached through a large room with low ceilings and sealed windows. It had been designed and unveiled with much publicity as a state-of-the-art paperless office, a vast white space in which all-in-one tables, chairs and computer terminals stood at meaningful angles on an uncluttered carpet. But each work station had been turned into an encampment, barricaded with cardboard cartons and bulging plastic bags.

The boss alone was allowed privacy and obsolescence, his room fully furnished with filing cabinets, bookshelves and family photographs. He welcomed Nina into it with a hug, told her she was looking lovelier than ever, the audience figures for the phone-in were healthy, they'd sold a twelve-week series of the investigation programmes to a national network, so what about her other ideas, was there anything in them?

'To begin with, I've worked out how they do it,' she said.

'Sell the babies?'

'No, that's easy enough—'

'If you have a supply of them. Where do they come from?'

'There's always unwanted babies,' Nina said knowingly.

'How come, with abortions and cash for single mums and all that?'

'Well, a few come from birth mothers who've come to a financial deal with desperate parents, but not many, now there's no stigma attached to being a single mother. Not like when I was a kid. I often used to get called a bastard.'

'What else, then?'

'A few of these babies seem to be coming from abroad. Being rescued, you might say.'

Nina thought of her recent encounter with Ginny Carter. Tracked down via Harry Anson's recollections of Claudia's gossip, Ginny had begun by denying everything. Ian was her own child born of her own body. But she'd weakened. Everyone needs to confess eventually, Nina had realised, promising, and meaning it, that she would never tell a soul what Ginny told her about her tummy-padded months, her journey to a strange town in Ireland and her triumphant return with her very own baby.

'We'd tried to adopt, for ages and ages we tried,' Ginny had explained. 'But we were too old—I was just forty—and too middle class. The social worker who did the home study said she could see we were ambitious and we'd put pressures on a child and she made an unfavourable report on us. We were desperate. Then someone put me on to the other agency, I mustn't say any names, but they're our saviours.'

As Ginny talked, Ian had rampaged. He

was on a different scale from his 'mother', at the age of five already a tall, square chunk of masculinity. He would be an attractive man one day. But Nina did not see him as an attractive entity at present. She didn't think she wanted children, had never felt the aching of empty arms that was beginning to afflict friends of her generation, hadn't worried about the biological clock. Sitting in Ginny Carter's messy room she suddenly thought, My own children would be different. A vision of a miniature version of Harry Anson flashed across her consciousness. Or a tiny Nina with an unblemished cheek.

Stop it, stop it, she told herself, what's come over you?

Ginny Carter was talking about the loving home she'd given to a child whose life would have been awful otherwise— 'those refugee camps, it doesn't bear thinking of.' And Ginny's own life had been transformed. Nina would understand why it had to be kept strictly secret, even though nobody had done anything really wrong. It made you believe in miracles.

Brian France said, 'Couldn't do it openly. He was a friend of yours, wasn't he, that guy that tried?'

'Zed Lyons, yes, he was.'

'So how do other people work them into the system?'

'This bit's incredible, enough for a programme on its own,' Nina said.

Brian poured himself a double espresso from his personal machine, but did not offer Nina any. 'Go on, then, girl, astonish me.'

'It's all a question of being plausible. I was surprised myself, I must say—did you know they don't require documents when you register a birth?'

'That's ballocks for a start, I had a computer print-out when Mandy was born.'

'Yes, you're always given one in hospital and usually if it's a home birth the midwife or doctor lets the registrar know, but there's no legal requirement.'

'You mean I could turn up and say I found the kid under a gooseberry bush, gissa birth cert?'

'That's right, so long as you sound convincing. They'd want back-up if you were an obvious nutter, or you looked shifty and like you were planning to get fraudulent benefits. But otherwise, I'd say the baby came so quickly there wasn't time to get help or my mum helped or something. And if I'd padded my tummy for the last few months so the neighbours weren't suspicious, then gone away and quote had it unquote and registered it in the district where it's quote born unquote ... there you are with a citizen of the United Kingdom, entitled to all usual rights, passport, everything your own real child would have, without any adoption orders or ward of court stuff.'

'Have you got this on tape?'

'Certainly have—not only someone very senior at the Registrar General's office in Southport, very helpful he was, but also Mr so-called Cliff Jones. And someone I can't identify, I've got an actor to read her words telling me exactly how to do it.'

'This is a programme on its own, Nina, and then there can be another about the birth mothers, lots of emotion in that, there's the making of a whole series here. You'll have to do some PR, write pieces for the tabloids and glossies when the time comes. Get the punters listening. But, Nina, why do these people bother? Why don't they just adopt?'

'Because not everyone's accepted as adopters by the social services—Zed wouldn't

163

have been. And even if you are allowed to, the birth mother can change her mind before the adoption's finalised. This way, even if she does change her mind, you can just say she's a complete stranger, you've never set eyes on her before and she's deranged or deluded. If you look respectable or normal enough no court's going to start ordering blood and DNA tests, not if you've got your own legal birth certificate, and still less if a doctor or midwife wrote and told the registrar you'd had a baby.'

'Got a bent medic on tap, has he, your Mr Cliff Jones?'

'I'm hoping to trace him too.'

Brian spat out his wad of chewing gum and unwrapped another. 'Bloody do-gooders and their non-smoking office. Did you say abroad, Neen?'

Damn. He would pick up on that. Nina didn't want to answer, she knew what she'd be starting. Tell Brian France where she was beginning to suspect the source of supply was and he'd expect her to go. Insist she went, in fact.

The story's got everything it needs. Why don't I just leave it at that, let him think the babies are born to girls who don't want abortions? It's half true.

But only half.

'You'd better listen to this bit,' she said, switching the tape on and fast forwarding until she found the relevant section.

Bill, taped on the afternoon phone-in: 'What can they do to me? Bronwen's not here any more and I'll be paying to support that poor little bugger for ever anyway.'

Brian said, 'Yah, I heard it first time round. Good radio. D'you get his number?'

'Not officially,' Nina said, waiting for the explosion, but Brian ignored her breach of station rules. 'Listen to this.'

The quality wasn't so good, just a private call with a tape recorder beside the receiver; she didn't play him the beginning of the conversation, the introduction, Bill's gulps and silences. He'd talked more easily, though still disjointed, after a while and then Nina'd asked exactly where the baby had come from.

'They showed us a photo of his home village, we were going to save it for him when he was old enough to understand, it was some kind of army stronghold that had been a crusader castle once and a Roman fort before that. Bron liked that idea, she said it was historical continuity.'

A pause for weeping, before Nina probed further and Bill went on, 'We were told he'd been taken to one of those camps, right up there in the thick of it, up in the mountains beyond—we were saving the poor kid from—well, conditions in the camps—you know what it's like over there. We were going to make him a home, give him a life. What's that? Illegal? Course it was *illegal*, but what would have happened if anyone had found out? He wasn't a charge on the state and it would have been inhuman to send him back—quite apart from the fact that he's legally ours. As far as the law's concerned he's our own, naturally born son. My God!' A laugh and then a sob. Nina's soft tone.

The man went on, 'How? They told us what to do, it was easy. Bronwen said she was pregnant, made herself look fatter, then I had to work in Ireland for a couple of months and we said the baby'd come so fast there wasn't time to get a doctor. Registered as Bron's and mine. Foolproof. Yes, Nina, of course I could prove he wasn't mine if I wanted to, no problem, you can even get home DNA kits now, but I'm responsible, I don't mind paying for the kid in his home, I'd pay for the rest of my life, I'd pay ten times as much, if only Bron ... well, there it is.'

Nina got up and walked over to the window where she stood with her back to Brian France to prevent him seeing the unprofessional tears which came into her eyes every time she heard the tape. He, apparently unmoved, said, 'So where d'we go from here?'

'What d'you think, Brian?'

'Would you fancy going out there, it's safe enough since the Dayton Peace Accord last December, you could find Mr Cliff Jones's source of supply and talk to the girls.'

'Oh no, not that, I couldn't possibly,' Nina said. She felt exactly as though a solid dark curtain had dropped in front of her, barring her from the future Brian France was looking at. Her voice and hands—one unconsciously fingering the scar on her face—were trembling, and she felt a physical sensation of chill as the blood drained from her cheeks.

'Only when you've got your mind round the idea,' Brian said.

'I can't.'

'Wouldn't the boyfriend let you?' he jeered.

The boyfriend would probably be all for it, she thought. Harry had made it perfectly clear that he thought Nina's work was perfectly pointless. Light entertainment, wallpaper for the mind, junk food: was it worth while? Pride would have made her walk smartly away from any other man who implied such a thing. But there was something about Harry. Not just that she was beginning to think about him at inconvenient moments, finding his image, often censorious, intruding into her life. Not just that he was one of the few people she thought cleverer and more able than she was herself. Not just that he was a better lover than any man she'd ever slept with and had returned her to the semi-permanent state of unfocused lust she remembered being in at seventeen. No, it was something to do with an invincible and, once recognised, potentially infuriating rightness. He was, she suddenly realised, a good man—which was more than she had ever thought about any other man. She wanted him to approve of her, to think she was worth admiring, desiring and—oh, yes, she thought, that's what I really want. I want him to love me. Harry X Nina.

13

They were due to join up with the convoy in the late afternoon, but had a puncture after their first rest-break. Claudia knew how to repair punctures in theory and both Mary Ellen and Sheila had done it in practice, but the tools provided would not shift the rusty bolts. In the end some Canadian soldiers in a NATO patrol stopped to help, but by then they were more than half a day behind schedule, and had missed the planned rendezvous.

'I hope they've really waited for us, because it sure isn't safe on our own, even now,' Sheila said.

On they went, driving in a muddle of routine traffic such as would be seen in any other European country, mingled with shabby, stinking rust-buckets which would attract police attention back home. They were all tense and unrelaxed, jumping at every backfire, but Claudia tried to pretend there was nothing to be frightened of, this was hardly different from going to Italy or

Spain, as she and George had sometimes done in the old days, travelling tentatively in a strange country, cautious of foreign laws and traffic, but safe.

Yet the knowledge of conflict coloured her perceptions. Any aeroplanes or helicopters seemed threatening, their clatter ominous. A column of smoke ahead could be a bomb crater; then they came close enough to see it was a heap of burning tyres. Those people, crowding along a side road, might be fleeing refugees. They were workers coming out at the end of a factory shift.

'Look,' Mary Ellen said. 'A circus,' and then the acrid smell, which had briefly seemed to be that of blood and graves, merely signified ill-kept animals. The outsiders moved smoothly along in their bubble of foreignness; Claudia watched an alien world through glass and wondered whether she could ever feel easy in it. Every fifty miles or so they passed through checkpoints, slower though no more alarming, but for the casually gun-toting officials, than a toll-booth on an autoroute. They were worried about the schedule, being hours late and still far from any designated resting place, but at least they passed without more trouble than frustrating waits. They were travelling along towards the road which, once out of Croatia, the British army had called 'Route Diamond'. Mary Ellen, who had been that way before, said it was also known as 'the aid trail', and Sheila said, 'We call it Ho Chi Minh's.'

Making conversation Claudia rashly asked Sheila about her experiences here, and in horrible detail she described the piles of massacred bodies she'd seen, the raped and murdered women, the sacked villages and slaughtered soldiers. 'Soldiers—that's what they called themselves, but without arms, how could they be? America and you Europeans wouldn't let my people have any weapons to defend themselves, lambs to the slaughter they were. Still are, actually, poor sods.'

Mary Ellen, having been so glum and sulky, was becoming nervously excitable and talkative, probing Sheila about her life and interjecting needling remarks to Claudia. Sheila, it seemed, was a sociology graduate. Mary Ellen described her own aborted dissertation. 'Not that Claudia'd know what we're on about, she's too posh to understand.'

Sheila, peace-making, asked, 'What d'you do, Claudia, when you aren't doing this?'

'Well, I'm just a housewife, really.'

'Some house! Some wife!' Mary Ellen mocked.

What can be wrong with her, she's behaving really oddly, Claudia thought anxiously, she's so twitchy.

'Lady high and mighty, that's our Claudia, rolling in it she is,' Mary Ellen said.

'I'm not, really,' Claudia said weakly. George paid Claudia's bills and didn't query them, but never gave her cash, because he always went through the housekeeping accounts to see what could be set against tax. In his world wives had 'money of their own'. She said, 'Things aren't really so easy.'

'I'd just help myself, in your place,' Mary Ellen said.

'Oh Mary Ellen, you wouldn't,' Claudia protested.

'I have too.'

'When did you ever do that?'

'F'rinstance, when I was still married, one time, goody goody little member's wife, butter wouldn't melt in my mouth, there was some poncy lunch with his posh constituents and the hostess was collecting for the new hunt kennels. I can see her now, carrying round this papier mâché kennel with a coin-slit in the roof, rattling it under my nose. When I went up to the bog I saw her own coat and bag slung on her bed, so I took a couple of notes from her purse, folded them small and fed them into her own collecting box. Serve her right.'

Sheila was pink with embarrassment. Half turning her back on Mary Ellen she asked Claudia, 'So what's your husband do?'

'Well, there's a farm to run, and various companies—'

'She doesn't have any idea what he does all day, or all night either,' Mary Ellen interrupted. 'None so blind as them that won't see and Claudia doesn't dare look, do you? Anything rather than end up like me, out in the cold, having to look after yourself, managing the best you can, doing things you'd never have thought you ever could—what's the time? Can't we get a move on?'

'You drive, then,' Claudia said in a thin, faint voice, thinking the activity might shut Mary Ellen up. What can have come over her? What is all this about? The way she's talking, she must really hate me.

'A silly bitch like you,' Mary Ellen went on in an almost conversational tone, 'you deserve what you get.'

'Don't we all?' Sheila said in a falsely jolly tone. Claudia said nothing, thinking her silence was exactly the passivity Mary Ellen seemed to despise. She never did say anything: not to George, not to the women in his life, not to his snooty relations, not, in the old days, to her own oppressive family. Stop it, she told herself, don't even think the words. There would be no end to them.

'Look, we're coming to the next checkpoint,' Sheila said.

'About time too, look how late we are, we should have got here hours ago,' Mary Ellen muttered. She's just nervous, Claudia thought. So am I.

For the first time they were not waved through on the strength of their flourished passports, but waited and waited with the engine on to keep the heater going as they inched forward behind a rankly odorous truckful of whining sheep. It was a grim place where the road passed through a cutting in the hill, iron grey rocks with

174

mud streaks, looming like prison walls.

By the time they reached the sentry box it was dusk, already chilly and still damp. Handing their papers into an outstretched palm, they watched the precious documents being taken away into a dimly lit booth. Some men pored over them, raising their eyes to examine the women's faces through the windows. Sheila drew her headscarf across her face.

'They'll never recognise me,' Claudia said. 'That passport photograph's hopelessly out of date.'

It was impossible to tell what was causing the delay.

'Perhaps they want a cut,' Claudia said.

'What of?'

'Money. A bribe.'

'Better not try that here,' Sheila said.

'This is ridiculous,' Claudia said. 'They should be glad of our coming, bringing all this free stuff.'

'Depends which side it's for,' Sheila muttered.

Two men came out to the truck and gestured a command to open the rear door. The women watched the examination of their load. The men seemed puzzled by the teddy bears and kangaroos, and took some out of their polythene wrappers to shake and prod. One man brought out a knife which he flicked open and used to slash down the petunia-pink fabric. Small foam balls of stuffing fell out on to the road.

'What do they want anyway?' Claudia wondered.

'I think they are checking for substances,' Sheila said.

'What sort of substances?'

'Drugs.'

Two of the men climbed into the truck and began to hand down sealed boxes.

'Oh no, must you?' Claudia groaned. She got out and went towards the men saying, 'It's relief supplies. Food.' She made miming gestures of eating, putting her hands to her open mouth and rubbing her stomach.

One of the boxes was slit open, the flaps pulled apart. A tightly packed row of tins was revealed, flat, oblong with rounded corners: sardines. Idly Claudia picked a couple out. The next layer seemed to be something different, metallic cylinders from which an acrid, oily smell came. She put her hand towards another sardine tin, saying, 'They are leaking.' But one of the officials grabbed the tin from her hand to replace both it and the other two, and then lifted the boxes back before repacking the rest of the cargo. Claudia stood to one side, unable to decide what she should do. Could that really have been ammunition? Were there weapons in those boxes? How did they get there?

You don't know what real guns and ammunition look like, she told herself. It's nothing like the sporting guns George uses. You don't know what they sound like when they are fired, you know nothing about it whatsoever. If you make a fuss now you'll be stuck here indefinitely.

Gun running. Arms dealing. Using the charity of which she was herself the figurehead as a front. It was impossible. Inadmissible. A mistake. It must be to do with Jake Konin. He'd been up to something. In Rotterdam, maybe in Munich, so possessive he'd been about loading the boxes. She'd never really liked him. He took advantage, she thought indignantly, he conned us.

What to do now?

Better to leave Sheila in blissful ignorance, drive on and deliver the consignment, most of which was surely much-needed relief supplies as promised, hand it over, get shot of it, turn round and make for home. What on earth had she got herself mixed up with? Best not to be sure.

The men were telephoning inside the booth.

Claudia beckoned Mary Ellen out of the Australian girl's earshot. In a low voice she said, 'I think that Jake set us up. There's something wrong with those crates. He must have known.'

'What?'

'I think,' Claudia whispered almost inaudibly, 'there's guns in there.'

Mary Ellen put her fingers over her mouth. 'Not drugs, then?' she murmured.

'Did you think there were drugs?' Claudia was seized by the terrible thought that Mary Ellen was implicated in this, that she was using the charity's reputation to smuggle contraband. I'm out of my depth here, God knows what's going on. What shall I do? she wondered.

Back out of earshot the men seemed to be arguing over the passports and documents. Eventually Claudia slid back the door, jumped down and walked towards the booth. She smiled at the three men still huddled inside it. They were not in uniform, but wore jeans and nylon shirts,

178

with black leather jackets hung on chairs. The cubicle was thick with smoke and very warm.

One of the men was working back through Mary Ellen's passport, a dark blue stiff-covered little volume with the royal coat of arms stamped on its cover. Reading the inked handwriting upside down Claudia could see that the next of kin was given as the Rt. Hon. Peter Wood MP, PC, the address, the House of Commons. Beth's name was still entered on her mother's passport, date of birth—must be '75, Claudia thought, though that uncrossed 7 looked like a 9.

'Is there a problem?'

'Yours?'

'No, the red one's mine.'

The man opened Claudia's modern European Community passport, read the computer-generated text, glanced from the picture to her, and closed it again. He resumed his discussion with the other men, ignoring Claudia as though she were not there. She went back to the van and got on to the bench seat beside Sheila. 'I think they think we're VIPs,' she said.

'If only. Then we'd be spared all this hassle.'

'I used to be treated like a VIP on official trips with my ex,' Mary Ellen said. 'It sure beat waiting round at checkpoints.'

'Look,' Sheila said, 'they're coming over.'

One of the men threw Claudia's and Sheila's papers on to their laps. Holding on to Mary Ellen's he snapped, *'Komm.'*

Uncomprehending, the women stared at him.

'Du. Komm mit mir.'

'He's telling you to go with him,' Sheila whispered.

'Me? Why?' Mary Ellen said. 'What's wrong with—'

He drew a revolver from his hip holster and pointed it casually at her.

'What on earth—?' Claudia began.

'You'd better do what he says,' Sheila muttered.

'It'll be some query about my passport,' Mary Ellen said. She climbed over Sheila and on to the ground. The other two women watched her, frozen in fear.

'What's happening, what's going on, can't you ask them, Sheila? You speak the language.'

Her voice hoarse, Sheila leant out of the window and began to speak. With an inattention that was almost more frightening than an angry response would have been, the man pushed Mary Ellen, not into the little booth, but on beyond and behind it, and out of sight.

What shall I do, what's best to do? Claudia's thoughts skittered round like a panicky rabbit. I can't just watch them take her away. She opened the driver's door and shakily swung her legs out. Would they even support her weight? 'We've got to find out what's going on,' Claudia whispered. Awful images chased through her imagination: murder, rape, torture. Why did I ever come?

'Don't get out, Claudia, can't you see he's aiming that gun at you?' Sheila sounded hysterical with fear.

Moving very slowly, as much from terror as in the need to seem unaggressive, Claudia climbed down to the muddy ground. She held the palms of her hands out flat in front of her and began to speak gently to the other men, asking where they'd taken her friend, but the long barrel of the gun was swung round towards her and the gesture was unmistakable. Get in or I shoot. She stood indecisively still, and heard the gun click. Hastily she climbed back into the driving seat.

One of the men shouted, '*Geh weiter*—go on.'

'We can't. We can't go without our friend,' Claudia dared to protest.

'You go—you go now. *Jetzt, sofort, geh*—'

Mary Ellen had disappeared. It grew darker. It was very cold.

Sheila whimpered, 'We'll have to do what they say, we can't just stay here.'

'Without Mary Ellen?'

'They think she's someone important, they think her husband's an MP, she might be a hostage but they won't hurt her, but we're no use to them, Claudia, don't you see, we've got to get out of here. We'll be coming back this way, she'll be here for us to pick up. I'm sure she'll be here then. If we don't do what they say they'll shoot us.'

A nightmare of argument and incomprehension. What shall I do, I got Mary Ellen into this.

A loud crack came from somewhere nearby. Sheila screamed, 'That was a gun.'

'Oh God, oh God, what shall we do?'

'They've killed her!' Sheila whimpered. 'They'll kill us, come on, Claudia, drive, let me drive, they'll shoot us too.'

182

14

Her hands were shaking almost too much to drive. Claudia felt like a criminal, like Judas, a betrayer. Sheila began to gabble.

'Maybe it wasn't her, it mightn't have been, it'll all be OK really, it must be, they prolly only wanted to talk to her.' She was trying to convince herself, her voice thin and terrified. 'And what about us, what are we to do, we haven't a hope of catching up with the others tonight, I don't know what to do, I wish I'd never come, Uncle said it was just a drive up the road to join the rest of the convoy and someone would give me a lift back. Where are they? They should have waited for us. They were told to wait for us.'

Numb with shame and remorse, Claudia tried to rally Sheila—and herself. 'We didn't have any choice, they'd have shot us if we hadn't gone on.'

'But we've missed the convoy.'

'We might find them round the next corner. Perhaps they wanted to get out of sight of the frontier post, it might have seemed provocative to have waited right beside it.'

'We shouldn't be alone here, we've got to be together for protection. There's a bloke from Auckland, he stayed at the hotel last week—I thought we'd be with them. Maybe we ought to turn round,' Sheila said.

The girl's only come to chase some New Zealander, Claudia realised indignantly. She said, 'Of course we'll go back, but not till we've got someone with us with the authority to get Mary Ellen out of there. There'll be someone with the convoy when we reach it. I'm sure there will. There's got to be.'

The weather was getting worse and the road was rough, no longer a highway but a winding mountain track with an uneven, broken surface. It could never have been perfect. Now, after months or years of neglect, it was rutted and scattered with stones. Nobody had touched up the white warning paint on the cliff sides, replaced missing cats' eyes or repaired the metal barriers on the sharpest bends.

They passed only two cars going in the other direction and were overtaken by one, going dangerously fast, which sprayed the windscreen with muck as it went by.

Sheila crouched against the door, sniffling. 'I never thought it was going to be like this,' she muttered.

After about an hour they came to a row of rusty barrels with planks balanced across them. A roughly painted arrow pointed to one side, directing traffic into a side track. They turned cautiously on to its rough surface.

Claudia drove very slowly. It began to rain more heavily. Silver stripes were illuminated by the yellow beam. She wound the window down and smelt the wet leaves, the resinous trees, the settling dust.

Useless or untrustworthy though Sheila might be, Claudia was glad not to be all alone to envisage the terrifying apparitions of this strange land, Dracula and Frankenstein's monster and all the forest demons of archaic European legends. Or the contemporary bogeymen; clones of those who had taken Mary Ellen away.

Driving. Driving. Forcing onwards.

There is a sheer drop on the right, a jagged rock wall on the left.

Where are we?

The van inches forward on the uneven surface and the awkward camber. She leans forward, peering through the continuously remisted windscreen, seeing only a short stretch of the road ahead. There is hardly anything to show where the road ends and plunging eternity begins. Her hands grip tight on the wheel, her right foot poised as gently as if there was thin glass rather than the metal accelerator beneath it.

Onwards, slowly slowly, in indistinguishable nowhereness. There seems to be no reason why this should ever end. For all eternity they would be driving beside a deadly fall.

At last, over the top of some pass or hill, the road turns downhill, very steep, the surface even less easy going than before, the bends sharp. She keeps the gear low and her foot over the brake, peering painfully ahead. When the headlights are full on she can see little more than their reflection on the sheets of rain. Dipped, they illuminate a very short way ahead.

A small animal runs across in front of the van and she brakes and feels the beginning of a skid. It is easily corrected, but then she slows down even more, crawling along and flicking the lights up and down.

They have not come much more than twenty miles from the checkpoint.

And then—

A horizontal line crossing the vertical lines of the rain. A rope. A thin wire stretched tight across the road between tree and tree.

Does her foot hit the brake? Does she wrench the wheel to one side?

No time, no time to react before a blast of unimaginable force sucks the air from her mouth, the hearing from her ears.

Silence, clamour, darkness and pain. There's no sense to be made of it as sensations and fear swirl in a disorientated consciousness. Visions, dreams, memories?

Were there figures moving in beams of light, carrying, lifting, holding guns like a vision of dread? Shooting? Had she seen this, clouded by chaos and agony? Or dreamt it, afterwards, since ...?

Another image flashes before her mind's eye. She sees the van, but she is not in it.

It is halted on the mountainside. And then it moves.

Inexorably, the front wheels slide sideways and on over the edge. How long does it take before, more violently, unstoppable, it crashes heavily, down, spinning free, the lorry angled and then twisting, bouncing off the trees and jagged rocks, down and down until, when it meets the ground, it is engulfed in fire.

Loud voices, raised in disagreement. A series of deafening reports. What is it, what are they saying? I don't understand.

A smell. Burning. A noise. Gunfire.

The clouds obscure everything again.

Then comes another flash of consciousness. She is lifted by ankles and shoulders, a harsh grip that makes her cry out in unbelievable, unprecedented pain. This can't be happening. It is happening.

She is swung and flung on to something hard. She is in a cart or van. Being moved elsewhere.

Where from? Where to? Who?

A nightmare.

This isn't really happening.

I'm dreaming, I must wake up.

It can't go on like this. I can't.

Someone will come soon. The emergency services. Sirens, bells, flashing lights. Busy, competent, well-trained people. They'll

know what to do. They'll look after me.
'What's your name,' they'll call, and 'Can
you tell me what happened?' and 'Get a
line in.' Someone must rescue me.
Help. Please help.

15

'British women die on mercy mission.'
'Stately home owner dies in former
Yugoslavia.'
'MP's ex killed.'
'Bad end for do-gooders.'
The news came through quickly, a
variation on the familiar litany of bombs
and bullets. A United Nations patrol had
found the burnt-out shell of Handyside's
lorry. A mine had been detonated under
the lorry before it plunged down the
mountainside. The destruction was such
that there would have been no way to
identify the individual victims or even send
any sad casket home. It was known that
the two British women had been on board
with an Australian companion. The Irish
soldiers who bulldozed the remains had

said a mass over the mound of earth.

Mary Ellen Wood and Claudia Anson were not the first aid workers to die in former Yugoslavia, far from it, but the status of one and former notoriety of the other made them much more exciting news than most.

It was at such moments that Nina was reminded of the unsettledness of her affair with Harry Anson. He went to Ansons to be with his family, and his phone calls were brief and uncommunicative.

Wounded, Nina turned to assembling and rearranging the material she had already collected about Mary Ellen Wood. Her fate would make a brilliant programme as well as an awful warning; an example of what happened to other wives whose love and money were entirely invested in a man who let them down. Nina collected her material, trying all the while to subdue the personal guilt she still felt about Mary Ellen's fate. Other journalists' obituaries of Mary Ellen all concentrated on the period before her divorce.

Articles about Claudia were more straightforward. Her life had been so very conventional, an archetypal lady-of-the-manor. Admired if not beloved, Claudia was to be commemorated as George Anson's female ancestors had always been. In death at least she would be a Catholic, given a plaque and a requiem mass in the family chapel. There would be a tree planted in the garden and the portrait by Ward would be moved from the obscure passage where Claudia had hidden it, into the gallery with all the other family portraits. George Anson requested sympathisers not to write. Donations to Handyside's Bequest would be welcomed in Claudia's memory instead.

Beth welcomed and wept over the letters people wrote about Mary Ellen. She said she would take them back to Chile bound up in a morocco leather album. It became clear, when Nina talked to Beth, that she'd known nothing about her mother's daily life, although it was easy for Nina to follow its trail and work out how one could cope, left penniless. She realised many women must have found the same solution. There might be other Mary Ellens all over London. This programme would strike many people to the heart. What were Mary Ellen Wood's qualifications? Zilch. During a period of high unemployment and in competition with younger women

191

who had degrees and diplomas, Mary Ellen was never in the running to get any job she applied for. And assets? Her voice. Her posh appearance. For one purpose, at least, they'd been enough.

By the end of 1994 Mary Ellen was destitute. Every penny Peter had made over to her when they parted had been paid out to Lloyds. That financial calamity was the late twentieth-century equivalent to the South Sea Bubble or the Wall Street Crash, the ruin of middle-class people in previous generations. Mary Ellen still owed, though there was no way she would ever be able to pay, a small fortune. She signed on the dole and moved from the house in Islington to a bedsit, still turning up at her polytechnic until an efficiency drive excluded anyone without the card issued only to those students who had paid up.

Beth Wood, who had settled in South America by that time, was spared the truth; all she was told, in up-beat letters and phone calls, was that her mother had changed her address. What was the point of making the poor girl miserable when there wasn't anything she could do? Let her live her own life. And Mary Ellen told a fellow student she'd rather die than appeal to Peter. Recovered from the numbness which anaesthetised her at the moment of discovering the truth, she felt a disgusted shrinking from her former husband. She had believed he was her soul mate—literally her other half. When his faithlessness was revealed it was as though a handsome mask had been removed to show a stinking, deformed monster underneath it.

'I can manage on my own,' Mary Ellen asserted. And so she did. Nina found that she'd cleaned houses, briefly had a job as a car-park attendant and escorted travellers, delivering a grandmother here and a grandchild there. Arriving for a summer school at Trinity College, Dublin, Kevin Reardon had caught sight of her in the distance at the airport, queuing at the immigration control with a wailing infant in her arms.

But Mary Ellen's chief resource was to forage in the pastures of the prosperous. It was now that she discovered the true value of the clothes left over from the old days. Expensive though never fashionable, the dresses and suits took her everywhere unquestioned. She would load a supermarket trolley with desirable goods, and be offered titbits from free-sample displays, lunching adequately, if not well, off cubes of cheese or biscuits smeared with jam, before abandoning the trolley and walking out empty-handed. Even in her present straits she rejected pâté or salami; other students half her age had converted Mary Ellen to vegetarianism. But she could sample cherries or grapes as though deciding whether they were good enough to buy; and sometimes she was even offered a tiny beaker of wine.

Mary Ellen could hardly afford fires or hot water in her bedsit but at least she wasn't sleeping underneath the arches in a cardboard box. And every day, unchallenged, she could enter hotels to use their ladies' powder rooms. Not Claridge's or the Savoy, because the best hotels had attendants who wiped the lavatory seat after each user, filled a basin with warm water afterwards and watched as patrons clinked some change into the saucer. It was wiser to go to inferior hotels, and during the day to department stores, which had well-equipped washrooms and nobody to mind if Mary Ellen made free with their facilities. She found that liquid soap washed hair as well as shampoo and some hand driers had gusts of warm air which could be redirected upwards on to her head.

Eventually she had even come upon a railway hotel with old-fashioned bathrooms in the upstairs corridors into which she could lock herself for an hour's luxury. And the once good clothes were her passport into other resorts of the wealthy: art galleries, large receptions and publicity functions. Unless there was someone at the door asking for names or even invitation cards she could walk in, smiling at an imaginary friend on the far side of the room, greeting perfect strangers.

'Hallo, nice to see you again,' she would say, moving quickly on what looked like a purposeful course across the room, before accepting a glass of wine and helping herself to crisps and nuts, or, if she was lucky, miniature pastries and protein-rich quails' eggs.

Mary Ellen found herself deriving creative pleasure from an urban version of living off the land. Running into her former professor one day she gave him full details of her 'research'. She said she would write a book on the Human

Ecology of Capital Cities. It would be called *Serendipity, or the picking up of unconsidered trifles.*

'It really was a good idea,' Kevin Reardon told Nina. 'I'd already spoken to my own agent, we were going to fix her up a commission for it, money in advance.'

Meanwhile Mary Ellen would trek back to her little room through streets where bag ladies pushed their supermarket trolleys and old men combed through other people's dustbins. And she would not ask for help. Not from Peter, not from poor little Beth, not from anyone. She became a watchful, prowling predator, scavenging other people's leavings to keep herself alive.

It was wonderful material, and Brian France pushed Nina to hurry up, giving her a short deadline. But she was afraid of seeming unforgivably tasteless so soon after Mary Ellen's death.

Brian said, 'You need a killer instinct in our job, no place for shrinking violets, Neen, you should know that.'

Nina said the details were too intrusive and painful even for an investigative reporter to be happy using.

'S'pose the boyfriend wouldn't like it, is that it?'

'What boyfriend?' Nina replied coldly. But when she rang Harry she got a brush-off. He's treating me like a reporter, she realised indignantly. So that's what I'd better bloody well be.

She tried to make the programme as general as possible—what happened to abandoned women whose husbands' careers had also been their own?—but it was the details she'd unearthed about Mary Ellen herself that made the broadcast sensational: the voice of a supermarket floor manager, who had observed Mary Ellen grazing off free samples, her upstairs neighbour who'd watched her sallying forth on her hunting exhibitions 'dressed up to the nines', Professor Reardon, enthusiastic about 'living off the urban land'. Topped with an archive tape from the day Peter Wood's peccadillo was found out, and tailed with a wail from Beth, incredulous that her mother had been destitute and never told her. 'My poor mummy, if only I'd known.' The programme was entitled 'If only I'd known' and replayed and quoted in chunks for days afterwards.

16

Pain.

Fear.

I feel dreadful. I feel like death.

Death? All alone, with nobody to hold my hand, in this place?

What place? Where am I?

Recollection flashes like intermittent lightning across her clouded mind.

Lying on the road. The side wheels and walls of the truck loom above her. Stones dig into her back and the back of her head. Rain showers on to her face and hands, into the sodden fabric of her clothes.

A shadowy face above her, peering down.

A gun pointed at her head.

Has she seen that or dreamt it?

She is in some kind of cell. There is a narrow hard surface on which she lies in a cubicle the size of a railway sleeping compartment.

Travelling north on the overnight train. The wheels turn clickety click on their iron tracks, water drips from the wash-basin tap. The smell of sulphur comes through the open window from the steam engine ahead.

The man above her moves up and down in his own rhythm, pressing her skin on to the rough sheet, holding her long hair back against the pillow with one hand, with the other grasping her chin, her mouth under his as he gasps, groans and slumps.

They have been married for three months and her husband still desires her.

The boards above her head are not those of an upper bunk but a roof with cracks between its splintered planks. Stripes of daylight give her dim awareness of her surroundings. A hut? A shed? An attic? The walls are rough, once whitened stone blocks.

A child is crying. Others are shouting, muffled.

Where ... who ...?

A tin bowl of gruel, a plastic bottle of water. They train her with rewards and punishments, though nobody has hurt her. Yet.

Yet.

It is her own fear, her own craven desire to please, which teaches her to put on the blindfold, a black hood drawn down over her head, before anyone enters the cell. She survives by subservience.

Later, hours or days later, she wakes from heavy sleep and tries to rise and stretch. Pain shooting through her back and limbs is an immediate reminder. She falls back on to the wrinkled cloth before sitting up more cautiously.

'I got off lightly.' She whispers to give herself courage. Nothing's broken, all limbs movable, though painfully or stiffly.

I can see. I can hear. I am fed.

A winter evening, sneezing, headachy, feverish. 'I'm not feeling too well, I'll go on up early.' A hot water bottle, lemon and honey, aspirins and a familiar undemanding book, Georgette Heyer or Agatha Christie. Sweatily, heavily asleep she is woken by George climbing into his side of the bed. 'I am ill,' he says, husky but penetrating. 'I've got a temperature. I need the thermometer, ginger ale, another pillow, those American pills I brought back. They might do the trick if I get a good night. Make sure I'm not disturbed in the morning.'

'Take no notice and it will get better on its own.' So her mother always said to her. So she said herself.

My turn now.

She is cautiously testing hands and feet, arms and legs, when a hand appears under the edge of the ill-fitting door. She sees it in the dusky gleam that comes through a crack between the boards of the closed shutters. It is holding a flat metal container, and for a moment she wonders, almost with detachment, whether this is her death.

The container holds water.

The hand withdraws, and soon the fingers reappear pushing some cloth under the door: folded blue denim.

For a moment the hand is still there lying on the floorboard. A brown hand, not wrinkled or spotted but hard, ridged with bones and ligaments, the nails rough and cracked. There is a wide gold band on the third finger. The hand of a married woman.

A hand lay on her desk at Ansons. It had been on the oak bureau in her student room and before that on her mother's kitchen dresser holding down a sheaf of recipes. That bronze hand had long slim fingers, the nails clearly marked, the tip of the thumb curving outwards, with a jagged break at the wrist. It was a piece of shrapnel amputated from some statue during an air raid and given to her mother by Papa.

Even when Mama was not at home the hand was still there to point its fingers, to observe and admonish; even to reach out and touch, gently, coldly. Papa had told her so. She had been terrified then of its sinister, small magic though it lost its power later and became nothing more than a metal paperweight; she only kept it as a reminder that she was grown up now, out of its control.

Like the shrapnel, this hand, a right hand, seems unconnected to a body. As silently as it appeared, it withdraws.

A small bowl of water. A pair of jeans.

Her own trousers, clean, and her own jersey, shrunken, matted and showing faint brown stains where the blood soaked in.

Very slowly she takes off the strange, thin sweater and jacket she has on, and the roughly knitted grey socks someone had put on her feet and the length of woven linen in which she'd been wrapped. Her bedding consists of a couple of thin grey blankets and a tattered square of white muslin which had been folded under her head.

With infinite parsimony she manages to tear a narrow strip from the muslin and to divide that strip into three pieces. She dips them in turn into the water, and wipes her teeth first, front and back, in and out, scrubbing with a cloth-covered finger, and then her face and the rest of her body, removing grime and dried blood, sweat and filth until each piece of fabric is in its turn filthy.

This is how they washed the time they camped on an uninhabited island the Ansons owned in the Hebrides. They rowed across the sound in a dinghy to collect fresh water in a milk churn. And she learnt the army trick of washing in a tin mug, working from the cleanest to the more contaminated and contaminating parts of the body. He'd liked moulding, teaching her things then. Washing became an erotic demonstration.

She examines those parts of herself which she can see.

The torn skin is mending, bruises yellowed over a scattering of boils and insect bites. Her cleaner face feels taut, the lips dry. Her nails have grown. Three days' worth? Four?

She puts on her own clothes. A small comb is still in the back pocket of the trousers, a cheap blue plastic comb from a long disappeared Christmas cracker. It was nothing, an object without value; but it is of infinite worth here. With reverent caution, she drags it through her leathery hair. She shakes out the bedding. She wipes over some of the boards in the small cell with the remaining drips of dirty water.

She waits. And waits.

'What are you making such a fuss about? You've been alone often enough before.'

Living in her gilded cage with her mechanical, inanimate servants, she has been used to solitude. A captive wife. Wives lived vicariously. They escaped into books, other people's worlds to rescue them from reality, imaginary people to stop them being their boring, bored selves.

'Where did you go, who did you see, what did they say?'

'Can you come to dinner?' That ambiguous English pronoun, singular or plural.

'I'm afraid George will be away.'

'Oh well, in that case, another time.'

One does not die of boredom.

One does not die of loneliness.

One does not die.

Not yet.

She speaks aloud against the cold silence of her cell. I will wait, and obey and endure. I will survive.

17

'I heard the programme,' Fidelis Berlin told Nina. She'd left a note in Nina's box asking if she'd like to come in for supper when she got back, and Nina, who had found her cupboards were bare of anything except some sugar-free muesli, but no milk, and some Marmite-flavoured rice cakes, was only too glad to go downstairs to her neighbour's flat.

Dr Fidelis Berlin was not the sort of person ever to find her own larder empty. Efficiently she assembled the meal, unconsciously humming as always. For once Nina recognised the tune, something from Holst's *Planets*. Fidelis served pasta, pesto, parmesan and rocket salad. She didn't mention her own or Nina's work while they ate. They talked about a bird-watching weekend Nina had been on in Norfolk, and about a new abstract painting by Wilhelmina Barns Graham on which Fidelis had committed an extravagance at a private view, and about a collection of poetry she'd been sent by one of Dora Wartski's protégées.

'And how's Harry getting on?' asked Fidelis, who had run into him and Nina in the summer, at an open-air Kenwood concert.

'Fine, I think,' Nina said. She and Harry had gone back to talking two or three times a day, though she couldn't help noticing he never mentioned his family. She added,

'We're both working so hard we hardly ever manage to meet.'

'That's an important job he's doing.'

'Don't I know it—the trouble is he's so full of *noblesse oblige,* he takes it to crazy lengths.'

'An old-fashioned English gentleman.'

'I suppose so,' Nina agreed. 'It's like he's subconsciously paying for his own good fortune in being born that way.'

'You make him sound very admirable.'

'Oh, he's admirable all right,' Nina said crossly. 'He won't ever sell out to Mammon the way I have, but I sometimes wish—'

'Nina, what do you mean, Mammon? Your job?'

'Well, I can't make out a very good case for myself as an altruist, doing my entertainment broadcasting, can I? It's not as though I'm doing anyone any good or broadening their minds or even keeping them informed any more.'

'But you're making good programmes. I was very interested by the one about Mary Ellen Wood,' Fidelis said. She poured jasmine tea and offered a plate of almond tuiles, before going on thoughtfully, 'Bag ladies, that's what less tough women than your Mary Ellen become. That's what the bogey in the corner is for so many of them, all those good wives who've never qualified to look after themselves and turn into embittered ex-wives.'

'Specially MPs' ex-wives.'

'I know, I remember talking about it once with a front-bencher. He was Labour, but the others would have been the same, dismissive, totally without sympathy or understanding. He asked why they don't get jobs as cooks or housekeepers. I told him most women in that position lived in dread of being cast out of the home, the tribe, their own place in the world.'

'It must be a generation thing, though,' Nina said. 'Younger women like me, we know we've got to be self-reliant.'

'But that's exactly what your Mary Ellen was, really resourceful, I admired her a lot by the end of your programme and you can see why she was an asset to that charity, she was a good coper. All the same I do wonder what made her do it all, given that she had a daughter to turn to. It must have been a miserable way of life.'

'I came to see her as a very unyielding person, very wholehearted. Everyone seemed to agree that she threw herself into being whatever she was at the time, a politician's wife, a mother, a student, a scrounger and then a relief worker. Apparently she always became devotedly committed to her causes, so when she started driving for Handyside's charity she wouldn't ever stop or take a break. You have to admire her.'

'I thought I detected an implication that you felt guilty about her for some reason?'

'Did that come through in the programme? I did, actually, I felt awful about Mary Ellen, the part I'd played in ruining her life—along with other reporters, of course.'

'There must be many people whose lives have been ruined by reporting; some also by you personally,' Fidelis, who was not one for disguising uncomfortable truths, remarked.

'Ouch.'

'It's the law of unintended consequences.'

'Maybe,' Nina agreed. 'But that was the first time I realised my gain wasn't worth her pain.'

A former patient had sent Fidelis a bottle of rare old Madeira, and she poured some into two lily-shaped glasses with bubble twist stems.

'What about the other one? Claudia Anson?'

Nina told Fidelis the story of how she had seen Claudia Anson on the same occasion as her last sight of Mary Ellen Wood. 'She looked very straight up and conventional, and that's how Harry makes her sound. I didn't really think much about her then. But I did hear her say that she had no intention of driving relief supplies herself ever, so I was really surprised later when the gossip columns said she was going to.'

'How did they know? Gossip columns always get facts wrong,' Fidelis said.

'No, there'd been a press release circulated from Handyside's Bequest, I saw it—and anyway, she did go. She went to her death.'

'I suppose she couldn't have backed out after that, she'd never have been able to change her mind so publicly once it was expected of her, it would have done the charity enormous harm— Oh, do you mind if I just answer that, I'm expecting a call from— Hullo? Fidelis Berlin.'

Nina went to load up the dishwasher. She enjoyed being in this homely flat where there was so much in common with the

Wartskis' house. They and Fidelis must have bought their equipment at exactly the same period, for both had several identical gadgets, furniture and light fittings. Red Magistretti chairs, Festival of Britain style china, these blue checked table mats. Nina was wiping the quarry-tiled surfaces when Fidelis came through and said, 'That's enough about past programmes. What are you doing now?'

It was the same every time they met. Nina intended not to talk about herself and her own concerns—after all, why should Fidelis care for them?—but the older woman was one of nature's confidantes. I wonder who she dumps on, if she ever feels the need to dump, Nina briefly wondered, before launching into an account of her babies-for-sale investigation. Telling it to the silent, sympathetic Fidelis made her put it in order in her own mind, more so than when talking to Brian France, who was interested in good broadcasting, not scrupulous accuracy.

An illicit organisation was selling babies to willing purchasers. The purchasers believed, it was to be hoped, that the babies had been put for adoption willingly, or that their relations had all perished.

Nina supposed that some, at least, of the bona fide charity workers in the babies' countries of origin knew what was going on, but more than that Nina hardly knew. She had gone to see the relevant officers of several of the charities involved, mostly harried, hassled people indifferent to their own comfort or appearance because the needs of their clients were so urgent. Laurel Berryman at Handyside's was the exception. Nina's appointment had been, as it turned out, a couple of days before the news broke of the death of Mary Ellen Wood and Claudia Anson, and she had no reason to mention them.

'She was absolutely terrifying,' Nina told Fidelis.

'You, terrified? I can't see it,' Fidelis laughed.

'No, honestly, you should have seen her. Stick thin, dazzling blonde, with a brilliantly pink and white skin and impermeable cosmetics and she probably has a personal hairdresser popping out of a cupboard between meetings. As for her clothes, she'd not have looked out of place on a catwalk. And so cool. Like I said, terrifying. God knows what she sees in George Anson, because he's rock between the ears by all accounts.'

'I expect she sees his position and his house in him,' Fidelis said quietly. 'Long lineage and lots of money have often made up for personal deficiencies, as English history shows. Have you met him?'

'Once, with Harry, but George didn't know we were involved. He's out of it a lot of the time, he's an alcoholic. But he was sober when we met and I thought he must be the stupidest, dullest, most conventional man I'd ever met, a nullity.'

'Is that what Harry thinks of his brother?'

'He'd never admit it, but he did once say the only original thing he'd ever done was fall in love with Claudia and marry her.'

'And regret it.'

'Harry didn't say that either.'

'And was Mrs Berryman any help about the illicit adoptions?'

'Oh no, she batted that straight back at me too, full of management speak about their systems and fail-safes and precautions against smuggling of illegal immigrants in one direction or contraband in the other. The funny thing is I'd not even thought about smuggling till she said that, but then I started thinking that must actually

213

be how it's done, using bent so-called aid workers.'

'Have you been able to work out where the babies come from?'

Nina replied, 'Obviously it has to be eastern Europe, and those who knew thought it was from former Yugoslavia. That guy who called himself Bill had been shown a photo of some village where the military had taken a crusader castle plonked down in a Roman fort.'

'It ought to be possible to identify that.'

'Yes, I've tracked down some possibles. Laurel Berryman had some ideas, I told her I'd be going out to follow the story up, but I don't really know if I can face it.'

'You may not be ready for that.'

'No,' Nina agreed. 'It—the idea terrifies me, actually.'

'Going to see what's happening in the camps—to the children, I mean?' Fidelis asked.

'Yes, because the babies I know of—not that I do know of very many—are European, described as Caucasian whatever that really means, but they're quite dark, some of them.'

'And how long has it been going on?'

'How can I tell? The oldest child I've heard of, that's the one landed on poor Bill, he can't be more than about five or six.'

'Yes.' Fidelis put her glass down and rose, to walk across to a table of flowering pot plants and begin fiddling with their leaves. 'I heard the phone-in with poor Bill and I've been wondering whether to talk to you about it ever since, though I didn't realise you were already following the subject up.'

'What, Fidelis? Tell me.'

'The fact is I really oughtn't to.'

'Why not?'

'The usual confidentiality, but I'm going to mention it, all the same, I'm sure you'd never use anything I say.'

'Of course not.'

'Because the thing is that I have been professionally involved with one of these children. It was an unusual case and it ended—well, I could never make up my own mind whether it was a sad or happy ending. And the consequences—well, let's say you might be the person to cope.'

'You're speaking as a shrink, I suppose.'

'Horrid word, as though you were swollen-headed. No, Nina. Not that. I

215

may be a psychiatrist but I've never worked as a professional shrink, as you call it, not even a soul-doctor. But I'm still capable of seeing you're dragging your feet, you aren't ready for the place where your story's leading you. But when you are, let me know and you can go and meet these people, and hear their story.'

18

Alone, lonely, solitary.

Who'll miss me? Not George. Not a son or daughter. There's nobody to care.

Selfish. Thinking about myself.

Think about Sheila. Dead. Killed.

What about Mary Ellen? That shot—she must be dead too.

My fault, Claudia thought, a punishment. We shouldn't ever have let her go, we shouldn't have driven on. And she'd never have come here but for me, it's all my fault, she was poor and hungry and I didn't help her out, I just sent her here. I never thought. I never thought at all, I should have known better, I did know what it's like being poor.

Claudia had been educated in self-denial herself, her puritan parents so committed to their missionary vocation that their own daughter always seemed to come last in their priorities. Middle class but always dressed in cast-offs and never given the money for school trips or subscriptions, Claudia had hated the austerities of her childhood. She'd been Hannah then, a name from the Old Testament which went with the unsociable austerity Claud Brown imposed on himself and his family. Only when she escaped could she opt to use her classical second name.

The Reverend Claud Brown was a huge, solid man with a long square jaw and prominent teeth. He had sparse, sandy hair and fierce watery eyes. He had a bath once a week, and had a distinctive, musty smell, reminders of which in later life would make Claudia involuntarily cringe at the memory of that rough coarseness against her, a suffocating sensation of being in his power, of confinement. She remembered him holding her down to spank or slipper. Of further forced intimacies she had no conscious recall. Hannah Claudia fantasised about luxury and artifice. She

217

wanted to know people who did not always share the truth, so seldom flattering to others, so often critical; why couldn't she live amongst those who said things that were kind or complimentary instead?

She used to gaze in museums or shop windows at objects designed solely to give pleasure, at paintings and ornaments and clothes which seemed to symbolise centuries of sophistication and were part of civilised lives led by cultivated people. She longed for a softer world where she'd be surrounded by love and beautiful things.

I knew what Mary Ellen's life must be like, but I never helped her, all I did was send her to her death. I deserve all this now, whatever happens to me. I'm being punished.

The Ansons would say she was being *tried.* They often used the expression—Mrs Anson, Claudia's mother-in-law, and George's sister Milly and especially Andrea Chandler who had gone through a phase of wanting to be a nun and mortifying the flesh by sleeping—as her aunt was now failing to sleep—on cold, bare boards.

George never cared that Claudia was a heathen but his relations never forgave her for not being received into the Catholic

Church. Why hadn't she? It would have been the last rebellion from her own background, and was the only one she couldn't quite make. Father, God, God the Father—someone or something wouldn't let her.

That God was punishing her now. Her sin had found her out.

'Sin, what sin?' The last whisper of rebellion surfaced in her mind. But she had always known what her sin was, the abortion so lightly arranged after she'd met George, so endlessly paid for in her subsequent sterility. 'God is not mocked,' her father's voice whispered, over and over again.

At last, at long long last, a pinkish light leaked into the room. For a wonderful moment Claudia thought she was waking from a nightmare. Then she heard her sandpapery tongue peel itself from the dried-out soft palate. She pushed herself on to her knees and then her feet, balancing uncertainly and stiffly like an old woman.

When they came again she was meekly, weakly, waiting with the hood over her head. She heard the scraping of wood against wood and even through the dark cloth sensed sunlight on her skin. The barred shutter had been opened.

Hands moved over her, prodding, palpating. It was painful but reassuring. This was some kind of doctor.

Duncan Croft was their doctor. Duncan had a beer belly and called her lassie. Prone, her feet in stirrups, immobilised and helpless as he pushed his instruments and fingers inside her, she was a captive audience for his reminiscences about getting drunk at Cambridge, larking around at boarding school, or before that playing doctors and nurses. She never dared tell Duncan that she'd heard it all before and always hated the child he was revealing to her, who grew into the man she'd fallen in love with. The boy he described as his childhood friend was not a person she would have wanted to marry when he grew up.

Duncan's hands had been rougher than this man's, whether or not he was a doctor. He raised and lowered her arms and legs, moved her head from side to side.

A voice said something indistinguishable. Irresistibly, she burst out, 'Can you understand English? *Parlez-vous français? Sprechen sie Deutsch?*'

With a sudden movement of her free

hand, she grasped the fabric of the hood and pulled it away from her face.

She lay still, blinking in the unaccustomed light that streamed in from the window opening.

The man had grizzled, crinkly hair and a dark complexion. He could be an Arab, an Israeli, any kind of eastern European. He wore wire-rimmed spectacles which slid down a narrow, curved nose. His lips were drawn in above a toothless mouth. He was wearing a suit made of some thin, slightly shiny blue cloth, with a fawn shirt open at the neck. His hands came towards her face and he peered with impersonal concentration into her pupils. Involuntarily she shrank back on to the thin pillow, but he only wished to draw her eyelids down. He had not shaved for a while and his breath smelt of garlic.

A woman was there too. She had pulled a scarf up over her chin and nose so all that could be seen were very dark eyes below a thick fringe of dark hair, and an unmanicured brown hand wearing a wedding ring. In case it was the woman who delivered yesterday's washing materials she smiled at her, trying to convey thanks and harmlessness. The skin round the woman's eyes crinkled briefly. Then other footsteps approached, heavy soles running up wooden stairs, and the woman shrank back into her reserve.

A soldier came into the room, a young man in battle fatigues with a handgun and no holster on his belt. The 'doctor' and the woman both retreated into a corner of the room. The soldier swept the gun around the room.

'You Sheila. You!'

Claudia was too petrified to speak and he roared, 'Why are you come here, in my country, why?'

'I came to bring relief supplies.' Quavering, hardly audible. Speak up, make it convincing. 'Help. You know, food, medicines—'

'To what people?'

'For the refugees.'

'What refugees, what people?'

'Everyone. Anyone.'

He shouted, 'You know this, you lie to me. You lose my guns, where my ammunition?' His gun had a dull, oily sheen. He was holding it the way a child holds a new toy.

Perhaps it was one of the guns which had been in the van. I brought that here, she thought, and I don't know who they were for. I brought *guns.*

Tears filled her eyes. She whispered, 'I didn't mean to, I meant to bring life not death. It's all gone wrong.' And then, weakly, with hatred for her own pusillanimity, she said, 'Please, don't blame me, someone else put them into the van, I didn't know anything about it, it wasn't my fault.'

'They kill you too,' the man said. 'They kill you Sheila and Englishwoman. It is plan, women die. But they take my weapons also, my guns!'

'Englishwoman,' she whispered. Me? Mary Ellen? Where was she? He thinks I'm the Australian girl.

'To her, bitch, goodbye,' the man shouts. 'English, Dr Owen, Croat lover! Serb whore!' Gathering saliva in his mouth, he spat violently, and went on, 'All Croats Killers! Serbs assassins! Why no guns for Muslim? English, I shit on English.'

Who was he? Not Mujahedeen. Who was he fighting?

The other woman said something in a low voice. Was she trying to protect Claudia? All she achieved was to provoke and anger the man with the gun, who

223

swung it carelessly against her before gesturing to the male civilian to follow him, swinging out of the doorway and clattering away.

The woman's forehead was pouring blood over her suddenly blanched face. She made ineffectual dabs with her hand.

Gently Claudia pulled the scarf away from the stream of blood and pushed the woman to sit down on the pallet. With incongruous efficiency, Claudia performed the first aid she had learnt at a Red Cross class which she had attended to encourage some of the estate workers to do so.

Winter evenings, three or four years ago, the village hall. Muggy and cold at the same time with the only heat coming from an antique coal stove in one corner. The walls were hung with posters for the local elections, and at one end was stacked the scenery for a pantomime. Jack's beanstalk loomed over the wounded dummies, a background to merriment as strangers performed intimate pretences on one another's limbs. Pressure on the bleeding point, Claudia remembered, infection from foreign bodies, the recovery position. She bit at the hem of the woman's scarf, a large square of some artificial fabric, and managed to tear strips off it. She made a pad to go over the wound and bound it firmly into place. Then she tried to mop up some of the spilt blood with the remaining rag.

The word the woman said and repeated could only mean 'Thank you'. Claudia smiled and made a deprecating gesture.

'Kanita.' The woman's voice was husky and tremulous. I believe she's concussed, Claudia thought. With the palm of her hand on her breast she said it again. 'Kanita.'

Kanita rummaged for something in a skirt pocket and brought out a small disc which she handed to Claudia with a gesture of someone returning lost property. The disc was a medal issued to Australian soldiers after the last war, someone's heirloom. 'Sydney,' she said, and kissed her own fingertips. 'Sydney, Australia, it is good.'

She thinks I'm an Australian.

Claudia opened her mouth to explain she was British, and then paused. She was better off as an Australian. Even Enver, the hotelier in Split, had spoken harshly of Brits. The soldier might have killed her if he'd known who she was. The British were not popular in his country, seen as arrogant bastards who had just stood by idly when they could have joined in on the Muslims' side, or as rich bitches who were indifferent to the needs of a distant land.

And then, with a rush of hot shame, clapping her hands over her mouth, Claudia realised that Kanita thought she was Sheila, the Australian girl. Sheila must be dead. She had not survived, killed in the crash or the explosion or the fire. Claudia could not bring herself to meet Kanita's eyes. But she said, 'Yes. Yes, Australia good.'

A shout and some childlike screams came from below. Kanita started up, staggered and fell against the door frame. She looked close to fainting. Her eyes seemed unfocused. Claudia stopped herself from pushing the other woman back down, with her head between her knees. Kanita shuffled unsteadily out of the door. There was a pause. Shall I go too, will they shoot me if I leave here? Claudia's thoughts were too slow. Kanita stretched back to put something on the floor and then shut and locked the door again.

She had not closed the shutters. She had left an empty blue plastic bucket and food on a makeshift tray, a wooden crate of the kind used for exporting fruit, with flat slats and shallow sides. It had a picture of an apple stamped in faintly coloured ink on one side, pale green, rosy pink. Claudia's mouth watered.

There was water in a litre bottle, plastic, palest blue. There was a small, blunt, stainless steel spoon, with a vestigial fantail pattern on the tip of the handle. There were two apples, with rusty spots on their shrivelled skins. There was an enamel plate, white with a red rim, its glaze faintly cracked with a map of light discoloration. It contained cold cooked rice. There was a thick cut-glass bowl, about two inches across, in which lay a pool of apricot jam, glutinous, thick. She lifted the bowl and allowed her tongue to touch the sweet, smooth surface. And again. I must not eat it yet. I must make it last.

Jam on the semolina pudding Mama cooked when she was small; thin, slimy jam with a curiously musty taste. It was made of marrows or carrots and insufficient sugar. She never liked the food, never understood what an achievement it was for Mama to produce it from the inadequate, rationed ingredients available in England in the

1950s. She never appreciated her mother as she deserved. Orphaned, isolated, looking after a small child in a foreign country, knowing nobody except her much older husband. I wasn't ever kind enough to Mama, there was never time to forgive or understand her.

It was still early. Narrow beams of warmth fell through the ceiling boards with dust motes moving in the light.

Time and the hour run through the longest day.

Never so sincerely meant, though often said. In queues, in traffic jams, in buses; during sleepless nights beside George when she lay counting his snores, counting sheep, counting backwards from three hundred.

How she wished she could recite the poetry learnt at school, or even the multiplication tables. The Kings and Queens of England. The siblings of Napoleon. How little she remembered of what she had once been taught, how scantily furnished the rooms of her mind.

Aloud, she said, 'This too will pass.'

Harshly clearing her throat she spoke again. 'One day you will rejoice to remember even this.' *Et haec olim meminisse iuvabit.* It was a Latin tag from a fountain in ... where? Not at Ansons, not at Milly Chandler's place. Some garden. What garden? Doesn't matter, it's not true anyway. How could this ever become a happy memory?

'While there's life there is hope. We're here because we're here.'

Why me?

But everyone asks, 'Why me?' Why her childlessness, his financial ruin, their air crash or brain tumour? There's only one possible answer. Why not me?

19

Brian France told Nina to cover the public meeting organised by Handyside's Bequest. 'Middle Temple Hall. They've got a judge on the board. Harry Anson's going to speak, you can go with him.'

How the hell did he know that? Brian France was as intuitive as a cat, Nina thought with a mixture of annoyance and awe. Then she wondered whether she would actually like it. Did she want to see Harry in a public context, the object of her professional task? One thing she certainly didn't want, and that was to be attached to Harry on that public occasion. She made a point of not mentioning the assignment when they went to the theatre together the previous evening, and the next afternoon Nina edged her way into the back of the hall as unobtrusively as she could. But her subconscious antennae were quivering. There he was, at the front, looking straight at her. They exchanged mutual, secretive smiles. The smell of sex wafted past and Nina sharply told herself it was imagination. She glanced furtively sideways to see if anyone had noticed, but she was sitting amongst other reporters and they were concentrating on identifying the cast.

'Look at Laurel Berryman,' the girl beside her whispered.

'She doesn't seem to be in mourning.'

'Like a cat that's swallowed the cream.'

'She's playing footy with George Anson,' another reporter said more loudly.

As people came into the great hall they were handed lighted candles to hold and pieces of green ribbon to tie round their arms as a symbol. On the dais stood two portraits, both oddly incongruous in the company of all the severe old lawyers on the panelled walls. One was of Mary Ellen Wood in the role of member's wife, taken by a fashionable photographer ten years before, showing her with big waves of shining, apricot-coloured hair, carefully made-up green eyes and darkened eyebrows, a half-smile with a gleam of teeth matching the gleam of pearl necklace and drop ear-rings. The other was a wishy-washy painting of Claudia Anson wearing evening dress and the Anson tiara on her brown hair, done by a fashionable painter who had concentrated on clothes and jewellery rather than personality. Wreaths of laurel leaves had been pinned round both pictures.

The Ansons had turned out in force. Peter Wood was not there, but Mary Ellen's daughter Beth, sobbing incessantly, was sitting at the front with her husband.

In the light of the candle flames an Anson prelate said a prayer. Then George Anson, in what should have been his wife's chair, his voice slurred, went to the next item on the programme, an appreciation by Harry Anson of the late lamented chairwoman and by Beth Mendoza Wood of her mother.

Harry began by describing the horrors consequent on what he sardonically called 'the New World Order'. The litany included continents—Africa and South America—and countries: Cambodia, China, Turkey, Indonesia, Iraq, Iran, Ireland. All of what used to be called Yugoslavia, much of what used to be the Soviet Union. Afghanistan, where he was to go himself next month. And so on and so on. 'It would be easier to list countries where terrorism and murder are *not* the norm,' he said.

Then Harry turned to the particular, speaking of the disinterested benevolence of those, like Claudia and Mary Ellen, who risked their own lives to save other people's. He spoke fondly of Claudia, his brother's wife.

His experienced voice was listened to with sombre attention. When he stopped there was no applause. Silence filled the dark-raftered hall, the flickering lights bringing life to the portraits around the walls, judges and dignitaries in their proud robes seeming to share the sympathetic emotion.

Beth Mendoza rose to her feet, gulped out a few incomprehensible words and was overcome by emotion. Her husband helped her back to her seat and George Anson said, 'I'm sure we all sympathise very deeply with Beth, this is a dreadful day for all of us. Perhaps you'll feel able to speak about your mother a little later, Beth, but for meanwhile Mrs Laurel Berryman's going to bring us up to date about the charity's aims and methods, and why it has to send supplies and their drivers into such dangerous places.'

Laurel Berryman's golden hair was dressed in a glossy mound above her very white skin and strongly marked brows and lips. She wore a short-skirted, narrow grey suit, with high-heeled, grey suede shoes. 'Valentino', Nina scribbled down, remembering the untrendiness of Claudia Anson's expensive London clothes.

Laurel was a practised speaker, familiar with her theme. So she should be, a professional administrator could be convincing about any organisation she worked for, she'd have used the same techniques to fundraise for sports centres or threatened art treasures or anything else.

The tragic loss of Claudia Anson and Mary Ellen Wood. The world-wide need, the wealth of Western nations, the goodwill of their citizens; what money would buy, what good outside aid could do. It was all correct, informative and impersonal. 'Much she cares,' the woman beside Nina wrote in capital letters on her pad.

Then someone got up to ask a question.

'Hi, everyone. I'm Kevin Reardon, I was Mary Ellen's tutor at poly, and her friend too. I had a lot of time for Mary Ellen, she was one tough lady who had a bum deal, if there was ever anyone that knew all about being short of food she was the one.'

A louder wail from Beth.

'Sorry, girl.'

'It's not true,' Beth gulped. 'She had lots of money, her flat's full of nice things.'

'Nice things from the old days,' Kevin said gently, and Juan Mendoza stood up and said firmly:

'You are mistaken, Professor, we find she lives comfortably, she has money. She has a bank account.'

'Maybe she came into some then, but I know your mum had a really bad patch and I guess that's why she decided to help feed starving people even poorer than her. Those women, Mary Ellen and her mate Claudia, they set off to help victims of war but they never expected to join them. They were outsiders—ordinary people if you like.

I bet they never knew what they were letting themselves in for. But somebody else did know. It's not as though what's happened to them is anything new. In the last few years lots of aid workers have paid for their goodwill with their lives. Sean Devereux, shot by a gunman in Somalia. Nurse Valerie Place, murdered in an ambush near Mogadishu. Frederick Maurice, killed in Sarajevo while travelling with an International Red Cross convoy. The United Nations Children's Fund has had more operatives killed this last year than in its whole forty-year history. Save the Children lost three staff members. Now listen, people, what I'm saying is, none of this is secret, everyone involved must know how dangerous this work is these days. Oxfam gives flak jackets to workers in former Yugoslavia, Save the Children's issued a survival guide. What I want to know is, how could you ever send amateurs into that obvious danger, all alone, without training or protection? Why did you do it?'

'Of course they were wonderfully brave, nobody's disputing that, but do remember, we'd never had any trouble before, and Mary Ellen has been driving for us as a regular. And of course they weren't supposed to be alone,' Laurel Berryman said.

'Yeah, Jake Konin went along too. And what happened to him?'

'He became quite ill on the journey, as you know, he had to be hospitalised in Split and then fly home. But now he's gone as the charity's representative to Sicily for a conference on famine aid, he's sent his sincere apologies, he asked us to pay tribute for him to our dear friends.'

'So he was safely laid up in Split while two unprotected women went on alone.'

'Three. Let's not forget the third woman who disappeared that day.'

'Who was equally unqualified by all accounts. You must have known perfectly well Claudia'd never been out before and even Mary Ellen wasn't a pro. Did you lay on the emergency training for them, like the big charities and news organisations do? Or did you just send them out unprepared?' Professor Reardon was holding a thick sheaf of newspaper cuttings. Everyone in the hall would have read them, the story had been lavishly covered. There were news stories, obituaries, think pieces, eulogies, and interviews with Sheila Kazaz's family, with Jake Konin himself, with the NATO personnel who had found, pieced together and disseminated the information about the lost lorry and its drivers.

Laurel Berryman said, 'Our transport was part of a whole convoy of trucks, with experienced personnel.'

'But they weren't with the convoy and they were inexperienced.'

'They got separated. We don't know how or why.'

George interrupted. 'This isn't the occasion for an inquest, Professor Reardon. That's not why we all came tonight.'

Laurel Berryman was about to sit down, when someone at the back of the hall called out, 'I've just got one question to Ms Berryman if I may. Hawker, the *Sentinel.*' His was a well-known name. Hawker was famous for exposing scandals and destroying people in the process. Readers who were not themselves and would never be in the news admired him. Others more at risk feared him, as the just perceptible frisson which his name provoked showed. Nina craned to hear him more easily.

'Mr Hawker. Yes, of course.'

'Ms Berryman, do you have a personal

connection with former Yugoslavia?'

'Certainly not.'

'One of the drivers, who left the convoy in Split, was Jake Konin.'

'Certainly, but why do you mention him?'

'Is he a member of one of the warring factions himself?'

'Certainly not, he's a Brit. Like me. Or you, Mr Hawker.'

George Anson snapped that this was neither the time nor the place for such questions, upon which Hawker said he'd find answers on those matters later and changed his angle of attack. 'Ms Berryman, did your drivers know exactly what was in the shipments?'

'Of course, as I told you, it was food mostly, plus of course medical supplies. Humanitarian aid.'

'I'm asking you this,' Hawker said, his gravelly voice menacing, 'because I've heard a different story. Can you assure me it wasn't drugs rather than medical supplies? And not food either. Guns.'

Laurel Berryman shouted over the chorus of gasps and exclamations, 'That's a complete lie.'

'Slander, libel, how dare you, sir?'

George Anson spluttered, laying his hand on Laurel's.

Hawker went implacably on. 'It's what I've been told, on good authority. So just hear me out. What do you say to the suggestion that you're using Handyside's Bequest as a front to provide goods that rebels and dissidents can't get legally? Are you breaking the UN embargoes? Smuggling? Dealing in arms? I've got statements. Eyewitness accounts. I've been told in every convoy of lorries there's one you don't want the customs to look at. Do you deny it, Ms Berryman? Are you so sure it's libel? Sue me if you dare.'

20

Claudia placed the shallow wooden box upside down on the bed-platform, and on it the upturned bucket. Clinging to the shutters, she raised herself enough to be able to look out of the window. At first the sight of the wide blue sky was enough. Sky, birds, high, white clouds.

Then she tried to see still more, pulling

herself up on tiptoes for the brief moments her weakened arms could sustain. She was looking down the slope of a steep roof. It was dilapidated, with gaping holes between overlapping, heart-shaped slates.

Within the angle of her vision at ground level was a yard surrounded by a high stone wall with its own little sloping roof of slates, and rows of rusted rings set at a convenient height for a horse's harness. There were two high nail-studded doors in the wall. The surface of the yard was broken and pitted concrete between slimy-looking cobble stones. A row of small brown birds was sitting on the wall. She watched as they rose simultaneously into the air, and wheeled about, and flew off into the invisible distance.

She exhausted herself in the delight of having something, anything, to see.

Where am I?

Nowhere. I've fallen off the edge of my world.

Claudia exercised her voice.

'Think yourself lucky,' she said aloud. 'You might have been born in time to be imprisoned in a concentration camp.' Her ancestors had known their enemies. Did that make a difference? Claudia had no idea at all who her own gaolers were.

She had been bombarded with advice before setting off. What to read, who to speak to, how to learn all there was to learn about the politics, history, causes of conflict in the Balkans; how to distinguish the issues, rivalries and hatreds.

'I don't want to know,' she had said, mindful of Laurel Berryman's words when she was being interviewed for the job of the charity's director. 'Anyone in need deserves our help.' All Claudia knew was that in the eastern parts of Europe, where once the Austro-Hungarian Empire and later the Soviet Empire had ruled, on the continent from which her own mother had once escaped, individuals were killing and dying.

'I meant so well,' she murmured. Her help was to have been humanitarian not partisan. Without labels.

Now Claudia, peering fruitlessly from her height, tried to believe she would be no better off for knowing who her captors were.

'I am a prisoner, that's all.' She tried words out. Captive. Hostage. There was a priest's hole at Ansons; in it Claudia had occasionally, briefly perceived a lonely dark shadow hunched, sitting, waiting. There was a dungeon under a building which had been converted for stables in the eighteenth century. Near the west lodge were the remains of the parish pound. Familiar concepts which had never properly registered on her imagination.

This is what it's like to be a prisoner.

Later on Claudia began to berate herself. Twit, twerp, bloody fool. Why did I come, why didn't I turn back? I should have known what would happen.

No, I'm here by accident, a series of accidents. I know perfectly well that I never wanted to come in the first place. Doing good unwillingly, I did bad. But then, just think how many women escort relief supplies without ever encountering any problems. I've recruited them myself, and interviewed them and sent them smiling on their way, like Laurel sent me, and they've all returned safely as planned.

But I was driving something else.

Guns.

Who knew? Did Jake Konin know, did he con us? I'd never have thought so ... perhaps he was full of well-meaning ignorance too.

Mary Ellen knew there was something

else in the cargo. She thought there were drugs.

There was a thriving trade in ripped-off medicines to war zones. Everyone involved with relief work knew that. It was a cruel scam because the drugs were not quality controlled. Sometimes they were straight fakes—water masquerading as antibiotic, talc as powdered drugs. But not always. In some cases it was the only way to get medical relief into places that couldn't afford it. Give Mary Ellen the benefit of the doubt. She probably had the best of motives.

But the men at that checkpoint knew what we really had in there. They'd been waiting for us, it was a way-station on the weapons' journey.

It was meant to be just me and Mary Ellen. Two expendable women.

Has Mary Ellen been expended? Or saved? What happened to her? And what about me, they tried to kill me, now they're going to kill me too!

She shook and moaned, her bowels loosened. But after a while, Claudia whispered, 'Calm, keep calm, you're still alive, perhaps that's part of a plan too.' Whose plan? What had happened? Did things go wrong when the main road was blocked and we were diverted into the mountains, was that when everything went awry? Or was that all part of the plan in the first place?

There was a wire stretched like a booby trap across the road. There was blood.

The image of a neck, sharply butchered, spouting blood ... shouting ... gunshots. No, not gunshots, not then. Something else. A bomb? A rocket? And men.

Shutting her eyes she saw it in tiny, vivid images, as though on a miniature screen. Men, their heads wrapped in cloth. Muj, she heard in her head, someone's voice saying they were Muj. They thought the truck was Western with immodest women driving it, they stopped it and found the weapons.

No. They must have come for the weapons. The officials at the checkpoint saw them. Or was it another gang? A rival faction?

Were they plundering the contents or were they the people to whom they had been despatched? How do I know? Why should I care? What difference does it make? The van was gone, burnt up now, and so was that poor girl.

The van had plunged over the mountain. And someone had brought Claudia here.

She shut her eyes again, trying to escape the memory. And then trying to remember. How long between stopping, between the van being brought to a stop, and its plunge over the mountainside? At some stage—was that when?—she'd been flung clear, or lifted out. Had she heard anything, seen what happened? Think, Claudia, bring it back ...

No, it wouldn't come.

Had the Muj come to take the weapons away from those who'd been expecting them? Is that what the soldier meant when he mentioned me—the Englishwoman? If the people who were meant to get the arms were supposed to kill us ... It was hard to think of oneself as an intended victim.

But it's not oneself, it's whoever happened to be driving that particular vanload, it didn't matter to them who it was any more than it matters to the hostage takers.

But that can't be right either. Claudia remembered her own voice. 'They think we're VIPs,' she'd said.

She made herself take slow, deep breaths, dragging them in against the

245

raw discomfort in her chest. She made herself lie down.

The sun had moved right across the sky before Claudia saw a human figure, thin and short-haired in trousers and an orange shirt, a boy or a woman, who walked quickly across the yard and into one of the sheds and came out carrying a heavy can—oil? milk? water?—bending far sideways, one arm dragged down by its weight, the other thrust horizontally outwards for balance.

What would happen if she called out?

Did they all know she was here? If they knew, would they care? Did Claudia's presence impinge at all on the inhabitants of this strange world? And theirs on her? How to express it?

One day someone would categorise emotions and feelings, she thought. The data would be fed into a computer to enable the humans of the future to save themselves the trouble of describing what they experience. Number one, love—sub-divided with letters and Roman numerals: sexual, filial, parental, passionate, platonic. No. Number one, fear. Physical fear. *Timor mortis.* Love came second to that, followed by number three, hatred.

Claudia tried to analyse what she was feeling at that moment, as well as that primal, primitive, primary fear. It was a less universal emotion, it would be far down the list, enumerated in double or even triple figures. Displacement. Outsiderness. Not belonging. Being an extra in other people's own worlds. That was the invariable, inevitable emotion she had busily, by always being busy, kept at bay throughout her adult life.

Oh God, what's that? Nightmare screams. Frenzied shrieks mingled with shouts, gasps, yells.

Disorientated, she tried to get out of the locked door. Then she climbed on the box again, and craned to peer down from the window.

In the dim light the yard seemed empty till she saw a figure lying on the ground, a short-haired person in trousers and an orange shirt. After a while someone moved into her vision, a woman with a scarf over her head, who knelt on the ground. When her hands lifted the head, blood spread from it across the ground.

Below, out of vision, she heard shouting and squeals: terrified children. Two running figures dashed out into the yard.

The kneeling woman half rose. Claudia heard the roaring rattling crashing sound of gunfire and knew it was an automatic weapon, a machine gun, rat-a-tat-tat. The running figures fell to the ground. Those children had been shot. So had the woman.

The children were still. Blood was splashed all over and around them. The woman had been wounded. She tried to raise herself to her knees, Claudia heard her call out. Was she asking for mercy, for help? Then the gun fired again and she lay still.

Claudia stood there clinging to the window sill as though turned to stone. She couldn't drag her eyes away from the bodies.

Later a man with a cloth wound round his head, carrying a gun, moved out from under her vantage point, into the yard, across to the people he—if it was he—had killed—if they were dead.

He lifted his foot and nudged one of the children over. The face had been shattered into a wet, red mess. She watched the soldier look at his boot, move to the woman, and wipe it carefully and thoroughly against her skirt.

There was another movement. Someone

was coming into the courtyard. Another child.

'Oh no, please no, not again, no more.'

But this time there were no shots, only shouts. Other children followed, a procession, cowering, hand in hand, pushed and prodded along by soldiers.

There were five soldiers, each carrying a gun. There were two other adults, a woman and a man she recognised: the doctor.

They were herded, shoved, across the courtyard, just to one side of their murdered companions. A toddler carrying a baby, a small girl pulling a still smaller child by the hand, scurrying, skittering, huddled in fear and obedience. Each child came out in turn, and saw what was on the ground, and shied away to one side. But they kept moving. They had their hands raised above their heads, and they went where they were told.

This is what the children of the ghetto did. The children in Nazi extermination camps. This is an image of our times.

There was a lorry. They were pushed into the lorry. Its engine started, turning over, revving, and, at long last, driving away. Claudia could not see it move away behind the wall, but she saw the old men and women who tried to follow it, their hands held out to the children. Not waving.

And then the screams and cries of bereft adults faded into the night's silence and light faded from the sky.

Later, hours later, Claudia's selfish misery began to outweigh pity and fear. The same old thought: I might as well be a ghost myself for all the good I am—I'm insubstantial. Irrelevant. Here, like everywhere else. No wonder I felt more at home with ghosts than real people. No wonder I made myself ghosts for company.

In the spring of 1993 Claudia had begun to catch glimpses of an unfamiliar apparition, one not recorded in the books about Ansons and unlike all the others she'd seen. It was a little woman in a dark coat with a collar made of a curly short-haired fur, a cloche hat drawn down over her forehead, thick grey stockings and low-heeled shoes with a buckled bar across the instep. The shape appeared so vivid that Claudia didn't immediately realise it was only in her mind's eye.

Claudia was feeling unsettled and tetchy

at the time so she interpreted the vision, at once pointless and unexciting, as just another manifestation of menopausal instability, and a far less inconvenient one than the hot flushes which pestered her days and nights. She saw the apparition at Ansons, in the distance down the garden, or in a group of guided visitors. On shopping trips in Gloucester or London she would catch sight of her in crowded streets, walking uncomfortably in those pointed shoes as though her feet hurt, or primly seated, ankles crossed and gloved hands folded on a leather bag, at the other end of a train carriage.

Later that year the woman's aspect began to change. She would be carrying a suitcase with tattered labels stuck all over its leather sides, weighted so as to drag her shoulder down, her clothes showing stains and tears. Claudia saw her limping and stumbling in a procession of other ragamuffins. Once, when Claudia was travelling by tube, she saw the other woman crushed in a crowd in a confined, dark space. This, unlike Ansons' own ghosts, must be a manifestation of Claudia's own otherness.

Claudia had thought of, but decided against, asking someone's advice. Whose would it be? The doctor? Never. Even if Duncan were the kind of man to be sympathetic to feminine hysteria, she could not trust him to keep quiet about it. 'Don't worry if the old girl seems a bit unbalanced,' Duncan might tell George. 'Women get like that. It's her age,' he'd say, and prescribe tranquillisers. Or he might send her to a shrink, and George wouldn't understand, he'd always disapproved of that kind of thing, regarding it as self-indulgent twaddle. Pull yourself together, have a drink. And another drink.

Claudia had written in her diary, 'I'm creating my own ghosts instead of telling myself I see the Ansons' because I'm guilty about my mother. I rejected her because I didn't want anyone to know where she'd come from. I was ashamed that she'd been a foreign refugee whose only chance in life was to marry an old man.'

Then the apparition swam into Claudia's consciousness in a different guise. She was standing behind a fence, thin and scrawny, dressed in a sack-like shift with her hair shaved off. Claudia recognised that her imagination had been invaded by horrors from former Yugoslavia, pictures of a camp in which skeletal men were crammed behind barbed wire.

Claudia was at Ansons when she realised who the apparition represented. She'd been laying the dining-room table as though for a banquet, to entertain George's friends. Laurel Berryman was coming so it was an answer to Claudia's prayers that the place looked its best, the herbaceous borders gaudy with summer flowers, the lawns velvet smooth, everything inside and out glossy, gleaming, sweet-smelling. She set out the luxurious linens and lace, the fragile crystal and sparkling silver, all the adjuncts of wealth and centuries of changeless security, and when she glanced at the sideboard to see the flower arrangements there in front of it was the pained, painful figment of her imagination. It was as though she were looking into a distorting mirror.

It's me, she thought. My subconscious has been reminding me what might have been. Don't fuss about George and Laurel, don't worry about what they get up to in London, just be glad of what you've got.

There was no time to think about all this. Laurel must see her as the perfect image of an English lady, and so must George. To him and to his other woman,

Claudia had to personify Ansons. So what if he came home no more than the odd weekend, or if he hardly spoke to her any more except in irritation or command, or if he was a drunkard, or if Laurel wanted him?

Suddenly, frozen as she stood holding a silver ladle, Claudia admitted the question, 'What if Laurel wants Ansons too?'

But the thought of a threat to what Claudia really cared about stiffened her. Laurel might want it but so long as Claudia lived she couldn't have it. And nothing else mattered.

She'd been so absorbed in memory that for a little while Claudia had forgotten where she was.

Suddenly tremendous rumbles and claps shook the building.

But it didn't rain. It wasn't thunder. It was bombs. Shells. Rockets. She was under fire. The house, the people in it, the town or village in which she was imprisoned, were being attacked.

Screaming without knowing it, Claudia was seized with wide-ranging rage. Why me, why here? How dare they leave me exposed up here, cowards skulking in some cellar. Then anger passed, drowned

254

in noise and terror. She hid in the illusory protection of the thin blanket, huddled with her arms round her head, hands over her ears, breathing in the fetid warmth of her own bad breath.

How do people bear it? I'll go mad. I'm going to die! She clasped her hands and tried to pray. As a small child she'd known how. Not any more, not for a long time. To whom? For what? Doubting even then, still questioning, her thoughts still slid away from ideas too profound for her.

'*Who* is there to hear? Who would listen to *me?*'

The teaching of Claudia's childhood came back to haunt her now.

'I've been such a sinner.' Superimposed on the puritan dogma of the uncompromising missionary was the ill-digested, nebulous influence of the Ansons' Catholicism.

Sins never admitted, never forgiven. Confession, even to herself, admitting it all, not glossing it over, that might bring absolution.

Idolatry. Ansons was Claudia's object of worship.

Lying. Fitting-in lies. Pretences so as to belong.

Cowardice. Why didn't she ever tackle George about his drinking, his unfaithfulness, his neglect? Because she hadn't dared.

Claudia huddled waiting for her doom. 'Let it be quick,' she said aloud. She tried to think of George as a widower. It was such a long time since they'd really been part of each other's lives. She tried to summon up the image of the young man she'd fallen in love with but could visualise neither him nor the stout, red-faced, bald man he'd become.

A louder explosion, the sky lit up. Whistling, crashing. Is the building rocking on its foundations? She was shaking. Soon she was screaming too, and moaning, and, as dust sprayed in through every crack, coughing and gasping. She cried aloud for help or mercy. But there was nobody to hear.

The attack tailed off towards dawn. When the sky lightened, the birds twittered their triumphant immunity. The air was thick. Was everyone dead? Would she stay here to die alone?

How often she, an avid, experienced reader of detective novels, had considered death. Death in stories, fictional, enjoyable, entertaining. Murder methods and suicide, motives, means, the abstract intellectual concerns of people who read crime novels, considered scientifically and entirely without feeling. Even now Claudia could hardly credit that she was really here, in this position, actually visualising—what? Something unthinkable. She thought, this can't be me. But it was. This was Claudia, crouched on the floor, exhausted and hungry, trying to face a reality from which she had always been insulated.

She heard the squeal of some animal and thought, I am caught in a trap too.

And nobody would come and rescue her. This was not like the adventures she'd spent so many years reading about. She wouldn't be saved by an Etonian with a Daimler Double Six or an English spinster from a cosy village or a private eye in a trilby and a grubby mackintosh.

All the same, she balanced herself to look out. Was she hoping for some knight in shining armour to gallop up out of the sunrise to the rescue of this damsel in distress?

The yard below was transformed into a pit of ruin littered with rubble. As she watched a shed collapsed, with a kind of

257

dainty slowness, settling its battered planks like spillikins on the ground.

Where is everyone? Are they all dead?

It must have been almost mid-morning when Claudia saw movement below her. A bent old man moved across the rubble-scattered yard to the doorway, pushed open its two high, arch-topped doors. It was like pulling back a stage curtain. Outside them was a new scene: a sunlit road, grass, a bush, dirt and dust, and people moving across, always slowly and in the same direction. A procession. A retreat.

Passing at infinitesimal speed, the trail of men and women moved out of sight. They were pulling carts or riding on small tractors, all laden with bags and boxes, old, bent men and women, as though everyone of fighting age had long since gone away. The children had been taken away, and now the old people had been driven out from the ancestral village by the night's attack. They were going to the relative safety of a town, as refugees.

She had been briefly distracted by what she saw from her own plight. Suddenly she remembered and shouted, waved, screamed, projecting her voice towards her escaping gaolers, but none so much as looked up towards her. Within, perhaps, an hour, they were all gone, out of sight. They had left her behind. Left her alone.

21

The house might have looked cheerful, or at least amusing, in summer sunshine. In a spring gale, the tossing evergreens and hurricanes of last year's dead leaves emphasised the ugliness of the three shades of dark brick, set in geometric but disproportionate designs, that the original builder had used to decorate the walls. Narrow, high windows, brown paintwork, the odd eaves, arch and turret combined into an unhappy whole and Nina found herself irrationally reluctant to climb the six steps to the front door and put her gloved finger on a tarnished brass bell. She half expected a member of the Addams family to answer it.

Footsteps squeaked along a tiled hall and towards the door. 'Who is it?'

'Mrs Patterson? Nina Gillespie. Dr Berlin rang to—'

'Yes. Come in.' She was a heavy-set, tall woman, wearing knitted clothes that clung to an ample bosom, with straggling pepper-and-salt hair, bedroom slippers and a miasma of depression hanging about her. Nina had done her share of interviews with people in despair—'How did it feel when you heard your son had died?'—but never learnt to feel comfortable about the intrusion. Now she had to overcome an immediate impulse to apologise and back away.

Mrs Patterson muttered, 'My husband will be back in a minute,' and Nina followed down a passage lined with school photographs of indistinguishable rows of boys in jackets and striped ties. Each oblong was framed in black, and labelled. Upcott House 1976, Upcott House 1986, Upcott House 1993.

'That was the very last summer, before we sold the school.'

Looking more closely Nina saw that a younger and happier Mrs Patterson sat foursquare in the middle of each front row beside a man with shiny black hair and a gleaming smile.

'That's Euan. My husband. We were joint heads.'

The doors leading out of the tiled passage opened on to a brown oak dining room, a grey metal study and a green formica kitchen before they came to a sitting room at the back of the house, with windows on to an overgrown, tattered garden. This room too was lined with dozens of framed photographs but they were all of the same subject, a bald dark-eyed baby who had grown into a curly-haired toddler. The room had been furnished as a nursery, with small, primary-coloured chairs and tables, a beanbag decorated with cartoon characters, a small climbing frame, a shelf of children's books. All that gear, although obviously not old or much used, looked like the stock of a second-hand shop. There was a sour, dampish smell. It was the smell, Nina thought, of despair.

A layer of dust showed how long it had been since a child had slipped down the short slide or sat on the rocking horse. The only well-used thing in the room was a wickerwork set of conservatory furniture, on which Mrs Patterson slumped herself down. She did not offer coffee or make conversation, but sat in a dejected heap, her eyes on a photograph album which lay open at her side.

Nina walked slowly round the room examining the pictures on the wall. Then she came to a framed document, an adoption certificate for 'Linda Patterson'.

Mrs Patterson said, 'We called her Linda, after my sister.'

The picture under the certificate showed Mrs Patterson with a child about a year old. She was showing the child a small, beribboned soft toy.

The front door opened and slammed closed. Heavy footsteps came along the passage. Euan Patterson had lost the black hair. He had an unkempt straggle of grey, a red, choleric face, fierce blue eyes. 'I got held up queuing at the post office. How d'you do. Has she told you everything?' Before Nina could answer he glanced at his silent wife and went on, 'No, she won't have. This whole thing has shattered my wife, it's been a catastrophe. That's why you're here. But you've got to go carefully. You may be a bright brave young newshound, Miss Gillespie, but the people we dealt with threatened us before the case came to court. That was when we discovered there's an organised trade in babies. They smuggle them out, some woman pretends to be the mother and brings them over. We aren't the only ones. I'll stop this happening to anyone else if it's the last thing I do.'

'I'm not really quite sure what did happen, Dr Berlin wasn't very specific.'

'Quite right and proper, client confidentiality and all that. Get out your notebook and tape recorder and I'll tell you the whole story.'

It began in 1994. The previous summer term had been the Pattersons' last at Upcott House, and by the autumn Marion was realising how dreadfully she missed the company of children. Until then she had never really minded not having her own, having been the guide, confidante and friend of generations of small boys. Now, at fifty-two, it was too late to have children or adopt any.

Or was it? That was the year of disaster in what was by then being called former Yugoslavia. Night after night the television screen was filled with pitiful pictures of the dead, the dying and the bereaved. Orphaned children gazed at the camera lenses. Wounded infants were pulled from flames, rubble and mud.

'You couldn't see those babies and not want to help,' Euan Patterson said. 'And we knew the right people, we'd always collected for Save the Children at Upcott, and some of the smaller charities too, Helping Hands and Handyside's, and of course the lifeboats. The boys always liked the lifeboats. Our boys' mothers were involved, we had contacts, so we let it be known we'd do what we could, take in children, anything.'

They'd been given the chance of looking after a baby rescued from the ruins of a village in central Bosnia.

'It had been shelled. They showed us pictures of it, there was nothing left, literally nothing but dust and devastation. A massacre, thirty-three corpses in the cellar, men, and women, nearly all old, because the young people had gone off to the war to work in the towns, it's the parents who stay on the land. But there was one young woman. Someone heard this wail and pulled a baby out from underneath her mother's body. She was about six months old, hungry of course by then but all right otherwise, except that she was all alone and unidentified. So she was brought to us to care for.'

They called the baby Linda, since nobody knew what her name had been, and treated her as their own; and within a year she became legally theirs.

'The social services weren't keen, they thought we were too old to adopt, but they couldn't find anything else to say against us and the judge was on our side,' Euan Patterson said. 'Actually, we discovered later that he'd had a nephew at Upcott so he had some idea of how well we'd cope.'

Marion Patterson muttered something and her husband said, 'What's that? Speak up, dear.'

'The judge gave Linda a teddy bear for luck.'

'They always do that with adoption orders,' her husband said in a low voice to Nina, and more audibly, 'He was certainly very kind.'

'She took the teddy with her when—' The woman's lips quivered and she clapped her hand over her mouth to hide it.

There was a silence, until Nina said gently, 'And then ...?'

And then: Linda's birth relatives tracked her down. An uncle, two aunts and a grandmother. Euan Patterson fetched an album of court transcripts and press cuttings to show Nina. The reporting was anonymous, nobody was supposed to know who 'Baby L' was, either in the name of Linda Patterson or Anoska Lovcen, as it turned out she had been called before. But anonymous though it was, the case had attracted widespread reporting, both legal and 'human interest'.

English lawyers acting for the baby's natural family said she had never been abandoned or lost at all, she had quite simply been stolen and they wanted her back.

The family's Bosnian lawyers showed that such an adoption would have been illegal in any of the former Yugoslavian republics, in all of which families that had been torn apart in the Second World War found themselves reunited many years later. In Bosnia, adoption of children by foreigners was a particularly sensitive issue. It could be equated to ethnic cleansing, if with the best possible motives.

Newspaper comment, free from the restrictions of the *sub judice* rule since nobody could tell exactly who was being discussed, said that on the one hand it was a case of cultural imperialism, on the other it could have saved the child's life.

A child-centred pressure group said there was never any justification for treating children as commodities, so a war zone could never be the right source for adopted or foster children.

In reply to all these points lawyers for the Pattersons said a properly completed adoption process was, by English law, conclusive and irreversible. Linda was the Pattersons' legal child now and she could not be taken away. Other newspaper comment said a secure environment in a stable country should never be exchanged for the poverty and danger which was all her distant relations could offer instead.

Expert witnesses gave evidence, among them Dr Fidelis Berlin whose speciality was maternal relationships with infants. Three days were taken up in court by discussions as to the best interests of the child, which are the paramount consideration in English law.

Would her interests be better served by returning to her roots with badly off blood relations she could not remember in a war-torn country, or by staying with the prosperous people she knew as her parents? By living where facilities were poor and education almost non-existent or by staying at the expensive school in whose nursery class she was already well established? By being taken away by strangers she did not understand or by staying with a family who had taught her to speak and start reading before she was even three years old?

The judgement ran to twenty-one pages. On the one hand, on the other, looked at this way, or contrariwise. This expert said this, that said that. Sympathy for both parties. But in the end the natural family prevailed. Linda Patterson was to be abolished, expunged, as though she had never been, Anoska Lovcen revived as though she had never been lost.

Marion Patterson was hunched on her sofa weeping uncontrollably at the recital of her tragedy. Her husband said wearily, 'The judge asked the other family to let us have contact. But when we tried to visit her they said it would upset her.'

'I'll never see my baby again,' Marion sobbed.

Nina made a little business about changing her tape and checking her notes. It was certainly a ghastly sad story, she thought, but the weight of misery in this house was too oppressive for a helpless outsider. She went and stood facing out to the garden while Euan tried to soothe Marion. There was a green woodpecker in that yew tree. It might seem heartless to take out her miniature binoculars. There were grey squirrels and several rabbits running across the rough lawn. The wind was getting stronger and a flutter of leaves rattled against the window.

'Miss Gillespie.'

'Nina, please.'

'You understand there's something wrong here. What happened with our baby.'

'You mean, when you were told she'd lost everyone, that she was lost.'

'Exactly. That was why the judge decided as he did in the end, he concluded she might indeed have been abducted, at the worst, but even the kindest conclusion had to be that proper inquiries were never made. Of course we didn't know that, we'd never in any circumstances whatever have done anything so cruel or improper. But the fact is that someone did. I don't suspect our contact, I've been a supporter of Handyside's Bequest for many years and I know it's run quite impeccably by Mrs

Berryman, in fact that's why we haven't taken it any further ourselves because they are doing such good work it would be a disaster if any criticism affected that. No, it was someone else, nobody who was directly part of the organisation. We took it all on trust and so did Laurel Berryman.'

Marion Patterson spoke from her sofa. 'And my heart is broken,' she said in a voice as intense, as tragic, as that of a great actress playing Shakespearian tragedy. Much as Nina pitied her, she also hoped the tape machine had properly recorded those five words.

22

Claudia lay stupefied by self-pity and terror. Nothing was real except her present position, as though her previous life had never been and there would be no future one. She was starving. Her limbs hurt. She felt ill. Neither unconscious nor fully conscious, Claudia realised she was in hell.

Nothingness. That was what hell would

be, Claudia's father had preached. Not a burning fiery furnace, not freezing, not the tortures of the damned, but empty, vacant, lonely nothingness for all eternity, a place from which God had turned his face away, withdrawn the light of his countenance.

Light stealing in at the window made her stir, and in its early dimness she began to revive.

Come on, Hannah Claudia, think. Get a grip. Do something. Nobody else is going to do it for you.

There must be some way to open this door. She threw herself against it, and rattled it, and peered under and round its edges. The hinges were rusted into place. On the other side a crack about a centimetre wide showed her squinting eye what was holding the door against her: a flat wooden bolt. It must be possible to move it. Somehow.

She tried, gave up, tried and surrendered. She made herself try yet again, persevering in the end as much from boredom as determination. Then, again and again, she pushed the end of the handle of the little spoon through the crack against the wooden bar, pressing it sideways.

A pointless exercise, chuck it, this is a

waste of effort. The spoon will break first. Why bother? Just wait. Admit defeat. Let the end come.

One more try. Claudia was about, at last, to give up, when she realised there had been a tiny movement. The puny pressure she was able to exert was having a minuscule effect. Hand sore, arm aching, she pressed and pushed; and knelt to peer through the crack, as the shaft of sunlight slanted from one wall round the room on to the opposite one. And at long, long last the bolt was free, and she pulled the door towards her and saw what was outside, a small landing, a bare wall, and a flight of wooden stairs going downwards into shadow.

But suddenly Claudia felt too frightened to leave her cell. She lay down again on the bed as though it were sanctuary. I'm tired out, she thought, I'm ill, haven't the strength to see what's downstairs. I don't want to know who's waiting. Who or what.

In the end, steadying herself with a hand against the rough stone wall, she forced herself to move out of the room and edge very slowly, inch by inch, down, and round and into the house in whose attic she had been incarcerated.

There was a row of doors in a passage on the floor below. She dared to peer into some of the rooms, which were deserted; two were completely empty of everything but dust and cobwebs. In one, mats lay crumpled on wooden benches, with a few thin covers on the floor. There was no other furniture or equipment. Everything was filthy. A few splinters of glass remained stuck in the window panes, a few flakes of grey-green paint on their frames. Some of the pink stuffed animals which had been brought in the charity's truck were in the room with the bedding, and an empty carton stamped with the Handyside's Bequest logo. Those bony, gentle hands, clasped in prayer, seemed to offer a sudden, brief reassurance.

Down another floor, the first floor consisted of a wide landing all round the stair well, with lots of rooms opening off it, most of them unused. One was some kind of dormitory, with thin coverings on the pallets. She counted to see how many children had been cared for here, and found nine beds had been used. Had she seen nine, the day before? Of those nine, how many survived?

Most rooms were empty and long unused, their plank floors covered with bird shit and feathers and pellets of mouse droppings. One smelt of stale sweat, with a rolled straw mat neatly on the floor, a thin brown jersey and a threadbare towel on wall hooks.

Treasure trove.

Outside the last door the floor had been scraped clean in a semicircle, by the door swinging open over it.

A large, airy, very light room, with a big window facing over the valley. Though shabby it had once had washed walls and a swept floor, but the night's bombardment had made everything filthy, dropping shrapnel and splinters from the cracking roof. On a high, narrow trestle table was a bucket half full of dust-thickened water and an empty charity carton: 'Powdered Milk Product, for Infant Feeding Only'. There were two plastic feeding bottles on the floor as though someone had dropped them and run.

There were four green, cracked plastic crates on the floor, each lined with thin grey fabric. Three were empty. In one, half buried by irregular lumps of plaster and stone, lay a baby with flies clustered on its eyelids.

Claudia lifted the baby from its cradle. Cold, slimy fabric fell away from its dangling bloodstained limbs. There was no need to listen for its breath, to wait for the warm touch of air on her cheek or the feeble fist to grasp her finger. She did, all the same, and patted the flabby back and breathed air into the fetid mouth.

Might it have lived if she'd found it sooner?

Claudia laid the dead baby down, and covered it from head to toe with one of the filthy cloths. She heaped debris over the crate in the vague idea of protecting the little corpse from predators until it could be properly buried in the comfortable earth.

Buried. There were bodies out there. Must I do it? she wondered in horror. Later, think about it later.

Then she went out of this deadly room, down another flight of stairs, stone this time, and into a larger room with an empty fireplace, overturned tables and short-legged little wooden chairs and the remains of a meal and upset bowls and spots of blood on the floor. An orphanage?

An old people's home? A hospital?

Claudia grabbed and ate a crust of bread with a smear of jam and tooth marks in it, and eagerly swallowed the water left in a tin mug. Then she padded through the hall and into rooms which might once have been larders, harness rooms, a dairy, a kitchen.

A kitchen! A table, on which someone had been writing: two sheets of lined paper, an incomprehensible language. A cold stove, a waterless tap, but in a scullery was a pump with a handle and a plastic bucket. Fumbling, trembling, she managed to make the primitive gadget work, filling the bucket to overflowing, and plunging her face into it, drinking the icy water like a thirsty animal. Would there be food? Oh, let there be food.

On a shelf beside the stove she found a tin with a picture of apricot jam on it, containing some grains of rice. In a wire-covered meat safe, a mouse-nibbled corner of hard, greyish cheese and a screw-topped jar containing half a dozen tiny brown olives.

Then she crossed, more boldly now she had been fortified by food, to the doorway. Only one half of a double door was still there, a heavy oblong of bleached planks studded with nails. She'd been in some kind of fortress. It looked like a reused medieval stronghold.

Outside the spring sun was shining, and though not objectively very warm it felt luxuriously so to Claudia in comparison with the gloomy chill of her attic prison. She experienced an incongruous slippage of reality, briefly feeling as though she were just stepping out into the first morning of a summer holiday after arriving in the dark, without any idea what to expect outside the front door of the hotel or villa.

But here the first sight was of ruination. This village street looked like London must have done after a bad night in the blitz. Rubble, dust, broken glass, twisted metal and jagged shafts of wood lay on the ground. A tree was torn in half. A wall had collapsed on itself, another's middle courses bulged outwards. There were raw rectangles in the ground: new graves.

And there—oh God oh God—what is it? A black, shimmering, mobile mound. Flowered material, a human hand. It was a body, covered with flies. Claudia could hardly bear to look. Peering out of the corner of half-closed eyes, she realised there was another body almost buried by a collapsed building.

Claudia thought, I'll walk away. Down the hill.

Go go go, she urged.

But she couldn't do it.

She knew she was going to have to see if anyone was alive in that courtyard. She was going to have to help.

Nobody would ever know if I didn't, she thought.

What could I do anyway, useless, ignorant, inexperienced, incapable Claudia?

Best to leave them. Best to escape while she could.

But while she was telling herself so, Claudia's feet had taken her into the house and down a passage and out again and her hand was touching whitened skin at a wrinkled wrist. They were all dead. There could be no doubt of it. Dreadful to realise that it was a relief.

A butcher's shop. The stench drowned pity in revulsion.

Claudia was sick, noisily, on to the ground.

I must bury them, she told herself.

Later. I'll do it later.

Staggering away, Claudia moved like

an old old woman, bent over, shuffling, moaning. Her legs would not carry her very far. She slumped on to the stony ground, her head down between her knees, and for a while, though conscious, was unaware and in a daze of horror and disgust.

When she pulled herself together there was still no sign of other life. The village was depopulated, deserted.

Oh—something moved, there, seen out of the corner of her eye. Momentarily she slunk back into the shelter of the doorway, peering out in terror for—for a cat: a skinny, tawny little creature. 'Puss, puss, here,' she cooed. The cat slid away. She shouted hoarsely. It mustn't go near those bodies. But it was out of sight. And if not a cat, then what? There had to be someone to clear up.

Must I? Yes, I must, but later. There's plenty of time. There might even be someone else. 'Come on, Claudia,' she whispered. 'Steady the Buffs.' That was one of George's sayings. Suddenly she was overwhelmed with longing for him, not for the hostile stranger George Anson had become but for the young man who had looked after her. What happened to us? she wondered, as so often before. What did it matter now? She began to walk. Which way? Turn left, the direction the cat had taken, and walk quietly, slowly, for she was weak after so many days of confinement, cautiously. What would she find—or, more importantly, who?

But there didn't seem to be anyone left alive at all. It was like a scene from a science fiction story, or a ghost town. But in a ghost town Claudia might have seen more apparitions than here in these deserted alleys and squares.

This had been like a little Alpine village, and must once have seemed snug and safe in its fold of the hillside. Now it was laid waste, randomly, viciously. Here a pile of rubble that had been a house, there one that seemed undamaged, built of concrete blocks with its top floor unfinished, rusty struts protruding from a flat roof, and with its wood store pathetically orderly beneath the front steps, and on them a small striped mat with a pair of men's brown plastic shoes neatly set beside it. Here was a burnt-out shop though outside it lay an unbroken plastic crate of soft drink bottles randomly spared in the bombardment. There was—oh joy—a single full one. Claudia unscrewed its plastic top and gulped down a whole litre of gassy, sweet liquid.

Then she walked further, to where, just before the open hillside, a cemetery lay, a field of gravestones, some topped with little turban-shaped twists of stone, others coffin-shaped, most painted a strong green and with the crescent-shaped carving of a sickle moon above the fading photographs. And oblongs of newly turned earth. Brand new graves.

Turning back from the graveyard, Claudia looked for a while at one of the intact houses. Should she just go in? Yes. She found herself in a conventional bourgeois home. Everything was covered with a thin film of dust and there was broken glass on the floor from two windows and a display case containing odd knick-knacks and a lustre coffee set, but that aside it looked as though a houseproud owner had just nipped down to the shop and would be back any moment. The floor was polished wood scattered with small Turkish rugs, the furniture was made of heavy wood and seemed too big for the room; on each table lay mats of white or ecru crochet, with others on the back and arms of a long crimson moquette sofa. Plates and framed photographs of picturesque old villages and minarets hung askew on a patterned wallpaper.

Beyond this front room was a kitchen, where a heavy table covered with an embroidered cloth stood among modern fitted units. Behind the broken glass of a dresser-style fitment, heavy glass bowls and ornaments remained intact. Claudia opened the fridge, but it was off and empty. She switched on the stove, but no light came on. On the wooden work top stood a spoke-handled jug beside a brass, tube-shaped coffee grinder. But there wasn't any coffee to drink, only its wistful traces to smell. In another cupboard the harsh smell of raw alcohol revealed a still. Slivovitz, Claudia thought greedily, but she could not find any.

Even the bathroom was modern. The lavatory flushed once and its cistern did not refill. No water or power then. But they couldn't have taken all the food in the village. Somewhere there must be fruit or chickens. Eggs. Root vegetables. And somewhere they'd have left warm clothes, blankets, beds.

Find something to eat. Then rest. First things first.

23

'Is that Nina, Nina Gillespie? I've got to talk to her!'

Nina didn't recognise the woman's voice and was surprised to recognise her own reaction to it. Relief. Why? Because she was afraid to hear a man. Cliff Jones. She'd been dreaming of his brutal face and unemphatic voice. He had frightened her more than she realised at the time, and now she was close to nailing him and his trade in human beings, he'd returned to haunt her. She was not usually shown the regular pile of anonymous letters, declarations of love and inexplicit threats. But sometimes she leafed through. A mistake. There had been one this week which could be from him. The radio station sent all the 'keep off or you'll be sorry' notes straight to the police. But that wouldn't be much help when it came to the point. Stop it, Nina, forget it, listen to this hysterical woman. She was gabbling. 'I need to speak to her, it's really important—'

'Stop. Listen. This is Nina speaking. Who's that?'

'Ginny. You remember, you came here, we talked about Ian—oh, my baby ...' Gulps and sobs down the line.

Oh my God, he's had an accident, something's happened to him, that poor woman. 'What's happened, Ginny, what is it?'

'I can't tell you on the phone, someone might be listening.'

'But is Ian all right?'

'Yes, thank God, but you've got to come here, Nina, today. This morning. Please.'

The Carters lived in a commuter village in Berkshire, in one of five hundred identical red-brick boxes marketed as 'executive homes'. They had two-car garages, driveways laid with square-cut cobbles and carriage lamps in the porch. The Carters' house showed the progression of its periods as clearly as an archaeological site, with the perfect elegance of a prosperous child-free couple overlaid by mess and toys and poster-painted scrawls.

'Come in, come in, Ian's at school, my Ian ...' More tears slid down Ginny's pale cheeks. She was a tall, plump woman, with

284

a deep bosom and fine brown hair; she looked as though every inch of her would be soft and smooth to touch, a cushion of sweet flesh.

'What's wrong, Ginny? Is it something to do with me?'

'It's—you're the only person I've ever talked about it to except for Tony and he's away, they sent him to a conference in Tasmania, and he'd be so upset too—oh, I don't know what to do.'

'Tell me what's happened, Ginny.'

'Look!' It was that morning's *Argus*, a page two news piece, illustrated with a shot of half a dozen rosy, dirty toddlers in an old-fashioned kitchen. 'Read this. If that's how we got Ian—they promised he didn't have anyone of his own in the whole wide world, we asked, honestly we did—well, I just couldn't bear it, that's all.'

On a bleak March morning Anya Jaksich, a student nurse, trudged to an orphanage near Belgrade to see her little brother Sergei. But baby Sergei was not there. 'First they told me he was out for a walk,' Anya said. 'When I returned the following day

285

they said he was at the baby clinic. I could not go every day and it was only after weeks of delays and lies they told me the truth, that Sergei had been sent to his new family in France.'

Anya was devastated. Her baby brother had been taken to the orphanage after the boy's mother was killed in a bombing raid, but Anya had been working to make a home for him so that they could live together.

The orphanage had never asked permission from Sergei's other relatives to give the baby away and they would not tell Anya where he had gone. Instead they told the desperate girl to forget her little brother.

Illegal adoption has become a booming big business in all the countries of the former Soviet bloc. Hundreds of wealthy foreigners break the law to buy children from corrupt orphanages or from destitute families unable to care for their newborn babies. There have even been recorded cases of abduction by masked gun-men.

Deals are often struck without the consent of the children's closest relatives.

The uncle of three girls sold by one Bucharest orphanage to a Sicilian family has taken the matter to court in a desperate attempt to bring them home. In Russia there is mounting evidence that the lucrative adoption business has attracted the interest of organised crime gangs.

And criminal organisations from the Western world are cashing in on the economic and social chaos that followed the collapse of the old regimes. Babies are being sold, traded and stolen.

As for Anya, she knows she will never see her little brother again. She only has one hope now. 'All I want to know is that he's all right.'

'It could be Ian,' Ginny cried. 'Suppose he was stolen from his real family! What if they're out there somewhere, missing him and longing for him, you'd never stop even after five years, you'd pine and pine for him all your life. Do we have to find them and give him back? But he'd be so miserable without us, he believes we're his mummy and daddy. Oh, Nina, whatever shall I do? And what have I done?'

24

The silence of that night was as frightening as the thunder of shells. Claudia thought she'd fallen off the edge of the world. What world? A world in which soldiers abducted children and old people were forced to leave their homes to find food and safety somewhere else. A world in which she was a nothing, unconsidered and forgotten.

She lay down on a sour-smelling mattress under a thin quilt and, for extra warmth, a dusty little carpet off the tiled floor. Someone had loved this little house once, as much as she'd loved Ansons and cared for it and cleaned it. She tried to think about the life its owners had lived here. They'd had electricity once, and piped water. It was like an English council house. One could make this cosy. When it's light, when I can see, I could spruce it up a bit, make it homely. But she dreaded the day and what she would have to do in it.

Sleeping at last, she was woken by a sound outside, a call. The words were incomprehensible but Claudia recognised the voice.

She rushed towards the door, calling, 'Kanita, is that you? Kanita!'

Here was someone Claudia need not fear. Now she'd be all right. There was hope. Of a kind.

Kanita was obviously extremely unwell, bruised and groggy from the blow she had received two days before. She must have come to the village in the hope of finding help for herself. Weakly, and in a language Claudia could not understand, Kanita made it clear that she was thrilled and relieved to see Claudia. There was no suggestion of guard or prisoner now, indeed Kanita's body-language showed she was pleading for something. For Claudia's help. She pulled and gestured for Claudia to follow her, walking unsteadily with Claudia behind or beside her, eventually leaning on one another.

They went quite far. As the sun rose up the sky they trudged painfully up the hill away from the village, along an unmade track bounded on one side by a crumbling wall, which led on to a green, treeless plateau with outcrops of light-coloured rock and no other habitation visible. The surface was rough, impacted stones and dried mud, with weeds growing on its edge. Kanita did not speak, needing every painful breath to gasp her way along, and Claudia felt equally weak and exhausted.

Claudia could hardly put one foot in front of the other, and the details of the landscape passed in a dull blur. I'm too old, she thought. It had been only as her years affected other people that Claudia had been aware of them herself. Workmen didn't whistle after her any more. George didn't want her. She was only middle-aged, she wasn't slowing down. But I'm not as strong as I was, she thought, and I've never noticed it before.

Carry on, go on, at least you're not dead. Think about something else. It's spring and you never noticed. Claudia saw wizened bushes leaning into rocks, reeds, several patches of a low-growing plant with glossy dark leaves, two thorny, gnarled old trees. Scattered over the ground of the field and the valley were clumps of flowers, yellow, white, a few blue and purple. Cistus, valerian, scabious. In the rock crevices a dwarfish cushion of leafy bush had tiny mauve flowers. There's the whine of insects. Birds. Wind. Sheep. An aeroplane.

Kanita was quicker thinking, and more accustomed to war. She grabbed Claudia's arm and dragged her under the inadequate shelter of a rock outcrop, shielded by a bush of broom. Slowly the plane flew over. But there was no movement for anyone to see, and after another circle round it flew away. Her breathing laboured and shallow, Kanita drew Claudia up and they carried on. But Kanita was faltering, the discoloured wound emblazoned on her deathly pale face. Arm in arm the two women staggered on.

On the mountainside ahead was an isolated house. As they slowly and painfully approached, Claudia could see it was, or had been, a farm, but apart from three tethered goats there was no other livestock to be seen now, only some weedy vegetables beginning to grow in a walled plot, and from nearby the comforting sound of chickens in an orchard of plum trees.

The house, like those in the village, was a concrete block left unfinished when the money ran out. It stood on a projecting spur, below a mountain peak.

291

The mountain had a bare, pinnacled ridge of silvery columns, and patches of orange marked what looked like fresher fractures of the stone. Below the ridge were desiccated slopes of sparse-looking pasture dotted with rock outcrops and dark bushes. Where the ground fell away below the promontory on which the building perched there were little, overgrown fields enclosed with boulder-built walls. Further below, stony scree tumbled away towards the misty, invisible distance.

Kanita staggered in tiny, last-gasp steps into the house. Claudia gagged at the miasma of sickness and incontinence. In what looked like an all-purpose living room, furnished just like the room in the village house, were two people, one an old white-stubbled man, asleep on a soiled bed against the wall. His mouth was open, revealing peg-toothed gums. Kanita slumped down by his feet, her eyes closed. The other, Claudia only noticed when he spoke. Lying at ground level was a black-eyed, bearded, youngish man, with a gaunt, drawn face and a sensual mouth. Both of his legs had been amputated above the knee and he was propped on a board which had pram wheels at its corners. And then Claudia noticed he had only one arm, in which lay a rifle, the fingers on the trigger, its muzzle pointed straight at her. In English Claudia stuttered some greeting and letting the weapon relax on to his lap he replied with some similar sound. Then he said in a weak husky voice, 'I am Alija, you are the Sheila.'

'But—that is, yes. The Sheila,' she agreed, clinging to the antipodean protection. 'But you speak English!'

'Little. Better German, until this war I in Düsseldorf am.'

'I'm afraid I don't speak German.'

'*Macht nichts.*'

'Where did everyone go?'

'To the town.'

'They left you behind?'

'*Sie sind alt.* Old.' He let go of the gun and with his one hand made a careless, dismissive gesture. 'The younger they go since long. Now the old also, they have fear.'

'But couldn't they have taken you with them?' Claudia asked, for a moment forgetting that she too had been abandoned by the fleeing villagers.

'They save themselves *mit die andere kinder,* other childs, also.'

'And Kanita?'

'She stay by us, Haric father'—he pointed at the sleeping old man—*'und die kinder.'* On cue, a wail sounded through the ceiling.

'Children? Upstairs?'

'Kanita is *schwester*. Sister.' The sister of Alija? Was Alija Haric's son, wounded in these cruel wars? Or did he mean that Kanita was the nurse, cleaner, carer, here? Yes, she must be a nurse of some kind, that must be why she'd been brought with the 'doctor' to check up on Claudia. Well, she was out of it for now, unconscious and probably concussed. There was an increasing chorus of cries but she did not stir.

'I'd better look and see.' Without waiting for an answer Claudia went out of the room, up the few concrete stairs, and into a room above. 'Oh my God.' There were makeshift cots in the room and the air was thick with the stench of stale body fluids. A baby, and a child who might be five or six, tethered into a chair by a couple of cords, nodding and jerking vacantly. 'Oh, what shall I do?' Claudia said aloud. She knew nothing about any children, let alone those with what she believed were euphemistically called 'special needs'.

What were their needs? Or the old man's, or the amputee's, or Kanita's own?

I can't deal with any of this, Claudia thought. She had always been protected by ever-present emergency and health services, by the invariable appearance of some competent person who knew, when she didn't, what to do.

Dozing while George drove, and jerked awake against her seat belt, disorientated, gasping, she was unhurt. George had a grazed forehead. The driver of the other car was screaming; he had broken his knee cap against the wheel mounting.

Claudia climbed out of the car and was cursing herself for not yet having been to first aid classes, before what seemed like dozens of people came running from neighbouring houses; a woman shouted, 'Leave it to me, I'm a nurse.' A man said, 'Don't touch him, I'm in the St John's Ambulance Brigade.' Another woman brought three mugs of steaming tea; followed almost immediately by the ambulance siren.

Other people had always coped for Claudia.

Not this time.

'But I can't. I don't know how,' the inner

wimp wailed. 'This isn't my problem.'

It is my problem, there's only me.

'But I'm no good, I'm useless.'

Pull yourself together, Hannah Claudia Brown! Her father's voice in her mind. Put your hand to the plough, he always said. They need you here.

Things to do, she thought, just as she used to make mental lists before going to the supermarket or picking up from the dry-cleaners.

Find water, cloths, food. Clean them up, bandage them, feed them. Somehow, anyhow, just bloody well cope.

25

Nina and Harry had quarrelled about her trip the previous evening. He was dismayed and she was indignant. 'I'd have thought you'd be pleased—you were the one who said I should be doing programmes that were more serious. Worthwhile was the word you used.'

'I know, I know, but that was before ...'

'Before what?'

'Before I ... before we knew each other so well.'

He can't say it, she thought, he won't say he loves me, damn him. He had never said that to her, or she to him, for both had been wary of a phrase they had misused before. But she wished he would. She said sharply, 'You're a fine one to talk. What about what you're doing—Afghanistan, for God's sake! I should be fussing about you, but I suppose it's fine for Harry Anson, just not for the little woman? What is this anyway? Since when did you tell me what I can do?' She tried to work herself up into a convincing fury, defying his assumed authority. But then she realised she was unconsciously fingering the scar on her cheek.

'I'm not, Nina, but I know you're dreading it really—be honest, aren't you?'

'What's that matter, if it's worth doing?'

'It's just that I can't bear to think of you—oh Nina, do you have to do this? Just for a potty radio programme? Light entertainment, in one ear and out the other? Is it worth risking your life for?'

'I'm going home. I don't have to listen to you denigrating my work.'

'I didn't mean—'

'Anyway, I've got an early start.'

'Don't let's part in anger, Nina.'

But Nina had never been good at swallowing her pride. She kissed him coldly on the cheek and went home in a fury.

So close to Easter Heathrow was crowded even at five in the morning. It was the end of the skiing season. Nina queued to check in surrounded by tall, healthy-looking people with too much hand baggage, their heavy boots clumping across the smooth floor and liable to catch an unwary stranger on the ankle, the kick followed by a blow from someone else's skis or overloaded rucksack.

There had been a time when Nina travelled light. That was when she was self-confident and optimistic. Now, forcing herself to think about it, to prepare, to get up and go, she had found herself unable to edit or excise. She had to take the heavy, bulky flak jacket. She couldn't go without the necessities no corner shop over there would supply: tampons, a mini-pharmacopoeia—God knows what ailments lay in store—iron rations, because she didn't want to be another mouth for

298

dwindling supplies to feed, a bed roll.

She paid for the excess weight of her baggage, and turned away to buy the papers before going through to the departure lounge. At least she did not attract stares. In the old days, when she was famous, strangers seemed to need to touch her. Sometimes people who had seen Nina on the screen gave in to an urge to reach out and feel her, and though she always wrote her autograph or even allowed herself to be photographed beside an admirer, she was frightened and felt threatened by such invasions of her 'personal space'.

So when, in the scrum of queuing strangers, she felt a hand on her back, Nina stepped sharply away from it before turning round, to see Harry Anson had barged into the queue behind her.

'What are you doing here?' she demanded.

'I've come to say I'm sorry.'

'Harry, look, you're holding up the—'

'Come over here, listen to me, I've got to talk to you—Nina—'

'It's not my fault,' Nina said. 'I've got to see this through.' Harry blocked her way, his arms folded. He was such a solid man, she thought irrelevantly, one could suppose him to be literally immovable.

'Do you really have to—oh, I'm sorry, I'm sorry, I don't mean it, consider that unsaid, it's only because I can't say what I really want to say here and it'll be so long until I can. Unless we meet out there ...'

'What d'you mean?'

'If I can get through with this Afghan business in good time, then I want to try and find Claudia's grave and organise some memorial since it doesn't look as though anyone else is going to.' Harry had not hidden his anger from Nina when George Anson had paid only brief lip service to regret for his wife, before moving Laurel into the London flat, Ansons and the rest of his life. 'Oh Nina, I'm kicking myself, I should have said all this when I had a chance.'

'Are you two going to get out of the way? Good God, it's Nina. And it's—we met once, in Dubrovnik, remember, Henry ...?'

Nina pulled herself back into professional mode. 'Harry, do you remember Zed Lyons—the photographer?'

'I always meet my friends at airports,' Zed said. 'Are you travelling together?'

'I'm on my own,' Nina replied. 'But

Harry—Harry. Goodbye. Good luck.'

'When we're both back—goodbye. Bye.'

On tiptoe she watched his broad shoulders part the crowd. Then he half turned and his lips made three words. Were they, I love you? Do it again, let me see again. But he was gone.

'You know, when I started in this game no TV person could ever work alone, all the kit needed a team of strong men,' Zed said.

'My gear's all in this small bag. But I'm working in radio now, not television.'

He said, 'I know, your boss is a friend of mine.'

'What about you?'

'I'm on a job for Magnum but I'll be meeting up with a hack from the Beeb. Wish we could all get together at the Pull Up For Car Men.' The facetious name had been given to a former transport café, a pair of chalet-style buildings with a large room downstairs and adequate, if unluxurious, sleeping accommodation, which, during the coverage of the war in Yugoslavia, the BBC had occupied. It had become a sort of club, a meeting place for reporters, but the world's interest had moved on since then and the club had effectively closed down.

Nina said, 'I'm doing a soft story, nothing to do with the war and I'm staying well clear of trouble. I don't think I'll be needing my accreditation card.' Her fingers went automatically to the scar on her cheek. She was furious to realise her hand was trembling, and snatched it down to shove into her coat pocket.

'All the same, you take care, Nina, you hear? Because too many of us have already come to grief out there.'

'You too, Zed.'

'Oh, don't worry, I'll mind my step.'

'You're all right, Zed, are you?'

'Yeah, if you mean about Daisy. It was a fantasy, I knew it all along really—how could I do this job with a kid?'

'You couldn't take the same risks, it's true.'

'But I go careful, I've learnt to calculate the odds, not least the odds of anyone showing the film I might have been killed taking.'

'It's old news, in a way, I suppose,' Nina said.

'The usual story, the editors got bored and the media moved on—but there it all is, all still going on. I feel a commitment to these people, far more than I did in the Gulf, or Vietnam or the Lebanon. Afghanistan ... anywhere else. This war has turned a news man's role upside down.'

'How d'you mean?' Nina asked.

Zed peered down at her from his six foot four. 'I remember a time when reporters used to be saying, "Let's get our boys out of here, what are we doing, it's wrong to be here." But in this war we've reversed it, not trying to get the boys out, but pressing to go on in. I was a pacifist once, but nobody could be after the last few years out there, you'd be made of stone to stand aside from this one.'

'But there's peace now.'

'So called and temporary. The moment NATO pulls out ...'

Nina glanced at the merry people around them, some eager to seize the last chance of a late skiing holiday, others setting off for a first taste of summer further south. None seemed to have any trouble in standing aside. In spite of all the efforts of Zed or Lord Owen or Cyrus Vance or anyone else, they had never been persuaded that it was their business. 'They can't imagine being involved, can they? Going hungry, being under sniper fire in their own back yard ... being wounded or raped ...'

'These are people who can tell themselves there's been peace in their time,' Zed said.

'Perhaps it's healthier to behave as though there's some sort of barrier between them and chaos,' Nina said. 'As though it could never happen here. Or to them.'

26

If anyone had foretold Claudia Anson's existence during these days she herself would have predicted a certain consequence: that she would not be able to manage and would not even try.

'I'd just lie down and wait to die,' she'd have said. 'I'd never have the guts to cope. I'm a terrible coward.' Then she would have added 'alas' or 'I'm sorry to say', self-deprecating for show.

Only by the most rigid control did Claudia prevent herself from spending all day and night crouched in a catatonic huddle in a corner. She made herself heave buckets of water from the spring. Directed by shouts from the two men, she managed to milk one of the goats, to forage, assemble food—one could hardly use the word cook—spoon it into the mouths of her helpless charges, push off Alija's one-handed, random touches and pokes and make her inept stab at nursing without the drugs or equipment she'd always assumed indispensable. She swabbed and straightened the old man, weak but not apparently wounded or ill; Kanita, delirious and sweating; the unsmiling, speechless infants whose only response was to wail or moan. She had to prop Alija on a pot or hold a bottle to his penis, and hurt pride made him mingle sexual or verbal aggression with his pitiful, unavoidable dependence. The old man Haric, if he was awake and conscious, spoke quite good English; it was he who told her the children were called Bor and Zivich, one was Kanita's son, Haric's grandson, the other the daughter of a couple who had fled months before, leaving their human burden behind. Only the helpless and the old had stayed; the old people would not leave the land until terror finally drove them away.

'The soldiers took children away.'

'Orphans.' Tears pearled out of Haric's faded eyes and he turned his face to the wall.

Alija was not Kanita's husband, but the friend of her husband. He had been in the army. That explained his wounds. Claudia did not like Alija, who watched her with scornful, jealous eyes and expected her to look after him like a body slave. And for the first time in her life, Claudia made no attempt to hide her own feelings. Why should she care what these people thought of her? She would do what she could for them out of common humanity, and because she didn't know where else to go or what else to do, but she didn't have to like them and it didn't matter a damn if they liked her. As the time went by she became ever more free with her language, swearing at them or shouting whenever she felt like it. They didn't understand. If they did, so what? She realised she actually liked yelling and cursing. It was a liberation.

Claudia, who would only a week before have fled screaming, instead threw a stone at a rat with apparent calm, disposed of spiders, and erected a rough wall across the broken rear doorway because she thought she'd heard the sniffing and scratching of some predatory mammal. She even collected a pile of small boulders as weapons against whatever the animal might be—a dog? a wolf? a bear? She began a new journal, scrappy notes, written with a cheap biro on the blank inside of cardboard packets of dried milk she'd fetched from the village. 'Place reeks, charnel house. Couldn't manage the necessary, too dangerous, will keep clear, not spread infection.' She had to justify herself somehow; but there was a limit to what one woman—even a more able and resourceful one than Claudia—could undertake.

On the third day Kanita was better. She knew where she was, took Claudia's hand and kissed it, tried to get up, but fell and had to stay lying on the frowsty cloths.

That night there was a storm. Thunder louder than Claudia had ever heard and lightning brighter. Fearful at first that it was another bombardment, Claudia saw Kanita was unafraid. A terrific flash lightened the whole empty room. The thunder followed quickly, as loud as a bomb exploding. Kanita put her arm round Claudia, maternally stroked her clotted hair, and pressed the other woman's head on to her own bosom.

'That's cosy,' Claudia murmured. Knowing nobody would understand the shameful statement, she added, 'It's better than sex.'

Claudia was of the generation which grew up into the post-pill paradise. Guilt, fidelity, right and wrong were meaningless words. Free sexual congress was the cement which held Claudia's college friends together, like the family meals she had sat through as a child, a ritual togetherness. Sometimes a couple would go round together for a few weeks in a psychic cloud of exclusivity and possessiveness. Mostly people shared. Claudia used to wish she did not have to be bothered with the obligatory sexual intercourse. It would have caused offence if she had refused without a very good reason, genital herpes or cystitis at least. And fucking was the price she paid for cuddling.

But her shame, a deadly secret, was that she never came. Only with Stavros, that one time on Korcula. He was not like the egalitarian students, he was a masterful man who reminded her of her father, he knew what he wanted. He didn't take no for an answer.

George had taken no for an answer and taken fakes for orgasms. Claudia couldn't hurt his feelings to say he wasn't satisfying her. She knew it was her own fault, she just wasn't passionate, and used to tell herself it was something she had to come to terms with, like her infertility. Claudia and George had fallen in love at first sight. But the earth never moved. And when he fell out of love with her it wasn't sex she missed, it was something a child could have given her, if only she'd had a child, simply a physical contact and warmth, a cuddle.

As the thunderstorm moved away, Kanita fell asleep and rain began to fall like a bombardment of pebbles. Claudia went outside to smell the cleansed earth. She squatted to piss and then took off her clothes to stretch and caper in the fall of icy water, naked and unashamed.

There was nobody else for miles.

She had always been an urban creature, ill at ease in the country, except at Ansons. Here, in objectively terrifying circumstances, she could have been excused for panic or agoraphobic reactions, but now that, for the first time in her life, there was really something to be afraid of she'd become calm, not starting at every squawk or squeak, not trembling at the touch of an insect or the sight of a rodent.

Alone and unprotected as she had never been before, sensuously enjoying the chill water pouring down her hair and skin, Claudia recognised that at this moment she, a captive, felt perversely free. Making practical plans for the next day—gather firewood, walk down to the village and find urgently needed linen in one of the houses—she went in to the two chairs which were her makeshift bed.

At dawn, while Kanita and the men were snoring, sunk in merciful oblivion, Claudia's eyes met the eyes of an intruder.

Her own worst nightmare: alone (as she supposed) in the house, naked in the bathroom or opening the door of a darkened room, someone is there, a dark figure appears reflected behind her shoulder. She looks through the uncurtained window and sees a face; whose? She opens the door and there is—who? She never knew. Bolting, locking, shuttering, Claudia had always taken precautions against an unknown foe.

The storm had passed, and the sky was clear and smooth, with one star twinkling beside a crescent moon.

Between Claudia and the sky, standing in the open doorway, the dim figure of a man, a strong smell of sweat, garlic and tobacco.

Who—why—? Has he come to kill us all?

Every instinct told her to freeze, submit, passively demonstrate her subjugation and his dominance. Don't make waves, don't provoke him.

It was as though she were watching another person, a fictional character, do something she had never done before and always assumed she could never do.

Leaping to her feet, seizing a decent-sized stone, she threw it as hard as she could at the man's face. He grunted, clapped one hand to his eye and turned away, followed by a silent shadow, a tall, thin, slinking, wolf-like dog.

It was a mistake. The man might have been a friend, he might have brought help. Or was he an enemy? Now he had discovered them, would he come back with his companions to kill them too?

Oh God, I must have been mad, I should never have done it. I don't know what came over me. I must have lost my mind.

27

Nina's interpreter, previously faultlessly punctual and reliable, was not waiting by the car. As she stood looking up and down the road, a man who had been waiting on the hotel steps came over to her.

'Miss Gillespie? I am your interpreter. My name is Yacoub.'

His pronunciation, even of Nina's surname, was faultless. He was tall and very thin, with high, prominent cheek and jaw bones, large dark eyes under straight black brows, stubbled olive skin and silver-speckled black hair. He was wearing clean, ironed jeans with an open-necked checked shirt and a leather bomber jacket. His very large, even and white teeth gleamed as he smiled and held out his hand.

'Haven't we met somewhere before?'

'Surely I'd remember it,' he replied.

He's gorgeous, she thought, but said coldly, 'What's happened to Lisa?'

'She's not very well today.'

'But she's been with me for days, she knows what I want.' On the gruelling round of refugee camps Lisa had not been told they were looking for signs of the trade in infants, but she had somehow managed to anticipate Nina's every need.

Yacoub said, 'That's all right, you'll be fine with me.' He took Nina's car keys, bag and video camera from her, unlocked the boot and stowed everything out of casual sight. When Nina flung her jacket on to the back seat, he picked it up, folded it inside out and laid it neatly on the floor, almost under the seat. 'It really doesn't do to leave anything showing. Anyone might take it. We are in lawless anarchy,' he explained cheerfully. 'Shall I drive?'

'Wait a minute, I haven't said you can come with me yet,' Nina protested.

'Don't you need a translator? Lisa said you spoke none of our languages.' He stood waiting for Nina's decision. She looked at him carefully, seeing a surface humility, with nothing in his stance to imply that he was anything other than a man who wanted a job. But Nina felt a suppressed arrogance, an impatience in him. She wondered whether it would be better to try to find some other interpreter as self-effacing and efficient as Lisa.

Lisa was a broadcaster herself when she had the chance, a country girl by origin, better educated than her peasant parents and pleasantly undemanding. She and Nina found a good deal in common, and it had even turned out that both had been at the same 'Free Press Workshop for Women' in Moscow some years previously, although they had not met then.

In those days the fresh wind of democracy had briefly seemed to be blowing for Yugoslavians (as they could still call themselves). Some old women had come too, who had been equal fighters with men partisans forty years earlier, though communism had halted their progress towards equality. But most delegates were young. They listened as women from America and Latin America, from Holland and Canada, stoked their hopes. That was 'bright glorious morning', Lisa had recalled, tears leaping from her eyes, a brief spark, quickly quenched.

'Where's Lisa now?' she asked, but Yacoub said he did not know.

Nina needed to get on but it wasn't a good idea to travel with a townee who despised the peasants. Nina had experience of such people, nearly always young men who were too arrogant and impatient to winkle out information. On the other hand she had realised that Lisa's contacts were limited. And Yacoub might be more of a protection.

Nina had made herself overcome her fears, she'd come back to this country and found it less frightening in reality than she had been imagining it all these years. Finally back on the horse that threw her, Nina was doing all right. But she had not found what she was looking for; she had hardly expected to. It would not be in this region of precarious civilisation that she'd see revelations of the heartlessness she suspected but in the backwoods, where petty warlords had taken control of small enclaves and pockets of separatism. In those areas of the country the situation was reverting to feudalism. A strong leader with enough weapons could protect those who, in exchange, paid their dues and did what he said. In their own small patches, until a stronger fighting band 'cleaned them out'—in the hideous, universal colloquialism—these temporary tyrants were monarch of all they surveyed.

Nina needed a good guide, though not one who knew the nature of her quest. She would never find the orphanages which sold their charges, or the strong men who dealt in babies for trade, unless she kept it secret that she was looking for them. She wanted to hear rumours, in this country where rumours always abounded, so she needed a companion who kept an ear open to hear them. The interpretation and recognition of clues was her business. It was how she had always worked before, all over the world, when someone might say, 'There's been a massacre in so-and-so village,' and Nina would go there herself with a camera man to check it out and, if it was true, tell the world.

Somewhere someone would mention another rumour: that infants dematerialised and money flowed in. Nina needed to be told what people whispered. Would Yacoub hear those stories, and repeat them? Would he accept that Nina was in charge?

But that was all rationalisation. It was not the real reason for Nina's hesitation. The fact was, she was not at all sure she could trust herself.

It was a long time since she had felt this: the physical jolt, analogous to an electric shock or a sharp kick, of the first contact with a man she wanted.

Until this moment Nina had been under the illusion that she had been there, done that, and never needed to again. The sexual imperative, so very strong in her teens and earlier twenties, was a dampened fire. This period after she parted from Carl had been a time of discovery, of finding out that she liked her own company and even enjoyed the freedoms celibacy brought. The new relationship with Harry was all the more exciting for coming after a time of abstinence. But it had restored to her something she'd put aside. Sex, just simple sex. That must be why she felt her treacherous body yearning towards this stranger while her mind warded him away.

There had been several other men (since Nina was fifteen and first had one) for whom her lust had been overpowering. Each time it was lovely, even glorious, until it became in retrospect ridiculous, but the flames had consumed other things in their path—friendships, even, and sometimes

Nina's vital self-respect.

Yacoub was watching her.

'OK,' she said. 'Let's go.'

'Shall I drive?'

'No, I'll drive,' she said. I drive, I am in control. I decide how far we go.

In parts of the country now called 'former Yugoslavia' the civilised relics of a European empire had outlasted the years of communist rule. The roads were still surfaced and had no more pot-holes than one could find in many other parts of Europe. Passers-by were neatly dressed. Children went to school with double-strapped satchels high on their backs, babies were pushed in buggies, fruit trees promised plentiful harvests in roadside fields, bulky cows swayed through flowered pastures.

But then would come a reminder of anarchy. A roadblock, lifted after Yacoub had a word with the casual men in camouflage gear who lounged with their cigarettes, passing Nina's money from his hand to theirs; a petrol station without any petrol; a street flooded from a high-founting water pipe without any attempt to repair the burst. There had once been a highly efficient administration here. There

might be again. Who could tell which way it would go?

Yacoub, whose excellent English turned out to be due to the fact that he was, in fact, British, talked about his first visit to his parents' country of origin, back in 1991, and how he now planned to stay, seeing, he said, the way England was going these days, down the toilet. He'd been glad to leave.

'Where were you living?'

'In Exeter. My father came over before I was born.'

'And your mother too?'

'Yes, from the Adriatic coast, but she left when I was still a kid,' he said, his voice frighteningly venomous. 'Still, it means I grew up with several languages and then I went to the Institute of Slavonic Studies at London University and learnt some more. Languages come easily to me.'

'Jolly useful for an interpreter.'

'I am not an interpreter by trade, Nina.'

'Sorry, I thought—'

'I told you, I'm just helping out my friend Lisa. I am a businessman. I deal in import and export.'

'Is it a problem for you, being away from work?'

'Not at all. No problem at all.' They were passing through an industrial area, shabby warehouses, fuming chimneys and shocking heaps of spoil, with rusty trucks on the road, spattering dirt on the gutter-hugging bicyclists. She drove cautiously, feeling his eyes on her.

It was late morning when they came to a town of cobbled streets built alongside a fast-moving river, with pavement cafés where people sat over meals and drinks while the shutters were put up over shops for an afternoon break. There had been no signposts on the road, and Nina wondered if they had been removed to foil invaders, as they were in Britain during the Second World War, or if it was all part of the former totalitarian secrecy. Yacoub, asked its name, uttered an incomprehensible polysyllable. Then he said, 'We're still some way from the camp you want to see, this is a nowheresville. Hick town. Nothing happens here, never has, never will.'

'All the same, we'll stop here for a bit.' Nina pulled up under a shady tree. 'Let's get something to eat.'

Sitting across a café table from Yacoub, elbows on the table, chin on her folded hands, Nina realised she'd never worried about being attracted to a man before. If it happened she'd let it happen. Before her celibate period she'd been a woman who loved making love. Sleeping with a man was fun but seldom momentous, a game in which two people's limbs or organs came into contact. Which limbs and organs they were was hardly of earth-shaking importance, merely a matter of degree. Now she had been resensitised to sex. Little did Harry know what he'd done to her. He'd made her into a creature whose every nerve ending quivered with perilous lust. If Yacoub's come-on had been more subtle she'd probably even have given in to it. He talked about his former girlfriends. An advertising executive, a dancer, a charity organiser. 'We always go on being friends,' he said. 'Never any unpleasantness.'

Make him earn his keep, she thought, and told him to see if he could pick up any useful gossip, while she sat on in the shade with her glass of harsh red wine, picking at the remains of dry bread, coarse sausage and corrosive pickles. What was—oh yes, nothing rare, a black-throated thrush. Yacoub was having a conversation with a man at the next table who had hardly taken his eyes off Nina since she arrived. Expecting to understand nothing, she suddenly realised they were talking Dutch, and having gone out with a Dutchman understood some of it. They'd met before. The other man was a travel agent, he'd come back to Croatia to see if the country was ready for Belgian groups to tour. At a conference, he was saying, when was it? Back in '91, at the beginning of the war. You got off with that amazing blonde. Were you in the business yourself, the travel business? I had a go at her myself, what was she called, Karen, Laura, something like that.

Yacoub glanced sideways at Nina, who was careful to show no signs of understanding. He said briefly that he was in import export now. Then he went across the square to talk to some old men who were playing chess on a paving stone board with chessmen on wheels.

Nobody spoke to Nina, but as she pulled out her telephone and managed to get a connection to one of her contact numbers, she was careful not to give anything away, only saying where she was and in which direction she intended to go. She would call again that evening.

But she knew if Yacoub had plans

for her, nobody could do much about it. Brian France, in his glass eyrie in London, Harry in the far corner of the continent, both were equally unable to come to her rescue. She vanquished a sudden, powerful urge to turn round and go home. Instead she sat waiting. The sun on her back felt soothing and pleasant. This pillared, canopied café terrace could be in Italy, the decorated stone house fronts were no different from some she had seen in Vienna, those dark, thin children could be Greek or even Indian; Nina's mind ran on vague and unconnected notions about the surviving influence of empires, Roman, Turkish or Austro-Hungarian; she wondered how many colonial administrators, homesick in exile at this far corner of whatever empire they served, had built for themselves some architectural reminder of home.

Yacoub walked rapidly back across the square, its paving stones polished shiny white and smooth by generations of use.

'Any luck?'

'Nobody knows anything. But the place is of course alive with rumours.'

'About?'

'Politics. War. Food supplies. Troop

movements, arms—and the football international. And hints of what you're looking
for, I believe.'

'How d'you know what I'm looking
for?'

'You've hinted at the missing children,
Nina, I understand where you're coming
from.'

Without replying, and easing herself on
to the painfully hot driving seat, Nina tried
to remember what she could have said that
Yacoub had so accurately interpreted. Be
careful, she warned herself, he's sharp.
But it was off-putting. She was no
less certain that he wanted to be in
bed with her than that she was going
to turn the key—there—and the engine
would fire—thus, but she was suddenly
positive that she would not give way
to the animal lust which had washed
over her that morning, and nothing, she
promised herself, would be said. No offer,
no refusal, no persuasion, no rebuff. Two
adults would work together in polite and
passionless co-operation. That was it.

That was the beginning of a curious
journey, coloured at the time and in later
memory by what Yacoub and Nina did not
say and do. All their conversations, all their

travelling and stopping and questioning, were directed to what they were seeing and finding. They took short nights in whatever lodging they could find (never luxurious, always separate), but otherwise worked and concentrated for hours without breaks. This was a way of life, tense, uncomfortable, reactive, into which she fitted easily. Nina Gillespie was back on the trail.

28

Nina's work was absorbing, so immediate as to leave no time for introspection and so objective as to leave her own self out of the equation. In collecting information for a distant audience, Nina automatically buried her individuality to become a characterless mouthpiece of truth. Tell it how it is, she'd told her audience of students in Cardiff. Now she was seeing how it was. Afterwards she realised Yacoub had made sure of that, purposefully, surreptitiously directing their travels.

Together they observed the uneasy peace that persisted within easy, perilous reach of an undeclared war. Some places were outwardly as unaffected as the little town where Yacoub and Nina had stopped that first day. Children went to school, men sat over their Slivovitz, women went shopping. And although what they bought was not what they might have chosen, at least they did go home with full bags and could put meals on the family table.

Within a few miles one could be in a modern version of purgatory: a school or football stadium, commandeered to house a few, and then more, and by now far too many people who had fled to safety, leaving their homes and most of their belongings, saying goodbye to their friends and relations, abandoning all the attributes of personal life, because terrible though the future they now faced might be, if they had stayed put there would have been no future at all.

Nina supposed that the first of the refugees had managed to find lodgings in normal houses, even to find work. But later they came in such numbers that they were herded into such shelters. It had soon become confinement.

With draped rags and bunches of wilting wild flowers the women created a pathetic simulacrum of domesticity. Children, so long as they did not go hungry, played. But the men sat sunk in melancholy all the time, indifferent to anything that went on round them, seldom reacting to the sight of Nina's tape recorder even when their wives clustered round her to tell their tales for Yacoub to translate.

'This one says she lost her brother and niece on the trek. Here is a lady who carried her own mother for many kilometres on her back. This child has lost his family. He is alone.'

Nina would make notes of the scene, record a few interviews, but always aware how few facts her audience would take in before they switched over to a game show or soap opera.

Some 'camps', with wood and block houses and even paved roads, were hardly distinguishable from ordinary villages in the same neighbourhood. But others were like the one they went to on day eight, a camp in a bombed village of ruined, roofless houses, roughly covered by tarpaulins or blue plastic sheeting stamped UNHCR. The shelters had been there for long enough to grow mould and the stench made Nina's head swim, before she forced herself to breathe deeply and get out of the car.

She walked around beside Yacoub and stopped to talk to a few people, but many were too disheartened to speak. There were orphans in this camp. One child, a girl of about nine, took hold of Nina's hand, her bird-boned fingers pressed against Nina's sweating palm, black, almond-shaped eyes staring up at her. A young woman came towards Nina with a grace and confidence that would have suited a metropolitan reception.

'Nina Gillespie, what a pleasure, what an honour. I watched you so often, with such admiration, when I was in London. You won't remember it but we met once, long ago at dinner with the Minogues in Hampstead. My name's Inea.'

She had studied physics as a post-graduate at Imperial College. In her own country she had been a university lecturer until having to flee. Now she was living in a tent supplied by the United Nations High Commission for Refugees, which she shared with her mother, sister, two nieces and a great-aunt who had lost her mind and believed herself to be back in the mountain villa she had lived in during her distant childhood; she spent the days babbling of cherry trees and river picnics. 'It cheers us up, really. She paints us word pictures, so delightful.'

'But you—what's going to happen to you? Will you go back to London?'

'My dear, of course I would, so gladly.' Her accent was regal, her voice high and silvery. 'But how can I leave my family? It isn't to be thought of.'

Nina scribbled notes, usually an effective way of distancing herself from the troubles she observed. Yacoub was on the far side of a dusty clearing talking, gesturing, cross-questioning a group of young men. Nina noticed Inea watching him, and said, 'That's my interpreter.'

'I have seen him, yes.' Inea's voice was chilly.

Nina turned so that Yacoub would not see her face and asked in a low voice, 'Do you know anything about him?'

'Very little. I believe him to be an expatriate who has returned to share in his nation's battles. He is said to be ardently committed to its cause.'

'Oh.'

'I am sure he's an excellent interpreter.

Now tell me,' Inea changed the subject as firmly and gracefully as a diplomat, 'have you seen the dear Minogues?' She smoothed the creased and stained material of her flowered skirt and added, 'They were always so hospitable when I was in London, I have the fondest possible memories of their home.'

The child who had attached herself to Nina spoke a few words of English.

'You carry me home,' she stated, and repeated the words as a question. 'You carry me home?'

That was what Michael Nicholson, the English reporter, had done. He'd taken just such a girl home, writing a name into his own passport under those of his son and daughter. Together the man and the child had flown to safety. One child, from so many. Better than none?

'You speak English very well,' Nina said evasively.

'We have good classes here,' Inea said. 'Myself, I am teaching mathematics.'

'You carry me home.'

'No,' Nina said, her voice hoarse with shame. 'No, I can't.' She resisted the impulse to shake the girl away from her. 'It's not allowed.'

Inea said in her light, elegant voice, 'Illegal, of course, but it happens none the less. It is a question of finance, like everything else. In this sad country, what you require or desire, one will sell you. A girl? A boy? A death? A living child? All, all is on the market here.'

Cautiously Nina said, 'Where would you go to buy a child? A baby?'

At that moment Yacoub appeared at her side. Gazing into Nina's eyes Inea replied, 'Yacoub can answer all your questions, I believe. Perhaps he will lead you to the answers.'

'What d'you mean? Inea—'

'It is so good to have met you again. I hope you will remember me to the dear Minogues.' Holding the child's hand, she turned gracefully and moved away.

Yacoub said, 'You've seen enough here.' A question or a statement? What is this man, she wondered, torn again between distrust and the reminder of the sexual attraction she'd been shoving to the back of her mind. These deadly camps were like death itself; they made one want life-affirming sex.

'You should have told me what you were looking for,' Yacoub said.

'Why?' Nina said.

'Because I know where to find it. I'll take you there.' Back by the car Yacoub said, 'Was that the first time it got to you?'

'What do you mean?' Nina replied.

'We have been going round these hell-holes for days and you've stayed as cool as ice, I thought you're more interested in the sodding birds than the people. You've had me ask the questions, you've listened to the answers and made your notes and pointed your recorder like the poor sods we saw were different species.'

'You can't let yourself feel emotional in this job,' Nina said, hurt.

'But you did this time.'

'It doesn't help if I got involved.'

'Yes, it does.' Suddenly, standing at the edge of the road, Yacoub was a looming, menacing figure. The person he had disguised in a cloak of helpful co-operation peeked through, showing someone of whom Nina was frightened—for a moment. Then he got himself under control again. He went on in a calm, almost academic voice, raising it when lorries swished by in their clouds of dust, not gesturing but fanning flies away with a flapping road map.

'Don't you think, perhaps, that it's because people like you remain so judicious in your reports, so unbiased, that people in other countries can tell themselves that the problems here are insoluble, that there's nothing they can do, that all sides are equally to blame? How are any of these people to win friends or allies, when the medium their message goes through is so determined to be non-partisan?'

'People take more notice of a balanced account,' Nina said, repeating an argument which was an axiom of her professional world.

'But they haven't, nobody's taken any notice at all. If they'd been listening, these wretched people we've been looking at like animals in a badly run zoo wouldn't be kept in these conditions, without enough food or medicine or even having the chance to fight their own battles.'

'But Yacoub, that's what I'm here for, to tell people.'

'Yes, but what do you tell them? I've listened to the reports you've recorded, all so calm, a little tasteful tinge of sadness in your voice, all so non-judgemental. That's the word you use, you lot, you reporters, isn't it? But your ever so balanced descriptions aren't going to make governments change their minds, they won't make anyone lift arms embargoes or even supply the food and medicines these people need. It takes something more than that.'

'Let's move on,' Nina said, getting into the car. She started the engine and moved off before asking Yacoub why he had said none of this before.

He replied, 'I kept waiting for you to show some feeling and acknowledge this human predicament, maybe, just once, become part of it. To realise you aren't any different yourself except for an accident of birth.'

'But I do realise that, of course I do, I'm concerned and involved—'

'That's just crap, Nina, none of you do, reporters, journalists, relief workers, supply drivers, you all go back to the safety you have come from, you swim through this sea of troubles in a psychic wet suit. How will you ever change Western opinions, your way? You'll go on dropping in and looking round and going away to your own fucking safety again until someone like you gets caught up the way my people are.'

As Nina drove towards the hills, Yacoub seemed to change gear.

'I'm sorry, Nina, I'm being a bore.' He put his hand on her knee, the first touch since that initial handshake. She shifted her leg abruptly and he removed his hand. He said, 'I was reading the paper you brought when you came, it was on the floor in the back. The *Sunday Times* books supplement. An interview with a woman novelist who writes what the journalist called Aga Sagas. Do you know what they are?'

'Yes. I don't like them much. Cooking, churches and kids and the regulation adultery. Just what the Nazis thought women ought to stick to.'

'She said people wanted to read about real life just as real people experience it, shopping in the supermarket and worrying about the children's exam results and visiting elderly relations.'

'She must be right because it's certainly a best-selling subject,' Nina said.

'It's a fucking unforgivable thing to say. Real life? Supermarkets? Exams? Where are the people of this poor bloody country to go for real life? The fact is you lot think they are already as good as dead.'

335

29

Claudia had been so busy and was so exhausted that she'd hardly thought about anything except keeping going from minute to minute. Yet the future could not be ignored. Kanita's hoarded food provided a sparse and deprived diet and soon there would be no oil left to heat the stove to boil the water to cook the dusty pulses and withered root vegetables left at the bottom of their sacks. Alija said they would keep alive eating leaves and acorns and grinding down the hard centres of corn cobs to make cakes with the powder. 'That's how our people lived in Srebrnica.'

Kanita was on her feet again, lurching from one hand-hold to the next. She moved from old and young man to the older and younger child, stroking and nuzzling each of them in an outpouring of affection. Claudia watched with a painful interest as the young man kissed Kanita's fingers and rested his face on her breast. Old Haric had cupped Kanita's cheek in his palm.

Nobody was ever going to love Claudia like that.

'I'm going out, you can manage without me for a change,' she said sharply. Without noticing the process she had become much stronger in the last few days, feeling, she now suddenly realised, not just well but far better than she had for ages. Perhaps a hard life was good for her after all. Her father would have said, 'I told you so.'

It was a beautiful day. She would hunt for plants Kanita might say were edible. She would see what was over the hill. Perhaps she wouldn't come back.

Claudia walked and crawled uphill on a mule trail. She was soon exhausted but still forced herself onwards and upwards, further than she had managed to go before. Perhaps there would be another village or farm just over the top.

Once she'd walked in hills like this on holiday in Austria with George and the Chandlers. Feeling lazy, and preferring not to spend every moment with Milly, she'd stroll up the easy path while the family climbed the long way round. She could almost imagine that round the corner she'd come upon a charming restaurant with umbrellas and checked table-cloths and friendly waiters, and order *citron pressé* and air-dried beef and have iced beer waiting for when the others' tall figures came into sight in the distance. They would gulp down the first blessed draught and go inside to wash their hands, and Claudia would read another paragraph of her thriller and smile at the couple at the next table and join in mutual congratulations on the wonderful weather, the unbroken sunshine; and they would ask to borrow Claudia's green Michelin guidebook and she would recommend the museum in the neighbouring town. And then Milly would sit down beside her and gossip about people at home and what was wrong with Ansons and somehow the catalogue of misdemeanours would be her fault. Here, alone in the middle of nowhere, Claudia suddenly realised she wasn't to blame. Perhaps it was the first time in her life that the ever-present, chronic guilt was lifted.

I've always appeased people, Claudia thought.

Papa. Mama. Always striving and criticising, nothing his family did was ever quite good enough, never up to the standard he expected. Never enough to meet Mama's dual need to appease him and to ensure that her daughters never needed to give such satisfaction themselves. She wanted me to be more free than she ever managed to be, Claudia realised, so much too late. That was why she was always pushing. 'Nobody else is going to help you out, do it yourself, do it well, better, best, stand on your own two feet.' Why didn't you win the prize, come top of the form, outdo all competitors? Or any competitors. Claudia, then still Hannah, never had managed to be any kind of living compensation for those dead forebears.

I hardly existed, Claudia thought, except as other people saw me.

George once had the words for it. Before they were married they stayed with his friends in an intimidating house where Claudia pretended not to be afraid of the dogs and horses and acquiesced in the kind of flirting which, twenty years later, would have been recognised as harassment. It was before sexual openness became the norm outside student circles. Claudia might sleep with her fiancé, but not admit it.

On the last night George came into her bedroom. She protested. Suppose the others heard? He was masterful. Claudia was his trophy. 'If I wake up you'll go out like a light.' A joke? Metaphorically at least, it felt perfectly true.

So she clung to George and his house. And what did he think, dream of, long for, regret? Claudia had no idea. She placated him, forgave him and eventually, so long as he wasn't there, managed to forget him. But she still knew that everything that went wrong was down to her.

Ghastly though everything was here and now, at least it was not all Claudia's fault.

It took her a long time to reach the green plateau above and at the end of the valley, listening to the ice cold water of the river in its narrow, deep cutting, the loud birdsong, the flutter of sulphur-yellow butterflies, and smelling the clean air and aromatic herbs. At last she found a way right up to the top of the battlement-like ridge. Her feet slipped on the scree and in the end she went forward on hands and knees, by inches. Exhausted but smug, she was excited. There could be anything there, on the other side.

But there was nothing. Nothing at all. No sign of life, no buildings or people or escape route, only grey peaks and troughs of sparse vegetation and slopes of tumbled stones down into the distance where trees began again, dark, forbidding conifers. A logging trail led through them, but all that Claudia could see was an uninhabitable, impassable wilderness. She was surprisingly little disappointed.

'What's come over you? Don't you want out of here?' she asked herself.

Another incomplete tag from her classical education. 'Know thyself.' The anxious diarist of the apprehensions of married life had never wanted to before.

At this moment, in this wasteland, Claudia could look at herself unmasked; and painfully stumbling back down the hillside on the aromatic, flower-spattered, springy turf, watching her lengthening shadow slide along beside her, she recognised what she was perversely feeling: elation, the kind of delight in being alive which some hallucinatory drugs induce. She remembered the mind-altering drugs of student days. She'd felt ecstatic, found the secret of joy; life was beautiful and valuable. But she was frightened by the loss of control and seldom took another dose.

At least I have discovered this, she thought, stumbling downhill. I can manage. I can change.

I may not like my companions but they are alive and I'm going to keep them that way. No ghosts here, no need for chilly expertise about Herend porcelain or Tompion clocks or any of the *things* that became my substitute for living people.

I've changed.

It seemed much longer going down than up. There were uneasy noises. Blasting? Distant rocket fire? The crack of gunfire? Somewhere else over the hill people were fighting. Better to stay in hiding out of the way.

It was late in the day, dim dusk, when she caught herself thinking, 'Nearly home.'

But when she got there—

'She couldn't look. And when she looked she couldn't take it in. And when she finally forced herself to believe the horror before her eyes, she knew it was all her own fault.

30

Nina Gillespie heaved the sat-phone from the back of the car. It was no bigger than a portable computer, but today it felt like a dead weight. She gave London a map reference and felt more secure immediately. What's happened to the brave reporter then? she asked herself, trying to get courage for irony.

A distant voice shouted, 'Your boyfriend thought you'd be with the other hacks down the coast. He sounded ever so disappointed.'

'What d'you mean, where's he gone?' Nina shouted but the signal had faded, leaving nothing but crackling in the handset, and she remembered she'd forgotten to recharge the batteries. Some days, nothing went right. Nina had her period, inconveniently heavy and painful, and as they jolted along roads which had seen no menders for years, she longed for hot water bottles and gin.

'I'll need to stop again quite soon,' she

said. 'Keep your eyes open for a café or something, will you?'

She came away from the stinking hole she had been shown by the proprietor to find Yacoub emptying a liqueur into his coffee. He passed her the bill without comment. Was it reasonable to be irritated, or was it just menstrual tension which made her resent Yacoub treating her as his mobile cash dispenser? The previous night, spent in what only the most charitable traveller could refer to as 'a village inn', Yacoub had stayed up late. From her room she could hear his voice and the high shrill giggle of the frizzy-haired waitress who had been eyeing him all evening.

As suddenly as she had been attracted to Yacoub Nina had come to be repelled, even frightened by him. But what could go wrong? Other people knew exactly where she was, and she had to press on, they were past the point of no return, even though she seemed to be stuck with a man who seemed ever more alien, continually reminding her this was his country, she could never understand it but he knew what was going on. When he spoke to other men Nina could see he was making sexual jokes about women in general and herself in particular. The men he spoke to would look at her sideways and brush their moustaches with their thumbs or nudge each other with their elbows, and make more openly lewd gestures.

A few days earlier they had left behind the towns that had once been popular with tourists, and would be resorts again when real peace came, towns which in the spring sunshine were pretty and even folksy. Now they had moved on into a less favoured area which had never been enriched by foreigners, although here too the only acceptable currency was still Deutschmarks and some houses displayed dangling signs saying *'Zimmer frei'*.

The landscape had its own charm, its light dolomitic limestone enriched by brilliantly coloured vegetation, but everything was sordid and neglected. Heaps of stinking rubbish lay beside all the roads, rotting and slimy after the previous day's rain, and crumbling, tumbling houses or sheds had not seen repair or paint for years.

The war had rolled through this region like a flood but new plants had already grown in the ruins of buildings, and the painted slogans had lost their original gloss. Old houses built of local stone had stood up better to attack than newer, blockwork boxes which, with a side blown off, a roof in fragments, looked like lifesize toys through which a bad, mad child had put a giant foot.

Yacoub said he had visited this area on his first trip to the country, after communism, at the very beginning of the war. 'I was involved in tourism then. Such optimism, in those days. Everyone wanted to bring in the foreign tourists, they were planning swimming pools, folk museums, designating new European cities of culture, establishing a new university. Oh well.'

The road went through villages where people from the losing side once lived, now deserted or cleared out, the fields and rotting fruit groves full of weeds, the only animals to be seen scrawny cats and menacing, slinking dogs. The next village, which had been on the winning side, would not be prosperous—never that, here—but was at least still a living organism, where food was grown and processed, cows grazed in the fields and babies were born, children taught.

They stopped for Yacoub to negotiate for petrol, its availability denied until he waved a fistful of dollars, whereupon a boy with a gun took him off to find a hidden store.

No curious knot of local people or children; nobody offering services or asking for a hand-out. Nina was alone on an irregular area of stony hard standing, a widening of the unmade track beside a house with shuttered windows and an open door swinging to and fro in the light breeze. Nina turned on the BBC World Service and heard Kate Adie reporting another massacre in Bosnia, three dozen people shot or hacked to death, their bodies left to rot in a deserted village.

The appalling item perversely cheered Nina up. That's what I'm doing here, she thought. She remembered Alastair Cooke, in his *Letter from America*, telling how cowboys murdered every single person in a village in the middle west, some time in the last century, and it was ten years before anyone else got to hear of it.

I won't let people be lost as casually as a crushed insect or trapped mouse, she thought, and slinging her bag and camera across her shoulders she locked the car carefully. She peered in and called through the open door but the house was deserted.

In the one dim room stood a three-legged metal and laminate table propped against the wall, on it a half-knitted garment in stripes of acid colours, the needles removed and wool unravelling. Two pictures torn out of magazines were pinned to the whitewashed wall: an ice-skater, all glitter and swansdown, and a fully rigged sailing ship. A mackintosh stiff with grease hung on a hook beside the empty hearth and there were broken Coca Cola bottles on the cement floor. The abandoned squalor in a once-cosy home epitomised everything Nina had seen.

'I found some petrol,' Yacoub said. 'Look.' He was holding two plastic fuel cans.

'Well done.'

'I know this road, shall I drive?'

His usual question; and this time Nina, by now thoroughly miserable with stomach cramps and back ache, agreed. She strapped herself tightly in, wedging her head against a folded sweater, and dozed as Yacoub pushed the vehicle, much faster and more jerkily than Nina would have done, onwards into the strife-ridden fastnesses of this harsh land.

Finding a place to spend the night

depended on significant details which weirdly paralleled their peacetime equivalent. The appearance of a place was measured, as though on the fresh paint and window box scale, by some index which Yacoub understood though Nina did not. She could see no flags or other signs of political affiliation on the possible resting places she suggested and Yacoub rejected, nor any reason to understand that the one he eventually made for would welcome him. At the time she did not feel up to questions or arguments, being too glad of an acceptable bathroom to quibble, and too nauseous to care that there was very little food on offer.

They were in a suburban villa, exotically placed at the edge of a primitive village. The outside turrets and balustrades decorating the fondant-pink villa could be matched in Brittany, Portugal or any part of Greece to which natives returned with their American or Australian-made fortunes.

The house was furnished with over-stuffed, stretch-covered chairs and shinily varnished wooden tables. Miscellaneous ornaments stood on every surface, an alabaster elephant, a shiny model of the Eiffel Tower, a biscuit tin in the shape of a London bus. Yacoub took the sat-phone away to recharge, saying Nina would need it working the next day, and put her into a front room, where she lay on a narrow, slippery couch while what sounded like a political meeting went on next door. There was a gabble of excitable voices; and Yacoub's, raised in emotion. Anger? Sorrow? Argument? Nina could not tell.

She was asleep when he came into her room. The hubbub had ceased. It was very quiet and dark. He said, 'Tomorrow you'll really see what's happening here. They've been telling me—God, Nina, if this doesn't make people understand why we need a proper supply of weapons, more than just a few crates of Kalashnikovs ...' His voice sounded emotional. Nina reached out for the light switch and saw his ravaged face. He reeked of alcohol.

'Yacoub, what's the matter? What's happened?'

He brushed his hand across his eyes. 'More of the same, Nina, what do you expect? And you'll probably wash your hands of that too.' With one hand he began to unbutton his trousers, with the other he reached out for Nina.

'No, Yacoub, I don't want—'

'You don't want this, you don't want that ... you've been throwing your weight around from the moment we met.' With his spare hand he scraped a fingernail down the scar on Nina's cheek.

'You're drunk. Stop it, stop now, Yacoub.'

'You'd be lucky to find a man now, you should be thanking me.'

'Get off me!'

'You can just shut the fuck up, just shut up. You can't get away with being uppity here, women do what they're told in this country.' He pushed her back on the couch.

No use yelling. His friends would probably hold her down for him. Keep him talking.

'I didn't realise you felt so committed to this country, Yacoub. You seem so English.'

'England's not a country for men any more. It's gone soft. How can you live in a country that doesn't let a man defend himself? Damned interfering cows breaking up families, neglecting their kids. Women still know their place here.'

He must have been saving this up. Should she just let him get on with it? There could be worse fates. Lie back and enjoy it?

No, not this time, not ever.

There had been other such occasions; in Africa she was saved when her assailant, a politician, was interrupted by an immediate call to the Presidential Palace. On arrival he was stripped of his government office and put in the basement cells, but released next day by the dissidents Nina was there to report on and established as President himself. But by that time Nina was out of the country on her way to cover an episode in Indonesia.

Even in the middle of London there had been an interview with an Arab prince whose aide pandered for him like a chief eunuch of old. It was not so much an assault, as total incomprehension. They thought her protests were part of a game. Nina'd had to use the bathroom phone to bring room service to the rescue.

'Hurry up, get them off,' Yacoub said.

Gambling on his prejudices she said, 'I don't mind if you don't.'

'Mind what?'

'I've got my period. That's why I needed to go to the loo so many times today.'

'Ugh.' He flung her away.

'It's only a bit of blood.'

'Filthy. Filth, I wouldn't touch you with a—'

He flung her away from him as another voice shouted, 'Yacoub!' It was one of the other men who'd come into the room, furious, pulling Yacoub back and emitting a long, incomprehensible tirade. Yacoub reeled out of the room.

By this time Nina was thoroughly awake. Midnight. Ten o'clock Greenwich Mean Time. She pulled out her miniature short wave radio and twiddled until she found the BBC World Service. A reassuring voice reading familiar words about Washington, Jakarta, Tokyo, Moscow; the bank rate, the test match, the car industry, the Princess of Wales. Stories in the future or conditional tense. The Foreign Secretary was expected to say, a government source would reveal, a report to be published tomorrow would show ... in Nina's trade it was called 'setting the agenda'. And one more. The marriage had taken place between Mr George Anson, widower of the woman relief worker who had been killed in former

Yugoslavia, and the director of the charity she worked for, Mrs Laurel Berryman. And that, said the calm, emotionless voice, that is the end of the world news.

31

He'd come back.

It was her fault.

The intruder. If she hadn't frightened him off—if she hadn't angered him ...

Guilt was self-indulgence. Escape. It let her off going closer and seeing ... seeing this.

They were dead. All of them. All dead.

There was no point in touching them to make sure, but Claudia did touch them where they lay in blood and shit and vomit, not cold yet.

What had happened?

Dully she supposed they'd all been shot, but didn't know how to tell. What did it matter? Kanita, that kind and saintly woman, old Haric, angry Alija, both the children. Dead.

It was a long time later that Claudia stirred from her sunken, shrunken squat at Kanita's side. Kanita's hand was cold and rigid.

Claudia's throat was sore. She realised in a kind of distanced surprise that she must have been shouting or wailing. The front of her shirt was wet. Not blood. Not rain—the evening sky was greenish clear, with a crescent moon and one brilliant star. She had been weeping.

Moving with agonised stiffness Claudia got awkwardly to her feet. Then she stood still, hands hanging at her side.

What do I do now?

There was a movement in the corner of her field of vision but she did not turn her head.

They've come for me now.

No, it wasn't them—whoever they were. It was a ghost. Mary Ellen's ghost.

That figures, Claudia told herself, I make my own companions. Again.

Mary Ellen who'd been shot at the checkpoint, as substantial-seeming as the Ansons apparitions that used to visit her; Mary Ellen, still in her jeans and khaki anorak, her sandy hair straggling round

355

her set face, the mouth sucked back into a thin line.

She wasn't alone.

There was a man. He was holding a gun, wedged under his arm, his finger on the trigger. It was pointing at Claudia.

No.

She opened her mouth.

Don't!

She couldn't make a sound.

And then the shot was fired.

32

In the morning Nina realised the only thing to do was behave as though the previous night's episode had never happened. Out here in the middle of nowhere she was not exactly at Yacoub's mercy, but she was vulnerable. But Yacoub's aggression must be put behind them both. He had evidently reached the same conclusion. Grim-faced, he climbed into the car at dawn.

'Nina.'

'Yes.'

'I was pissed.'

'Yes.'

'And I'd had bad news.'

His face looked ravaged and Nina realised that she was actually sorry for him. 'You just can't behave like that,' she said weakly. But unspoken between them was the awareness that things were different here. His educated British veneer had revealed the innate bandit beneath, the man whose pride resided in virility and physical strength. Anyway, what did expressions like 'sexual harassment' mean when society had reverted to medieval savagery? Where might was right, maidens were ravished. Certainly in modern Britain, Yacoub would be counted as a criminal, but elsewhere Nina would be thought mad or bad or stupid. In these badlands a young woman who travelled alone and unprotected was 'asking for it'. Anyway, she'd won. Put it behind me, she thought. And lock the bedroom door.

'Your bad news ...' she began.

'I'll show you.'

The sun was just touching the roofs of the houses when they reached the village. They had driven past abandoned fields and then along a great rocky defile, travelling up the hill on a rough road which twisted

357

in parallel with a fast-running river. They went over a ridge and saw above them the huddled houses of a mountain village, built at the top of a long green valley between the mountains. No smoke rose from the chimneys. There was no movement to be seen from this distance, except the sudden flight of a great flock of storks.

They went on, the road surface deteriorating.

'Is this a logging trail?' Nina asked.

'More mule trails, these days.' He swerved to one side of a crater in the rough surface. 'As you see, they mined it.'

On a little bluff just before the village was a kind of battered fortress.

'Romans, Crusaders, Turks, Hapsburgs —they all used it. Then it was a hospice,' he said.

'With children? An orphanage?'

He didn't answer. Nina became gradually aware of a heavy smell: charred wood and corruption. She looked at Yacoub in horrified question.

'We thought this was a safe haven,' he said heavily.

'What happened?'

'They took the children.'

'But why?'

'Why do these gangsters do anything? They're savages, one can't explain, it's animal behaviour. They took the kids away and shelled the village and then the few survivors were driven out.'

Nina knew it wasn't the first place where such things had happened. It wouldn't be the last. And Yacoub's people would do the same to their enemies, if they could.

They stopped in the empty central square. Startled by a movement under an arcaded house Nina saw two bloated dogs gnawing at something unrecognisable.

Years earlier Metromedia had sent Nina on a 'hostile environments course' where ex-soldiers taught journalists about lines of fire and the use of dead ground, as well as fieldcraft and survival skills. Her skin crawled with the fear of something being aimed at it, as she slowly climbed down from the car and hesitantly, reluctantly, walked across the square and into one of the narrow alleys leading out of it. This was—had once been—a highland farming community, with logs and the remains of winter fodder heaped in open-sided cellars under high, narrow stone houses. They walked past a car on blocks and two small tractors. There were carved balconies and well-made wooden doors; Nina had read that this area was full of woodworkers and joiners. Outside one house, on a ragged patch of grass, was a single, sodden, soft toy, a brilliant pink elephant. A red and blue tricycle lay on its side under a line of flapping and bird-spattered washing. A plastic slide had been overturned.

'These are brave fighters, warriors, if the British had let them have weapons everything would be different. I got guns, but never enough,' Yacoub said.

With repressive accuracy Nina recorded the evidence of atrocity. Then they went further, and down other alleys and into all the houses of the little community just in case anybody had been left there to tell the tale. But the only humans in the village were those who had died.

Later, much later, back in the car, Nina was bereft of speech, though she knew the necessary words would come when it was time. Heartfelt, useless words, discounted, ignored, less attended to than the game show they followed or the costume drama which came next. Her mind skittered away at an angle, unable to take in the immediate horror, remembering a speech

360

by the British Foreign Secretary when he said journalists' reports of what they had seen made it impossible for diplomats to be dispassionate. He thought reporters and diplomats should keep their emotions out of foreign affairs.

The brilliant sunshine was a mockery of the scene, casting hard jagged shadows on to the unpeopled ground. After a long time Nina said, 'You sent them guns?'

Yacoub nodded.

'In the relief convoys?'

'And drugs.'

'To beat the embargo.'

'Can you blame me?'

'How did you pay for them?'

'You know how.'

'Babies? Children?'

'Yes,' he said strongly, 'babies, children, orphans who'd lost everything. We got them families and homes, food in their bellies and a chance of education. Like you got yourself. And what's wrong with that?'

'You sold human beings!' Nina couldn't keep up the professional dispassion. 'Like commodities, things—Yacoub!'

'I never kept the money, not after the very beginning, not like some, I never wanted designer clothes or a house in

Chelsea, once I'd got involved here it was all for the cause, everything I've done.' His wide gesture swept in the ghastliness around them.

'You smuggled them into the UK?'

'That's right.'

'How?'

'Nobody questions accompanied kids. They'd go in on someone's passport, through Ireland sometimes, or by ferry, it was no problem.'

'But Yacoub, what about the children's families?'

'D'you take me for a gangster? Fair trade's one thing, that's how it began, I admit it, I was a businessman, but then it was the only way we could buy arms, but I'd never take kids from their parents, not if they had good homes. Don't you see, that's what happened here, they took the kids and then they bombed the place into the Stone Age. Look around you.'

Nina turned her eyes away as he dashed his hand roughly across his wet cheeks. Then, holding the mike to Yacoub's face she said, 'What was this place, who lived here?'

'This was a mountain enclave for our people to wait out the war, the old, and the kids, non-combatants. That's what we thought.'

In the still desolation a movement caught Nina's eyes, and Yacoub's at the same moment. With professional smoothness he whipped a Kalashnikov from the floor of the car. Automatically Nina ducked behind the jeep. Then she took out binoculars to look up the mountain.

A figure was stumbling and limping very slowly down the stony track, leaning on a rough walking stick. She had matted, ragged hair, blotchy and peeling sunburnt skin spotted with bruises, scabs and scratches.

It was—it couldn't be—it really was ...

Nina cried, 'Don't shoot, it's—my God it can't be, I don't believe it, it's Mary Ellen Wood!'

33

After the first emotional greeting, an embrace, some tears, Nina got out the first aid kit and began to dab and plaster the raw bleeding patches on Mary Ellen's skin, though the injuries seemed to be superficial. Mary Ellen refused to be taken down straight away to the house of Yacoub's relatives, instead insisting in a hoarse whisper that she had to show Nina what had happened, Nina was a reporter, she must tell everyone what had been going on here.

'And that you're alive,' Nina said, 'it's such wonderful news.'

'Yes, yes, but you've got to see for yourself, I can't tell you—get going, can't you, drive on—up there, towards the mountains ...'

Mary Ellen did not have much strength for talking. So it was Nina who reminded Yacoub about the two Englishwomen who everyone believed to have perished in the wreck of their aid lorry. He said, 'Sorry—you're—which one? You're Claudia Anson?'

'This is Mary Ellen,' Nina said.

'And you've been here all this time?' Yacoub exclaimed.

'Were you a prisoner?' Nina asked.

'Felt like it, or a hostage. There must have been a ransom demand,' Mary Ellen whispered.

As they approached they saw a huge

bird, Dracula-like, hunched on the ground. Mary Ellen screamed and lurched towards it, and the creature teetered a few steps along the ground before taking off into the air. Its wing span was two metres at least: a European griffon vulture.

Claudia Anson had fallen face down. Nina gently turned the straggle of greying hair to see the altered, emaciated face, with an expression of horror in the staring eyes. The chest was a bloody hollow. Oh Harry, Nina thought, and wondered how to maintain a reporter's detachment. It's getting to me, she realised. With mounting hysteria she flapped clouds of insects away from the body, but they came back and back. The vulture was gliding in a circle, black against the blue sky. Swallowing nausea Nina said harshly, 'Yacoub, you've got to find something to cover her with, anything.'

'Inside, you've got to see ...' Mary Ellen gestured.

Two men, two children, a woman, all dead. 'So Claudia died here, after all, and so recently,' Nina murmured.

'But she never stopped thinking about home,' Mary Ellen whispered. 'She went on about Ansons all the time, never stopped.'

'Sad. So sad.'

Yacoub said, 'Yeah, it's dreadful, but Nina, you've got to call London, this is a big story.'

'Later, I need to—what happened, how come you escaped this—this slaughter?'

Mary Ellen breathed her halting story: she'd been up the mountain, alone—nobody else had the strength to go with her, she was looking for food. And while she was gone ... this happened. Who? Why? She'd no idea. But when she came back, this is what she found.

'How long have you been here, what happened?'

'The lorry crashed, I don't know after that, it's all a blur, we found ourselves here, couldn't get away, nobody came ...' She broke off in a fit of dry sobs.

Yacoub said, 'Nina, you've got to do this story quickly, the world needs to know what's happening here.'

'I have to let them know she's survived. Your daughter—she'll be so happy,' Nina said, realising that in the middle of this ghastliness she too could feel relief about Mary Ellen, a weight off her mind; she'd never stopped feeling guilty about the consequences of Mary Ellen's ordeal by media. Yet how trivial that seemed now.

Mary Ellen spoke quickly, 'Can you send it now? From here? Do it then, go on!'

'And tell them about the orphans,' Yacoub urged, 'the abducted children— that atrocities have been committed here!'

'D'you know who took them?'

'The enemy, isn't that enough?'

Nina paused to arrange her thoughts; how could she elucidate for others an incomprehensible situation? God knows who took those poor kids away, she thought, or who shelled the village and drove its people away. But it almost doesn't matter. In this chaos there's one stable fact—woe to the defeated, God favours the big battalions, not do-as-you-would- be-done-by but be-done-by-as-you-would. They'd all massacre their enemies if they had half a chance.

But there had been too many atrocities on the air. Each hideous detail made a repetitive horror which Brian France didn't wish to broadcast. 'That's old news,' he shouted. 'Another village shelled, another massacre—sure it's awful, but give me more about the human story, listeners can identify with the Wood woman.'

So Nina concentrated on the new story, telling how she had witnessed Mary Ellen's resurrection. Mary Ellen whispered a few broken phrases. The piece was bounced into space and from the satellite, straight back to London. It was a sensational despatch. The distant technician who received it gave a long whistle. 'That Mary Ellen, she's the one you talked about before, the one that was so broke? No worries about that any more, this'll make her fortune.'

It hadn't occurred to Nina before. In the midst of death media deals seemed irrelevant. It certainly wasn't the moment to mention it to Mary Ellen. But it was true; the moment Mary Ellen arrived home she'd have offers from tabloids and publishers and agents and chat shows. She'd be famous all over again, but to her advantage this time.

'Done it?' Yacoub said.

'Yes. The piece will be picked up by all the other media, the whole world will know.'

'You sure?'

'Why?' Nina asked, turning to look at him. Yacoub was holding his gun.

'Hey, careful, that's pointing at—'

'Yacoub. Look.' Mary Ellen had hauled herself upright, shading her eyes to look down the dusty road. 'Someone's coming.'

They heard it as she spoke, an engine labouring up the hill towards them.

There was an army jeep carrying two soldiers in army fatigues, Brits; it was followed by a white United Nations land cruiser. First out was a European monitor in his white suit, followed by two armed men in camouflage clothes with pale blue helmets, then a man with a camera unfolded his skinny length from the back. It was Zed Lyons. Then another civilian got out: Harry Anson, wearing a dark flak jacket and plain khaki helmet.

Nina's relief and delight at the sight of Harry took her by surprise. But she couldn't resist the stubborn instinct to attack.

'Sir Galahad to the rescue? What are you doing here?'

'Pax,' he said, holding his hands up in mock surrender. 'I was following Claudia's tracks.'

Oh God, Nina thought, I'll have to tell him—show him.

Mary Ellen straightened herself at the name, and fixing her fierce, pale eyes on

Harry Anson said, 'She's dead, see for yourself.'

It was cruel. Harry knelt by the body with his hands over his face. Was he praying or weeping? Nina put her hand out towards him, but then drew back. She had no right to watch or comfort him. Turning her back she asked Zed what had brought them here.

'You told Brian France, he told me, I told Harry, he told the military,' Zed said with a simplicity that seemed out of place in this complicated situation.

The soldiers' presence needed no explanation. Protection was needed. These were badlands.

Zed had been looking alertly around him, his nostrils quivering like a hunting dog. He said, 'OK, Nina, what's the story?'

'Yacoub and I—where's he gone?' But Yacoub had disappeared somewhere. Nina spoke with chilly precision, a situation report.

One of the soldiers spoke urgently into his handset. Another, with a Canadian maple leaf on his insignia, said, 'There was an Australian woman up here.'

'Are you sure?'

'S'what the liaison officer said the locals told him. Their aid lorry was blown up, one woman was killed but some locals rescued the survivor and she stayed up here with them.'

'But shouldn't someone have checked?'

'Not our concern, ma'am, if an Aussie chooses to live with the locals.'

'But it was the Australian woman who died, and there were two women here, not one, Brits, why didn't the army—'

'Couldn't say, ma'am.'

The British soldiers, lieutenant and corporal, administered first aid and more. One found water, washed Mary Ellen with a nurse's tenderness and dressed her septic wounds more effectively than Nina had managed. Food was offered. Hot reconstituted soup? A nice cup of tea? Put your feet up, take it easy. No problems.

Zed was snapping away with a kind of ferocious dedication, distancing himself from the horror by recording it. It was what Nina had done too, a professional response to atrocity, one which enabled her to stop feeling the horror and pity, to stay outside the disgust, the smells, the incessant head-drilling reminder of the clouds of buzzing, scavenging flies.

The European monitor muttered memos into his tiny machine.

'Should we do something about clearing up, graves ...' the British officer asked him.

The other man had a weary, deeply folded face, his dark eyes experienced in infamy. He said in a French accent, 'We don't do it, but yes, this will be cleared. I ensure this.'

Harry's gaze had been fixed on the desolation around them. 'I'm taking Claudia home,' he said.

A sinister plastic roll was produced from the jeep and the young soldier said, 'I'll see to it, sir.'

'No, I'll do it.'

Nina couldn't watch Harry feeding Claudia's corpse into the body bag. She moved into the shelter of a bush, in the incongruously peaceful sound of bees, the scent of broom. Without any of the usual delight she observed a black redstart, a rare bird at home. She made another call to London. Should she say the army had been negligent? No, later, when she had the story clearer in her own mind. She delivered a brief update. She could already see the photos and films: the body discreetly unloaded into a hearse, the surviving woman returning to a heroine's welcome. Nina saw her own hands were shaking, and she felt sick and chilly in spite of the sun's warmth. It's getting to me now, I'm suffering from shock, she thought, I can't think straight, I'm losing it again like last time.

She shivered in the warm sunshine, going over the events of the day with her mind sliding off its usual straight and logical path. She was distracted by the infinitely desirable image of a sheltering bed, not her own or Harry's, but Carl's grandiose hide-out.

What had been going on here? An ambush; the load hijacked, the truck destroyed, one woman dead and two taken up here. Rescued? Or as prisoners? Hostages? But was it connected with the dealing in infants, that trade Yacoub couldn't see anything wrong with? What was wrong with it, actually? Was he a criminal? Or immoral? But gun running—that couldn't be right. Could it? What if it was the only way people could get the means to defend themselves, from—this, the atrocity that had taken place here?

The thoughts escaped analysis, like

mercury evaded one's fingers.

Listen.

A helicopter clattered out of the distance, closer and down, its camouflage livery reassuring.

The young soldier picked his way across to Nina. 'The officer's compliments, ma'am, and he's ready to hit the road as soon as the chopper's taken off.'

She made herself reply sensibly. 'OK. Where's Yacoub? Yacoub!' He appeared from behind the house and Nina said, 'We're going.'

'Not me,' Yacoub said.

'I know you,' Harry said, mopping his face.

The body bag had been tactfully slid into a cargo area and now the soldiers, and a woman in service uniform who'd leapt out of the hovering machine, were making Mary Ellen as comfortable as they could in its rear space. 'Here you are, luv, let's get this tucked round you.'

Harry said, 'No doubt there's a big welcome waiting for her, risen from the dead like this.'

'I'll have to do another story about tonight before the others can get at her,' Nina agreed.

'You'll cash in too, I suppose.' His voice was chilly and two simultaneous and contradictory images flashed through Nina's mind. In one, she was receiving journalism's top awards for her brilliant story. In the other she was giving in her notice to Brian France because Harry didn't want to marry a hack.

Yacoub leant in to Mary Ellen lying in the helicopter and said, 'You'll be all right, girl, just hold on.'

'Harry, this is my interpreter—'

Looking at Yacoub, Mary Ellen made a thumbs-up sign.

'Konin, isn't it, Jake Konin?' Harry said.

'Yacoub?' Nina said.

He said, 'Jake, Jacob, Yacoub, it's all the same.'

'Step back, please.' The rising helicopter was momentarily deafening and the wind shifted the inadequate coverings from the bodies that were still on the ground.

'Officer says we got to move, ma'am.'

'Yacoub, are you—'

Yacoub said, 'What difference does it make? You've seen what's happening here, so that's me done.'

'Nina, are you all right?' Harry was

shaking too, she could feel his hand quivering on her back.

God, don't let me faint. 'But Yacoub, you can't just stay here!'

'This is where I belong. I'll guard the bodies till my people get here.'

Nina slumped into the passenger seat of her car, Harry would drive. He seemed to hear her unspoken plea to get her out of here, and started the engine to drive off between the two military vehicles. The man who'd once been an ordinary Brit morphed in her mind, reverted to ancestral type, and it was a Balkan brigand she saw in the wing mirror as they bumped along the road. Drops of tears and sweat were sliding down Harry's cheeks.

34

He did make some attempt to inquire what had been happening to her, and she made a stab at telling him, but very briefly. Harry was in mourning and Nina thought he should be left in peace. She felt quite shattered enough herself by the sights of that day, and she hadn't even been fond of Claudia. Had anyone been, other than Harry?

The next hours passed in a daze: driving westwards in convoy towards the lowering sun, then into a scarlet sunset and quick darkness, and on and on, doggedly under the starry sky. With a start Nina opened her eyes.

'It's getting light already, you must have been driving all night, have I been asleep?'

'For hours.'

'I'm so sorry, Harry.'

'It's OK.'

'Where's the others?'

'We parted company, it's back to civilisation now.'

'Let me drive.'

'No need, we'll stop here.'

A hotel: geraniums in tubs, a row of flagpoles with rival allegiances flapping in the dawn breeze, expensive, clean cars on smooth tarmac, a uniformed porter. A room with a pair of queen-sized beds, television, which Nina immediately turned on to CNN, a marble bathroom, even a fluffy bathrobe. The luxury seemed intensely surreal, a few hours' drive from the refugee camps, the orphanages, and the massacred victims. When a black-coated waiter brought a trolley with a starched white cloth and silver-domed dishes and a delicious waft of coffee Harry too remarked on the oddity of the ambience. 'Remember the Imperial at Dubrovnik?'

'Where this all began.' Nina wasn't sure herself if she meant the tragedy of this country, or her meeting with Harry. He had shaved and bathed, but still looked gaunt, with shadows on the freckled skin under his eyes and in the hollows of his cheeks. She took great gulps of orange juice.

'There, she's arrived,' he said, and went to turn the sound up on the television. A plane landing at Northolt airport, a waiting crowd. It was raining in London.

Harry was restless, walking between the trolley—more coffee, a croissant buttered but not bitten—then across to the balcony, from which the view was perfectly peaceful, velvety grass leading towards a pinewood, then back to the mirror where he looked with menace, even hatred, at his own weary face, then back to stand in front of the television screen. Mary Ellen Wood, supported on either side by a nurse and an air steward, could just be seen through the plane's open door.

Nina wondered if she too was feeling '*déjà vu*' at being again faced by the ranks of hacks and snappers. And there was Beth, dashing up the steps of the plane, her arms spread wide.

Harry groaned and without meaning the words to slip out she said, 'You look haunted.'

He didn't answer her directly. Rubbing his hands over his face he said, 'They should have fallen into each other's arms, don't you see? Mary Ellen and Konin, whatever he was calling himself, they weren't strangers.'

Nina clapped her hands to her cheeks. 'I don't believe it, I must have been out of my mind, of course you're right, he knew her very well if they'd driven out together from London—but he asked her, I heard him ask which one she was, called her Claudia, he must have been putting it on. Why didn't I see it? But what was it for? When she turned up out of the blue, what—'

'Out of the blue?' he interrupted. 'Come on, Nina, that wasn't a fluke, it was a rendezvous. He got you where he wanted you, he'd planned it all, you were supposed to come upon Mary Ellen Wood and get your story on the air.'

Nina replayed the scene in her mind. Could Yacoub have been feigning his surprise when Mary Ellen came towards them? And then, when they went back together up the hill? Oh my God, that's it—'They needed me to report it,' she exclaimed.

And there Nina was, reporting it: her voice came from the television set. Brian France's rights manager had been quick off the mark selling that tape.

Harry said, 'You were an independent witness.'

'He made sure the sat-phone was recharged, I should have noticed, he wasn't usually so helpful—and then he got me up there.' Suddenly Nina was shivering uncontrollably. 'And then when I'd done the piece, just before you got there ...' The image of Yacoub and his gun, pointed, unbelievably, at her. She whispered, 'I think he was going to kill me. If you hadn't turned up just then ... but what about Mary Ellen? She wouldn't have stood by, was he going to shoot her too?'

They stood side by side in front of

the screen watching Mary Ellen's slow, supported progress, through the doorway and to the top of those steps. Yesterday she could walk.

'But I don't understand,' Nina said. 'Why was I there?'

'An independent witness, one whose words would be believed.'

'But who needed an independent witness, what for?'

'To report Mary Ellen's return from captivity. With you there it turned into a good story, you said yourself she'll get rich on it.'

The distant camera panned across the waiting crowd, mostly media people, but not exclusively. The tall, narrow, blonde-topped figure of Laurel Berryman—now presumably Laurel Anson—stood near the ambulance at the bottom of the steps. She was holding an enormous bouquet.

Nina muttered, 'I don't understand it, what about the others, the Australian girl, Claudia—'

'Claudia?' Harry said in a dreadful voice, his words drowning the bland commentary in which one of Nina's colleagues was charting Mary Ellen's tottering progress. 'I'll tell you what about Claudia, she went as a lamb to the slaughter.'

'Harry—'

'I should have understood when we were at Ansons that day, Laurel was already taking over. She knew Claudia wouldn't be going home again.'

'You mean Laurel arranged for the truck to miss the convoy, to crash?'

'It's a murder method with scriptural authority.'

'I never seemed to do much RE at school,' Nina said, suddenly wondering whether Harry would want her to turn Catholic.

'King David sent Bathsheba's husband into the most dangerous part of a battle to get him killed and leave her free to marry David.'

'But then Yacoub, Jake, he must have been part of it, he's a criminal, we shouldn't have let him go!'

'Us and whose army? He couldn't be arrested there, so long as he stays with his local pals he's safely melted into the background.'

The camera went in close on a small black girl with her hair in dreadlocks offering a posy of violets to Mary Ellen.

Nina gasped, 'Oh Harry, the baby

smuggling, the arms dealing, I told you he admitted it all, don't you see that means he must have been doing it through the charity, Handyside's, what a twit I am, call myself an investigative reporter!'

Laurel was in the shot again, coming forward to bend and embrace the pathetic little figure.

'A murderer by remote control?' Nina said incredulously.

'And the rest. Look at her,' Harry said. 'You don't really think she could ever have run her expensive life on the amount a charity paid her, she wanted money, and fame and status, she used Handyside's as a front to get them. And then she saw Ansons and wanted that. Mary Ellen was her tool.'

'Have you spoken to your brother?' she asked.

'Tried. Pissed as a newt.'

Far away on the other side of Europe an ambulance door was closing on the media's new heroine. Nina said slowly, 'But it's still a mystery, Harry, because if she planned to meet Yacoub and me how did they ever get it together? She was stuck up there, out of contact.'

'God knows. Let's stop talking about it.'

He drained the pot and gulped down the dregs. 'I'm bushed.'

And miserable. But Nina knew he wasn't ready for consolation. Sleep, not sex. He was unconscious almost before his head touched the pillow. Nina turned off the television, pushed the trolley of uneaten food into the corridor and hung a 'Do not disturb' notice on the door handle. He didn't stir as she slid in close to him and when she woke four hours later he was still lying in exactly the same position.

35

Harry was almost totally silent all day and Nina did not disturb him though usually they had so many thoughts to exchange that continuous chatter jumped from idea to joke to observation until silenced by passion. It could have been a beautiful drive in the landscape of classical dreams, but instead of its beauty Nina noticed the modern degradation. There was a lot of traffic going the other way, south and inland. They queued at one checkpoint for more than an hour; at the next it was the opposing traffic that had to wait while a Christian Aid convoy of lorries was slowly searched.

Nina was going to settle her ghosts. She kept unconsciously rubbing at the scar on her face. The next day they were going to return the hired car and fly home together. Neither of them had decided what the next step should be.

It was nearly twilight when they returned to Dubrovnik, already dim under the tall trees that made an avenue leading towards the city walls. They walked over the bridge above the moat in a faintly blue evening light that made the tiny cats grey, all the carpet vendors' wares richly beautiful, and lent a golden glow to the domed roof of the fountain. The paved Corso had filled up with evening strollers. The locals looked prosperous. Some tourists, mostly Germans, had dared to come back. A street photographer was snapping strollers with a Polaroid. *'Lachen sie,'* he called. 'Smile.'

'They've fixed it all up already, there's nothing to show for what happened,' Nina remarked in wonder.

'Nor for the last war, or all the wars

before, nor for the series of earthquakes,' Harry replied.

'You'd need to be sure what used to be here. I ought to remember some of it, I came here for my honeymoon.' She said it with a little gasp, making herself admit the reality that there'd been a time before Harry.

'We'll go to the South Pacific.'

She didn't take it in at first. 'I've never been—what did you say?'

'That's why. I'll take you somewhere neither of us associates with human misery.'

He really meant it. He wanted to marry her. He repeated and elucidated. Nina was engulfed with joy. She'd thought he didn't love her enough; or disapproved of formalities. Just in case he was making a sacrifice of his principles she said she'd live with him anyway, and he admitted this convention was his remaining touch of Ansonism. 'I always knew it wasn't going to last with the others—'

'Don't. Don't tell me about them now.'

'But this time I want to do it properly.'

'The whole bit? The chapel at Ansons?'

That, fortunately, he regarded as going too far. In any case, Ansons had been poisoned for him. 'I'm not going there with that woman in charge.'

They sat at a café table. I've had a drink here, Nina suddenly realised, with Carl. But it didn't matter. A whole new life beckoned.

The man who had taken their picture stood by their table offering to sell the print: Harry, more gingery on the cheap film than in life, every inch the English gentleman in his light linen suit and panama hat; Nina, her amber eyes very large and glossy black curls longer than usual after weeks away from home. Her hair had blown back from her face, but for the first time she looked with calm acceptance at the silvery line exposed on her sunburnt cheek.

He paid the photographer and then said, 'I've got something to show you.' He drew from his side pocket an envelope printed with the name of the hotel in which they had spent the previous night. 'I'd forgotten this till I was looking for the road map in the glove compartment this morning, the British soldier said he'd found it. It was in that house. He handed it over to me but I didn't look till today.'

She thought, this is what he's been

worrying about since the morning, he waited to tell me about it until he was sure we were a team. With a feeling of cold dismay she accepted the little package. It consisted of a few ragged sheets of cheap cardboard, the unfolded packaging of dried milk. One showed, on the outer side, Handyside's praying hands. The writing, in hard, faint pencil, covered every other millimetre of the surface. Full stops had made holes in the cardboard, some letters were indented through to the back.

A waiter brought resinated wine and the *Englische Platte* they had ordered, a variety of cold meats and pickles. 'It's Claudia's writing,' Harry said. A flower seller came and hovered by their table. 'Quicker to pay than argue,' he muttered, and bought Nina five red roses.

'I'm frightened to read it,' she said.

'It's her notes, a kind of journal.'

'She always kept one at home, didn't she.'

He didn't ask how Nina knew. 'Yes, but it was pretty dull, the weather, the new upholstery, menus, sometimes when she thought she'd seen a ghost. She used to let me look sometimes, when I was a kid.'

Still hesitating, Nina arranged the pitiful testament on the metal café table. 'It isn't easy to make the writing out. What does this say? Something about infection in the village.'

'Look at this first. No, listen, I'll read it,' he said. '"This better than solitude but H & A not gd. company, K still wandering. Exhausted & longing for real conversation. May never see a friend again, am forgotten here."'

'What does it mean? What about Mary Ellen?'

'There's other passages about her loneliness. But listen. "Long convn. w. Haric, he knows wh happened. Load really arms, as feared, plan to hijack en route, English woman to be killed, he meant **me**!" Look, Nina,' Harry interrupted, 'it's underlined, and see how wild her writing got, what d'you think she felt like, writing that down?'

'Does she go on?'

'"Arms as pay. But who wanted me dead? Won't think abt it now. Haric says enemy—who?—ambushed and fought over arms. One dead woman found, poor Sheila, but assumed I was her so rescued, brought up here, safe hide-out."'

Nina cried, 'Where was Mary Ellen?'

'She'd gone already. It's on this bit, after a list, "dill, rose-hips, sorrell", I suppose that was some of the wild food she found. Listen, Nina, this is where Mary Ellen was. "ME taken from truck at checkpoint, acc. to plan, explains why tried stop Sheila coming, I shld have been alone. Jake's illness fake? Mustn't brood. Found way to make Zivich laugh, Haric says first for months, simple peep-bo, boring, made Alija do it."'

'It's hard evidence,' Nina said soberly. 'All it needs is a handwriting expert. We can prove Mary Ellen wasn't there.'

'And even that she delivered poor Claudia up to what was meant to be her death. But this doesn't prove Mary Ellen shot her.'

'You don't really think that!'

'Who else was there? As far as I can see this is the last bit Claudia wrote. "Madness to attack intruder, idiotic, if friend have made enemy, if enemy, may come back with others. Wld never have dared before, good to be braver, but went too far."'

'What d'you think that's about?'

'It must mean Claudia's enemies did believe she'd died in the crash, which explains how that woman felt safe to go and marry my pathetic brother. But then someone came upon Claudia and her companions, not knowing previously they were there, and when Mary Ellen heard of it she had to finish the job, or at least make sure someone finished it.'

'Just in time for the rest of the plan, being discovered by someone who'd turn her into a heroine. Muggins here.'

'Who was punctually delivered by the third conspirator.'

They sat in silence in front of the spread of pitiful documents. Nina's eye fell on a few lines written at right angles to a closely covered page. 'Nobody will know me when/if I get home, changed, rude, decisive. George appalled! This has made new woman of me.'

Now it was fully night the evening promenade was over, and the crowds in the Corso dispersed, leaving other pairs of lovers to wander under the spangled sky. There were sounds of conversations and arguments; pop music and, from some courtyard, a chamber trio playing Beethoven. How peaceful it seemed. But when an aircraft broke the sound barrier above their heads Nina found herself trembling and sweating at the sudden thunder. Jumping up she almost pulled Harry along in her haste to escape from the little city.

So much had happened since the last time. I've changed. Claudia changed. Mary Ellen Wood went through as many changes as a chameleon, from politician's helpmeet to student to bag lady to smuggler and then, yes, then to murderer.

They were back at the car-park, it was time to go if they were to catch an early flight. 'Will they be charged, d'you think?' she asked.

'D'you mean Mary Ellen? Or Laurel? Or even Jacob Konin?'

'All of them, I suppose. Or any.'

'Where's the admissible evidence?'

A group of rough but clean children, none older than nine or ten, came surging through the car-park. Three of them swerved to jostle round the rich foreigners, holding out their begging palms. Before Nina or Harry could decide whether to make a hand-out the children were followed by a woman in jeans, running and shouting. The children coalesced again into a group and went on towards their bus. As the woman passed she said a word in Serbo

Croat, and translated it with an apologetic grin. *'Waisenkinder.'*

'Orphans,' Harry said.

Children who'd been left behind. Would they have been better off in some adoptive, foreign home? 'What are we going to do?' she asked and he replied:

'If not the law, then public opinion. You'll do your job.'

'I don't know how to explain what's happened.'

'But you can give evidence about it. You're a witness.'

'That's what I tell students, I'm there to speak for those who didn't survive.'

Running his finger down the side of her face, Harry said, 'You lived to tell the tale.'

This Large Print Book for the Partially sighted, who cannot read normal print, is published under the auspices of

THE ULVERSCROFT FOUNDATION

Other MAGNA Mystery Titles In Large Print

WILLIAM HAGGARD
The Vendettists

C. F. ROE
Death By Fire

MARJORIE ECCLES
Cast A Cold Eye

KEITH MILES
Bullet Hole

PAULINE G. WINSLOW
A Cry In The City

DEAN KOONTZ
Watchers

KEN McCLURE
Pestilence

a 6

X